Champion
of Sherwood

by

Laura Strickland

The Guardians of Sherwood Trilogy
Book Two

Champion of Sherwood

Cover Art by *Diana Carlile*

The Wild Rose Press, Inc.
PO Box 708
Adams Basin, NY 14410-0708
Visit us at www.thewildrosepress.com

Publishing History
First English Tea Rose Edition, 2014
Print ISBN 978-1-62830-179-3
Digital ISBN 978-1-62830-180-9

The Guardians of Sherwood Trilogy, Book Two
Published in the United States of America

"I ask of you, young man, only one thing, one boon, one favor if you would survive this night."

"Of course I will survive. How not? This is but darkness, and trees, and moonlight."

The man waved one of his hands. A creature appeared beside him, a pure white wolf with its hackles raised. Another subtle movement and he was suddenly flanked on the other side by a great white hart, its sides streaming mist. The trees overhead tossed their branches and Gareth felt the power gather, sharp and vital, around this being who faced him.

Fear such as he had never known—not even when awaiting the arrival of his father with the strap—engulfed him. "What do you seek of me? What boon, what bidding?"

"I ask of you but one promise, that you should follow what is in your heart." The man smiled again. "Does not a champion, a true champion, always follow his heart?"

Gareth had no answer for that either. His father had insisted a champion strove for perfection, to be faultless in all things and above reproach.

"My heart has been dead a long while." He did not know why he said that—it felt drawn from him.

"Nay, not dead," the specter told him. "Merely closed tight." Before Gareth's eyes his form wavered like a reflection in water, as did those of the creatures on either side. As Gareth stared, they shimmered and blended together until all that faced him was a brown hart, head high and rack displayed.

The spirit's final words floated to him even as the hart bolted. "Now run, my son. Flee!"

Praise for *DAUGHTER OF SHERWOOD*

"Laura Strickland creates a world that not only draws you in, but she incorporates it so seamlessly that Sherwood is every bit as much a character in this story as Wren and Sparrow. Throw in a love triangle that has you flipping the pages, and you have the kind of book that keeps you awake well into the wee hours, and sighing with satisfaction when you've finished the very last page."

~Nicole McCaffrey, author

Dedication

For my husband, Paul,
who has always been my champion

Chapter One

The village of Oakham, Sherwood Forest
Midsummer 1235

"Lark! Falcon! Will the two of you not give over with your nonsense and get out from under foot so I might get my work done?"

Half exasperated and half amused, Linnet directed the words, and a sharp glare, at the figures wrestling at her feet. "Grappling" might make a better description than "wrestling," she acknowledged, for what the two of them were about.

The pair, so unevenly matched, contrasted almost ludicrously—one fair-haired and lithe, possessed of quick, easy strength, the other small, dark-headed, and a veritable fury of energetic intent. At the moment, the dark-headed combatant had rolled atop the other and looked to prove victorious. Even as Linnet scolded her sister, Lark dug her elbow into her opponent's midsection, eliciting from him a gusty "Whoof!"

"That for you, Falcon Scarlet!" the victor crowed with satisfaction, sitting astride him the way a naughty lass might a recalcitrant pony. "I win."

Linnet, arrested and distracted from her chores, narrowed her eyes. Did she detect something beyond mere rivalry in the scene? Did her sister, Lark, allow her triumphant body to cling a little too eagerly to that

1

of the young man trapped beneath her?

Before Linnet could fairly make up her mind, Fal moved. With effortless strength he lifted Lark above him, swung her around, and slammed her against the earthen floor.

"No, mite, you have not won," he cried with obvious enjoyment. "Nor will you, ever."

Lark, furious, had no chance to reply as one of her flailing arms caught the wooden cupboard beside which she had been flung. Pots and crockery filled with the products of Linnet's morning-long labors toppled and flew everywhere. Three cries of dismay arose, Linnet's the loudest.

"Now look what you have done. How many times have I told the two of you to keep your wild antics out of doors?"

Her twin sister, Lark, sprang up from the mess apparently unharmed. She tossed Linnet a glare bright with defiance before she lit out and disappeared through the door of the cottage, which stood open to the summer air.

Lark's foe, Falcon Scarlet, got up more slowly and shot Linnet an apologetic look.

"I am that sorry, Lin. The tiny hell-spawn pushed me to it. I was not thinking."

"That tiny hell-spawn, as you call her, happens to be the person closest in the world to me. If she came from hell, so must I." Standing amid the ruin of what had been an ordered room, Linnet fixed Falcon with a hard stare and raised an eyebrow. "Do you mean to say I am hell-spawned as well?"

"Never." He leaned forward and planted a sweet kiss on her cheek. "You are heaven walking. Do not be angry with me."

Linnet sighed. Despite the many and virtually continual reasons he gave her, she found it impossible to stay upset with Fal for long. Sizing him up frankly now, she doubted any woman with red blood in her veins could. Falcon Scarlet was far too charming for his own good, and far too attractive. Even she, who felt more like a sister to him than otherwise, had to admit it.

Take now, with his fair hair mussed from his tussle with Lark, his greenish-blue eyes dancing, and his white teeth gleaming in a mischievous smile. His long, lean body moved with strong grace, and she caught a glimpse of tanned skin where Lark had managed to rend the front of his tunic. Was he not any maid's wild dream?

Well, perhaps not Linnet's.

"It is just that your sister has a rare talent for aggravating me. You know what an even-tempered fellow I am, usually."

Linnet had to admit that was so. And Lark did try the lad sorely.

"I hope you did not hurt her."

Falcon snorted. "Injure that imp? Impossible. She is the toughest and most terrifying person I know."

"Nay, Fal, your father is most terrifying." Falcon's father, Martin Scarlet—son of Will Scarlet, the legendary companion of Robin Hood—was a hard man, some might say devoid of mercy, and intimidating even to Linnet, who prided herself on her imperviousness to intimidation.

"Aye, well." For an instant Fal's sunny gaze clouded. "He has changed since Ma and Thrush died, and not for the better."

Linnet nodded. Nearly a year had passed since the Sheriff of Nottingham's men had come to Oakham looking for outlaws—or those harboring them—and burned half the dwellings to the ground with their inhabitants inside. Falcon's mother, Sally, and his young sister, Thrush, had perished. And his father had become honed, sharper, fiercer, and more deadly.

Linnet supposed, given all the grief he carried, she should not deny Fal his moments of tomfoolery, yet she had just lost a full morning's work. Among the three of them, all so close, she sometimes felt more a parent than a companion.

"Never mind," Fal said now, stepping closer to her and unleashing his full charm. "As the hell-spawn has fled, I will stay and help you clean up. Am I not a good lad?"

"You are a wicked lad, as ever. What of the tinctures I boiled down and bottled? What am I to say to your friends and neighbors when they come to me for a cure?"

"Say it is all Falcon's fault, and cure them with your beauty." His eyes wooed her now. He had stepped far too close, so she could smell the sunshine on his hair. Give Falcon Scarlet a chance, Linnet admitted wryly, or even half a chance, and he would always take full advantage. Since time out of mind he had sued Linnet's attention, and would not likely stop now.

"Run away with me, Lin," he whispered seductively. "You know you want to, in your heart." His gaze caressed her. "Or in some other place, still more interesting, about that lovely body."

"I do not want to." Linnet strove to sound stern.

"It is only a few days until midsummer," he

continued to persuade, "when lads and lasses get up to all sorts of wondrous wantonness." He widened his eyes in mock innocence. "I know I am up to it. Whenever I am near you, I am up—"

Hastily, Linnet interrupted him. "As if I would be fool enough to go anywhere with you."

He smiled persuasively. "Come, we will hare off to the depths of Sherwood and visit your parents."

"Oh, aye?" Again, Linnet lifted a brow. Her mother and father, Wren and Sparrow, along with Martin Scarlet, were the guardians who held safe the magic of Sherwood. Her parents lived the life of mystics and virtual hermits in the depths of the forest. An ancient place, the heart of Sherwood felt like another world to Linnet, even though she and Lark had been born and had spent their early childhood there. Sherwood's magic remained potent enough to touch them all. "Aye," Falcon whispered now, his lips but a breath from hers. "And on the way we shall catch the Green Man's ear and so pledge ourselves, and become man and wife."

"I have no wish to wed with you," Linnet said bluntly, striving to break the web of desire he wove so skillfully. Not that she had never thought about it. No woman could watch Falcon Scarlet draw a bow, move through the forest, or even ply a hoe without imagining what it would be like to be his. The lasses of Oakham followed him the way bees followed the scent of honeysuckle. Linnet had no idea how many of them had already tasted his sweetness.

"'Twould be like marrying my own blood kin," she protested. "You might as well wed Lark."

"Uff!" That backed him off a step and pricked his

ardor. "How can the two of you be so different, and you twins?" His eyes touched her again, and lingered. "You all woman and she more lad than lass."

"Aye, so." Linnet bent and began gathering broken crockery. "My father always says Sherwood blessed him twice in one blow, and in very different ways."

"You do not even look alike, save for the color of your hair."

True, also. Lark and Linnet had both inherited their mother's wild locks of deep brown. Lark had Wren's fierce eyes, as well, the golden gaze of a wolf or hawk. But Linnet had her father's dark eyes, thickly fringed with black lashes. Lark had been a tomboy from the time she could walk. She reached instinctively for the bow and wanted none of the knowledge Linnet sought, of herbs and healing.

Falcon seized both Linnet's hands, trapping a shard of broken pottery between them. "Why fight it, Lin? You know we are meant to be together, you and I. It is destined, ordained by the very magic of Sherwood. Why make me wait, unless you wish to drive me mad?"

"Is it ordained, though?" Linnet questioned, attempting to take a step back.

"We are members of the next triad, meant to guard Sherwood's magic," he said, suddenly grave, "you, Lark, and I. That is fact. And two of us will bond as only man and woman can, as did your father and mother. That you cannot deny."

Linnet's gaze challenged him. "What makes you think 'twill be you and I? Why not you and Lark?"

"Do not give me such nonsense." His fingers tightened on hers. "You know I love you, Linnet. I have since we were children and your parents brought the two of you out of the forest. Must I beg?"

Linnet had to admit the idea of Falcon Scarlet on his knees at her feet held some appeal. But never in her life had she been unkind.

"What you feel, my fine lad, is lust and not love."

"How can you say so? You do not know what is in my heart."

"Do I not? That is just it, Fal: I know you far too well. You truly are like a brother to me."

"If I am your brother, then my eyes should be put out for the incestuous thoughts I have of you. 'Twas difficult enough, Lin, when you were a girl and I watched you grow ever more beautiful. Now that you are a woman—" Something kindled bright in his eyes. "You must wed eventually, and you would not accept anyone else." He added a bit wildly, "There is no one else."

Linnet laughed and managed to pull her hands from his at last. "There are fine men in plenty, here in Oakham and all about Sherwood as well."

"There are." Falcon leaned close once more and whispered in her ear. "But none for you, Linnet Little. None, I say to you, but me."

Chapter Two

"So you decided to come home at last. Where have you been?" Linnet cast the words at her sister as Lark entered the cottage, bringing with her an air of sullen rebellion.

Linnet could sense Lark's mood most times. She did not know if that was because they were twins or because, as Falcon had said earlier, they were both members of the triad destined to one day guard the magic of Sherwood. Linnet knew her parents could sense one another's presence, catch one another's thoughts and, often, speak to each other mind to mind. She knew, also, they shared deep bonds with Martin Scarlet, the third member of the triad that even now held Sherwood's magic strong.

In any case, Lark's present mood assaulted Linnet, pricked at her senses, and virtually flooded the room.

Linnet had spent the entire afternoon in Lark's absence—both with Fal's assistance and without it—tidying away the mess made earlier and calculating her losses. Without question, Linnet ran the tiny dwelling the sisters shared in the village of Oakham. Never in her life had Lark tended a hearth; rarely did she prepare a meal. Thinking on it now, Linnet had to admit there was some validity in Falcon's estimation of her sister.

Lark would have made a fine lad. A bundle of pure fierceness in a small frame, she rarely backed down from anything and fought, always, with her whole heart. She could shoot an arrow better than most young men in the village, or beyond, and was no poor hand with a sword or sling. Long had she made herself one among those who went raiding and preying upon the travelers of Nottinghamshire. She was even a favorite of Martin Scarlet, who, Linnet would have said, favored virtually no one.

Now Linnet appraised Lark with a single glance: hair escaped from its braid and tangled, bare feet filthy, burrs caught in her clothing.

"You have been in the forest."

Lark flung herself down beside the hearth, somehow managing to display both arrogance and grace in one movement. "I had to be sure he was gone before I returned." Her voice, husky and smoky, reminded Linnet of their father, Sparrow Little. Sudden longing to see her parents tugged at her, as it so often did.

Wren and Sparrow had bidden their daughters choose, when they became old enough: life in the peaceful depths of Sherwood or in the quickened pace of the village at Oakham. Both had chosen the village. But for many years they had spent time, summers mostly, absorbing the ancient magic that dwelt, like their parents, deep among the trees. Linnet never doubted the love that dwelt there also, but she supposed all in all it had been a strange upbringing.

Not surprising, perhaps, that it had produced an unusual pair of women.

With that thought in mind, Linnet eyed her sister again. "Perhaps it is time you visited Mother and Father. It might do you good."

Lark gave Linnet a stare so sharp it might strip bark from a tree. "You say I should go? Why me, and not you also?"

"I have things to do here."

"Aye, and midsummer is upon us." Lark's golden gaze, now directed like a weapon, increased in heat. "And so you will not leave him."

"Him?"

"Falcon Scarlet." Lark spoke the name like an epithet.

"I do not know why you let him get under your skin so," Linnet said, exasperated. "Nor, quite, why you torment him so often."

Lark's lips twisted in a grimace. "Do you not?" She added with false sweetness, "And I thought you such an intelligent woman."

Surprise seized Linnet an instant before understanding. She abandoned her chores and sat down at her sister's side. "Lark, never say that you—" She found she could not quite speak the words.

Lark glared still harder. That stare said many things but screamed the truth only when it fell abruptly.

"Oh." Bits and pieces of wondering and conviction fell into place in Linnet's mind. "You—and Falcon?" To be sure, she had teased Fal with that very prospect but had never guessed what lay in her sister's heart. And that made a bold testament to Lark's skill at deception.

"No," Lark said bitterly, "not me and Falcon—just me." With miserable defiance, she added, "He does not see me, Lin, save as an annoyance. He has never really seen me."

A hard and undeniable truth. Dismay washed over

Linnet in a rush, for if Lark had gifted Falcon Scarlet her heart she faced an uphill battle, indeed.

"Why did you never tell me, Lark? All this time—how long?"

Lark shrugged irritably. "Forever. Does it matter? By any road, I should think you would have guessed. I would think anyone would guess, even a fool. Even *him.*"

"Falcon Scarlet is no fool." Whatever else he might be, Fal possessed a quick mind, which, in Linnet's estimation, numbered high among his other attributes.

She reached out and touched her sister's arm. She could feel Lark's tension, and the force of her spirit battling, within. "Lark, is this indeed why you are forever pestering and tormenting him? Why you plague him so mercilessly?"

"Why ask senseless questions if you already know the answers? His annoyance is better than no attention from him. And at least when we wrestle I can touch him." An incredible expression—one Linnet had never seen before—invaded Lark's eyes. In it combined desire and longing so intense it made Linnet catch her breath.

"Oh, Lark," she whispered.

Lark shot her a burning, rebellious look. "There is no hope for me, and I know it. 'Tis but a matter of time before he speaks for you." She broke off and then asked bitterly, "Or has he already? Do not try to deny it, Lin. You are a terrible bad liar. I can see everything in your eyes."

"He thinks he wants me. I am not so sure."

Lark raked her with another glare. "How could he fail to want you? You are everything a woman should be, soft and graceful, with healing in your hands. Not like me—a tiny, misbegotten throwback to our ancient ancestors who lived underground."

"You have your own beauty. Someday a man will come along with the wit to see it."

"I do not want 'a man.' I want Fal Scarlet."

"Well, then, love, perhaps we could work on your appearance just a tad, do something with your hair, and put you in a dress."

"Me, in a dress?" Lark had just forced an incredulous laugh when they both became aware of an uproar outside the house, the sound of many voices raised. A hand pushed the cottage door open and a head appeared—that of Falcon Scarlet himself.

"Come swiftly, Lin. One of our raiding parties has just returned. They have a prisoner—and a plum picking at that. He is injured, in need of tending, so my pa says."

Both young women leaped to their feet. Linnet's heart began to pound for reasons she could not understand.

"A prisoner?" she echoed.

Fal's teeth flashed in a wicked smile. "A Norman, and high born, to judge by his fine clothing. 'Norman git,' my pa says, and no doubt worth a high ransom."

He withdrew, and the sisters exchanged speaking glances. Lark swore and ran out ahead of Linnet, who paused to gather supplies, her hands suddenly unsteady.

This could only mean trouble of the worst kind. "May the Green Man be with me," she muttered as she hurried out the door.

Chapter Three

"Silence, you stinking pile of Norman offal! You will speak when you are asked a question and not before, or are you too stupid to understand?"

The words came accompanied by a blow, and not the first Gareth de Vavasour had received from the man who stood above him. It knocked him sideways into the dust, and he gritted his teeth against the ensuing pain. Determinedly he fought to remain silent; he suspected his left arm must be broken—better that than his right, his sword arm. But his injuries had not kept these feral bastards from binding his wrists behind him, and the agony of any movement made him want to retch. He battled that down also. He would not give these Saxon villains the satisfaction of witnessing his pain.

His uncle, Robert de Vavasour—current Sheriff of Nottingham—was right about these serfs he said infested his domain. He had told Gareth they lived, bred, and behaved like vermin, without scruples or morals. From all Gareth had seen this afternoon, he could but agree.

And this ruffian who now stood over him seemed the worst of the lot. Tall, with a wild mop of gray-blond hair and an even wilder beard, he was head of the band that had seized Gareth on the road to Nottingham. He bore a face full of scars and the fiercest pair of eyes Gareth had ever seen. They fairly spewed hate.

Gareth wondered how many of his party now lay dead—killed by the band of outlaws who had taken him. In the company of a strong troop of soldiers, Gareth had been escorting a shipment of tax money and valuables, bound south from York, while journeying to join his uncle's home guard at Nottingham. He had seen at least two men fall. Who would have thought mere peasants brandishing staffs and stolen swords could fight so well?

He did not doubt he now found himself in the very depths of trouble. At best, he would be held for ransom. At worst, the scarred madman looming above him would give in to the desire that shone from his eyes and cut Gareth's throat.

Where was he? Thrown down at the center of a village, he had no way to tell. It looked a poor place of wooden houses and wandering chickens. Folk came streaming from every doorway, precisely like the rats his uncle had described, and stood staring at him. Small children with their thumbs in their mouths blinked, as at some new entertainment.

Gareth strove to keep the disdain he felt from showing on his face. He supposed a thing like his imminent murder would prove exciting to such cretins as these. Ah, but he did not want to die! He had far too much he longed to accomplish first.

Even as that conviction took form in his heart, he listened to the discussion taking place over his head.

"We took them on the York Road," cried one of the younger men proudly. "A stout company they were, but not stout enough. We fell upon them—whack, wham! And what were they but a band toting the Sheriff's treasure? We took a coffer filled to the brim with coin and a smaller casque crammed with jewels."

Gareth closed his eyes briefly and choked down his humiliation. From whence had they come? The trees that bordered the road? The ground itself? He still could not tell, and he had been on watch. The peasants had seemed to materialize from the air of the dense, hot afternoon, to appear out of the green leaves overhead.

"And this prize." The fair-haired madman kicked Gareth in the side, not gently.

"Aye, he will be worth a bit, will he not? Along with the Sheriff's ill-gotten hoard."

"The King's taxes," Gareth said in a voice like dust. He lifted his eyes and directed a stare at the evil faces that surrounded him. "You have transgressed against your king. That is treason."

They laughed—the last reaction Gareth expected. Aye, when his uncle sent for him, he had indicated the task at hand—chasing down and eradicating the miscreants who infested Sherwood—was a fierce one. Gareth recalled how the letter had gone.

Now that you have finished your training and have some service under your belt, I beg your foster father release you. I need your assistance in Nottingham in eradicating a plague.

And so Gareth found himself in the center of the contagion and not likely to get away out of it alive.

"Aye, and what are you worth, my fine peacock?" The scarred visage came closer as its owner bent and seized Gareth by the hair. "Tell us your exalted Norman name."

"We could torture it from him." The suggestion came, shockingly, from a woman, a rawboned creature with a ravaged face. "No more than he deserves,

15

Martin."

So—his captor's name was Martin, was it? Gareth tucked that information away in his mind for future contemplation. And he appeared to be headman of this pest hole.

"Nay, we cannot do that, not half," Martin replied, "else we would have nothing with which to bargain. I do not doubt this delicate flower would wilt under strong questioning. Whoever he is, I do believe de Vavasour will pay to get him back." The man smiled a terrible smile. "Whole, more or less."

"Takes a lot to kill a man," speculated a fellow from the far side of the human fence that now surrounded Gareth. "I dare say we could hack him apart bit by bit without killing him."

"I dare say. Put your knife away, Micah." For the last speaker had drawn a wicked blade. "We cannot so indulge ourselves, yet."

"Let me take one of his pretty Norman ears to send de Vavasour. A little bloodletting will do him good."

"He is already bleeding freely," the headman pointed out. "That wound to the shoulder does not look good, nor the one to his leg. He fought well," the man added grudgingly, "for a piece of shite."

He leaned down and once more virtually spat into Gareth's face, "Aye, that rankles, does it not? I suppose you are a fine champion among your own kind. Much good that does you against the likes of us."

Gareth was spared the need to answer by the appearance of a lad who pushed his way through those gathered to stare at him. Gareth's eyes narrowed abruptly. Nay, no lad this but a woman clad in a lad's clothing. Tiny, she was, with a head of wild, dark-brown hair tangled with burrs and a golden yellow gaze as dangerous as a raised weapon.

She looked like she wanted to flay him alive, and he would not put it past her.

What manner of folk were these that inhabited the fringes of Sherwood, who dressed their women as men and gave their children the spectacle of torture for amusement?

Before he could decide, a second woman appeared. This one wore the proper clothing of a peasant, a plain brown dress covered with a rough, tan smock. Tall, willowy and lovely, she carried a bundle in her hands.

She paused when she sighted him as if she had run into a wall, and her eyes met his with the force of a blow.

"By the Green Man's horns," she breathed. "Thank all goodness you have not killed him yet."

****

"This will hurt," the woman told Gareth, and he caught his breath. Each time she had told him so, it had proved true, and he believed her now. He braced himself for more pain and told himself he was nowhere near the end of his endurance. Was he not a proven knight? Had he not endured broken bones before, been tossed in the lists and taken many a hard fall?

Aye, but then he had only needed to get to his feet and weather his injuries. He had not been surrounded by a pack of carrion ravens.

True, he found himself, now, alone inside a dim hut with this woman. But he knew the scavengers still lurked outside—he could hear at least two men just beyond the door, no doubt guarding it, and talking to one another. The other noise outside had not abated.

Folk seemed excited by the proposed spectacle of his death.

But would they provide him this care only to kill him? The woman—Linnet, he had heard someone call her—had skill in her hands, quick and gentle. Already she had set his broken arm and now worked over the ugly wound at his shoulder, which brought her very close to him, indeed. She poured some vile-smelling liquid into the wound, and he caught his breath sharply.

She had not lied: it hurt.

"That will help keep the poisoning from setting in," she said with brief asperity.

"Does it matter? They wish only to kill me, that crowd out there. They will never send me to Nottingham, even should a ransom be paid." He stole another look into her face. Nothing like he had imagined a Saxon peasant, she was entirely surprising. Aye, some of their women were bonny and reputedly lustful, with bountiful yellow locks and still more bountiful bosoms. None of that fit this woman at all.

Her face floated above him, a pure, almost perfect oval. Most of her dark brown hair lay gathered under a head covering, but her brows soared like two dark wings over eyes so beautiful and unusual he scarcely dared look into them. Fringed by the longest lashes he had ever seen, they appeared liquid dark, bottomless and wild. In truth, she felt wild withal, despite her neat clothing, a foreign creature not meant for this place. Yet her hands remained kind and calm, her face serene—an intriguing contrast.

"They will not kill you," she said softly. "Though it will go better with you if you tell them your name so they can send word to Nottingham."

Gareth shook his head.

A slight frown marred her smooth brow. "A word of advice—you will tell them, sooner or later. Spare yourself their persuasion."

"Torture, is it? As might be expected of cowards."

She withdrew slightly. "If you think those people out there cowards, you know nothing about them." In defiance of her hard words, her fingers slid over his skin, applying some sort of unguent before pressing a cloth bandage in place.

To Gareth's surprise, he felt a prick of arousal. This was not the time, the place, nor the woman—beautiful as she might be.

Someone—a man—thrust his head inside the open door of the hut. "All right, Linnet?"

"Aye. I am nearly done."

Briskly now, her hands moved to the rent at his thigh. Once more he caught his breath, though not against pain this time.

The wound there, he knew, was a grave one—had it landed a bit farther to the left, he might well never lay a woman again. She tore the cloth further asunder, only to find she had exposed more than the wound. She tipped back on her heels, and a lovely, deep color swept her face.

Her eyes met Gareth's in a look so deep and dark it pierced him to his soul. A wave of feeling rose between them, bright and intense. So powerful was it, for an instant Gareth almost supposed he could sense her thoughts, every whit as entangled as his own.

"Ah," she said softly. "I will be as quick as I can."

"Aye," he said in a voice that sounded strangled. And just as well.

Chapter Four

"I do not want you alone with him again, Linnet. 'Tis not safe, nor proper."

Linnet raised her gaze to Falcon, who paced the floor of her tiny hut like a caged beast. Morning had come and with it a renewed sense of purpose. The village council had met, led by its headman, Martin Scarlet. And Fal had invaded her cottage with trouble in his eyes.

That was the problem with Fal, Linnet reflected even as she gathered supplies to take to her patient—he was far too perceptive and intelligent to miss much. She knew he had been standing guard at the door and then hovering in the doorway itself yester evening when that exchange took place between herself and their prisoner, and it had raised all his instincts.

Truth be known, it had roused a few of Linnet's, as well. She could not say exactly what had taken place between her and the young Norman captive. She only knew something had.

"Do not be foolish," she chided Fal now. "I am a healer. Of course I must tend him."

Fal shot her a wild look. "Let someone else do it. I do not trust you alone with him."

"And why, Falcon Scarlet, would you fail to trust me?"

Fal scowled. "Not you—I misspoke. 'Tis him I do

not trust." In the dim interior of the cottage, Fal's eyes glowed green-blue and nearly feral.

"What harm can he do?"

"Aye, now there is the question. He might easily seize hold of you and wring your neck."

"But he has a broken arm, as well as two other wounds to hamper him." He had a beautiful body, as well, and Linnet had seen more of it, last night, than she dared remember. A well-muscled chest sprinkled with light brown hair, smooth, tanned skin, and, below, muscular thighs. Ruthlessly, she pushed from her mind the image of what else lay below, which she had also glimpsed. But her fingers tingled again just thinking on it. The man might be a Norman and poisoned fruit, but he made a potent temptation.

Truth to tell, she had never before been so near one of her detested overlords. She had never gazed into one's eyes, nor caught his scent. She shivered even now in response.

Fighting the feeling, she spoke to Fal briskly. "I was not alone with him yester e'en. I knew very well you were there in the doorway. Come along with me now, if you will."

"I will, but Linnet..." Falcon came close and touched her arm. "I do not like this. You know what he is. He does not deserve your care but should be tied to a tree and left to die."

Linnet looked into Fal's face and said gravely, "This is not like you." She knew Falcon Scarlet to his bones. He was not a cruel man but for the most part a light spirit, full of joy. Now she barely recognized the expression in his eyes.

"That bastard and his kind killed my mother and

sister and have brought suffering to countless other good folk."

"Aye but not he, surely."

"They are all one. Never forget that, Lin—they are all one."

****

The interior of the hut was small and dim. A shelter for ailing beasts needing to be kept apart from other stock, it had been hastily cleaned out last night, save for some straw, and still contained an aroma of goats. As Linnet stepped in with Fal at her side, she saw the captive had been provided no comforts. He lay on the dirt floor with his good arm tethered to a spike in the wall. Linnet would not see a dog treated so, especially an injured one.

He started up when they entered but could not move far, the tether being cruelly short. In the morning light that streamed in through the door, he looked wan, his fine clothing sullied and torn. But his gaze met Fal's like a raised weapon and only moved to Linnet's face after.

What fine eyes they were—steady and bright, set under level brows, and of a color pale as clear water, a true gray. His hair spilled, mussed, across his brow, golden brown, straight, and shining with health.

Aye, and a privileged life he had no doubt led, Linnet reminded herself. No hungry days for him, and no pinched nights in winter, listening to children cry from want. As Fal said, she needed to remember what he was.

She glanced at Fal, for she could feel the hate streaming from him. He had drawn his knife and looked ready to defend her to the death. Her lips curved wryly.

Foolish men.

She went forward and set her bundle on the floor, appraising her patient as she did. He might wish to appear undaunted and fearless, yet she saw the lines of pain in his face and the way he coddled his broken arm against his chest. It had been brutal to tether him. With his left arm broken and that deep wound to his right shoulder, the strain must be nearly unbearable.

"Cut him loose," she told Fal.

"I will not. Tend him where he lies."

"Impossible. I need to change the dressing on that shoulder. No doubt being bound so has torn the wound open."

"Leave him lie, I say. It is no more than he deserves."

Someone came pushing in behind Falcon and blotted out the light, a tall, looming presence: Martin Scarlet.

He spoke in an ugly tone. "I cannot but agree with you, lad, but unfortunately he is too valuable to die, shite as he may be." Fal's father spat and the spittle landed beside the captive's knee. "Besides, he has a long day of torture ahead of him, and I would see him fortified."

The prisoner never flinched. If anything, his silvery eyes gleamed brighter in defiance.

"What is the sense in me tending him if you mean only to hack him apart again?" Linnet asked. She knew what happened to Norman captives. She had grown up amid what Martin Scarlet and her parents called a forest war, fought continuously. Despite repeated requests and demands for the rights Linnet's people felt they were due, the Normans kept the peasantry down through a combination of brutality and want. The Saxon folk fought back in any way they could, and there was very little mercy on either side.

She had seen Norman captives questioned before— soldiers, traveling members of the clergy, even nobles seized on the road. She had witnessed the work of this man now standing beside her. Martin Scarlet's hate tended to be checked only by his cunning.

Many a terrible thing could happen to this young man before he found his way back to his own kind, so long as he remained alive.

It turned Linnet sick inside. Deliberately, she turned her gaze away from those wide, gray eyes.

"What of the men who were with me?" the prisoner asked in his clear, steady voice. "Have you murdered them all?"

Martin Scarlet gave a tight smile, a terrible thing on his scarred face. "Not all. We spent the night questioning them, two of those who survived the raid in the forest."

The prisoner drew an audible breath but said nothing.

"One of them," Martin said deliberately, "is almost ready to speak. He does not endure agony well."

Emotion flickered in the gray eyes—anger and perhaps disdain. He must have heard the screams last night, Linnet reflected. They had kept her awake.

"Think on it," Martin told him shortly. "Or pray, if you feel so inclined. He may yet speak and spare you your own ordeal."

The prisoner reared back his head. "Cowards. Pagans, speaking of prayer. Have you no decency?"

"Decency?" Martin repeated the word. "Shall I

show it to you?" Deliberately, he delivered a blow to the captive's face that swayed him. "All the decency has been bled from us by your kind." He turned burning eyes on Linnet. "Tend him, lass. Be certain he does not die on us beforetimes."

Martin pushed past his son to the door. "Stay with them, Fal, and make sure he does not so much as look at her wrong."

The prisoner stared after him, livid weals springing forth on his cheek and blood welling at the corner of his mouth.

Linnet looked at Falcon. "Cut him loose. I must see to that wound."

Fal hesitated. Then, brandishing his knife, he stepped forward and cut through the tether that bound the captive to the wall.

The Norman made an involuntary sound as his injured arm dropped and pulled on his rent shoulder. He turned white as milk.

"Do your work swiftly, Lin."

"I will. But move out of my light. How can I see what I am doing?"

Fal stepped to the door and left Linnet in possession of the cramped space. She could still hear him breathing.

She dropped to her knees beside the prisoner and opened her bundle. Determinedly, she avoided looking into the man's eyes.

"Let us see that shoulder first," she murmured. Already, fresh blood soaked the rent fabric there; last night's bandages had bled through. Were this man not so young and strong, Martin Scarlet might well end up cheated of his opportunity for torture.

The prisoner said nothing but tensed himself when she pulled off the soaked bandages and examined the wound. If anything, it looked worse than last night.

After several moments' silent struggle, he suddenly asked, "Who is that man with the scarred face?"

Linnet's hands froze momentarily. Leaning forward to tend him, she found herself very nearly in his arms. Their eyes met and, abruptly, the feeling sprang up between them again, vital and real.

No, she thought to herself even as her spirit cried within her and her breath caught in her throat. *No, and again no.*

"He is our headman," she replied softly, as her fingers resumed their work. "You need not know his name."

A tight smile curled his lips. Fine lips they were, now surrounded by a growth of golden-brown beard. Linnet focused on them because she dared not lose herself in those eyes. "Need not know the name of the man who means to kill me?"

"He will not do that. I told you last night."

"I heard what you said, but I have also seen the look in his eyes."

"No speaking." Fal leaned in the door. "You will not talk to her."

"Get out of my light, Fal."

Falcon's golden head disappeared. Abruptly, there came another interruption as Falcon protested and was shoved out of the way. A small figure erupted into the shelter: Lark, with her eyes wild and her hair loose and flying.

"So he survives," she cried, her eyes all over the prisoner even as Falcon pushed in behind, "our noble prize, valuable beyond measure."

Falcon asked, "What are you talking about?"

Lark turned to look into his eyes. "One of the soldiers your father has been busy questioning all night has broken—babbled like a frightened child." She glared at the man who had gone so still beneath Linnet's hands. "It seems this fine buck is nephew to the Sheriff of Nottingham, and will surely bring us the highest price we have ever taken in ransom."

Chapter Five

"Surely they will not kill him now," Lark said with barely-disguised enjoyment, "much as Martin may wish to. He will be used roughly, no question, but returned to his accursed uncle in more or less one piece." She cast a look at her sister, who busied herself at the hearth. "I will confess, I looked forward to seeing his pretty head on a pike."

Linnet shuddered. It seemed she had been in a state of constant upheaval since learning the identity of the injured captive. Had he been a Norman soldier or even some other noble's son, the situation would have been bad enough. But the hated Sheriff Robert de Vavasour's blood kin? He might as well be the devil incarnate.

Damn his handsome gray eyes.

She said with asperity, "You should not gloat. His head on a pike, indeed—that is a man of whom you speak."

"No, Lin, it is a stinking Norman of which I speak. Never deceive yourself. Have you forgotten the things his uncle has done? Burned the cottage of a dying woman for a few pence taxes, for theft taken the hand of a poor widow with young babes to feed, imprisoned Derek Sawyer in that vile pit called a dungeon in Nottingham, and his wife left to grieve with a dead child?"

"I have forgotten none of that," Linnet said bitterly.

"But I am not certain the proper answer to hate is more hate."

"You have grown soft in doing your healing. You have lost your warrior's heart."

Linnet turned from the hearth and leveled a look at her sister. "And you have lost your womanly compassion."

Lark, who lounged on the floor, held up both hands. "Do I look like I ever abounded with womanly compassion?"

Linnet had to admit she did not. Lark might have been one of the lads who ran about Oakham, her hair once more braided and confined beneath a leather cap, her clothing a smaller version of what Fal commonly wore. She looked all warrior.

Lark's mood changed with the swiftness of lightning. "Fal certainly does not think there is anything womanly about me."

"Back to that, are we?" Linnet asked, caught by the change of subject. "What can you expect when you dress like a woodcutter's son and go about with the men, drinking and swearing? There is that gown of yours, tucked away in the chest. I have said I will dress your hair for you. You do have lovely hair when it is combed out."

Lark met the suggestions with a bright, golden stare mutinous as that of any child. "You think to make me something I am not. Would you have me win Fal on the basis of a lie?"

"From what you have said, I thought you would win him any way you might."

Lark linked her fingers together and showed them to Linnet. "The three of us—you, me, and Falcon—our

29

lives are enmeshed like this. From the time of our births we have been meant to form the magical three, with two of us binding in the flesh and one binding to Sherwood itself. That is destined." Lark hesitated. "No, I have no objection to binding with Sherwood. I will admit, I feel at home there as nowhere else. The trees are my solace. But, sister, I want a real flesh-and-blood man between my legs."

"Lark!" Linnet exclaimed, shocked despite herself.

Lark's lips twisted. "Why should I lie about it? It is hard enough deceiving Fal, especially since if he plays stud to anyone it will be you."

Linnet abandoned her work and sat beside her sister. Softly, she confided, "The truth is, I do not want him."

Lark's fierce gaze flew to Linnet's face. "Are you mad? What more could you want?"

The image of a lean face arose before Linnet's mind's eye, shining golden-brown hair and that long, tanned body, gray eyes so clear she swore she could see her future in them. Impossible. Surely the Sheriff would not hesitate to ransom his nephew. He would be gone before she knew it, back to the privileged life he enjoyed, far beyond her ken. Better, far better, to forget about him now, and spare her heart.

****

"Your uncle is Robert de Vavasour, Sheriff of Nottingham, no? And your name is de Vavasour also? Gareth de Vavasour, we have been told."

Three men, headed by the fellow with the scarred face and merciless eyes, stood over Gareth on his tether. The second was the young man who had accompanied the healer, Linnet, to tend him. The third

Gareth had never seen before, but he stank. Even from his place hard against the wall, Gareth smelled the blood on him, and a reek of burning.

Ah, so they had brought their torturer. Gareth hauled on his courage and tried to ignore the way his balls crawled up toward his belly. He swore, whatever they did to him, he would not break. He was a Norman knight, and proven.

"He does not speak," said the third man, in the leather apron stained with gore. Was he a blacksmith when he was not hacking apart his betters?

"Aye, but he will," said Scarface with some satisfaction.

"Where are the men who were seized along with me?" Gareth asked. His voice sounded hoarse. He had been afforded one cup of water in all the time he had been held, and his mouth felt dry, his tongue thick.

"One is dead. The other has given us all the information we need."

"What do you want from me, then?"

"A token," said Scarface. "Something of yours to send to your uncle, that he will recognize."

Despair flooded Gareth's heart. He strove mightily to keep it from showing. "You may as well kill me now," he said.

Scarface kicked him. The blow, aimed at Gareth's ribs, pulled at muscles already drawn unbearably by his bonds. He received the punishment silently and glared into his captor's eyes.

Scarface grinned one of the most terrible smiles Gareth had ever seen. "Be of good cheer," he said. "The bastard de Vavasour, being your blood kin, will want you back. You will not enjoy our hospitality long."

Gareth's thoughts flew, seeking some way to use this to his advantage, finding none. Grudgingly he said, "My uncle barely knows me."

"Eh?" the torturer ejected.

"We have not met since I was four years old. I was raised in Leeds and fostered in York for my training. I was on my way now to take up service with my uncle when you interrupted my journey." His first station, and it came to this. Humiliation burned in him. All those years sweating and training, proving himself a worthy champion, and it availed him nothing.

"A fine lie, that, to save yourself," said Scarface disdainfully.

"I ask to be spared nothing. It is no lie."

"Send the uncle an ear," said the torturer. He drew a stained blade from his apron and fingered it contemplatively. "Or an eye."

Still Gareth strove to show this pack of dogs no fear.

The younger man spoke for the first time. "They took his weapons from him, Pa, when he was hauled in. He had a knife with a distinctive crest. Perhaps de Vavasour will know that."

Ah, so the Saxon buck with the wild hair was Scarface's son. Gareth eyed him as he might any opponent, sure he could take the fellow in a fair fight. Of course, that was not likely, given he was tethered and had a broken arm.

"Bring it," Scarface snapped and the younger man hurried off.

"I need the privy," Gareth stated. He had already pissed in the corner, but now another need became pressing. He was cursed if he would beg, but had these brutes no common decency?

Scarface tossed his head. "Bring him a bucket, Tim—he shall enjoy our finest accommodation. Never let it be said we offer fewer comforts than are afforded in the dungeons at Nottingham Castle."

The torturer went out.

Scarface took a step forward and seized Gareth by the hair. "So, my fine cock, it is just the two of us alone, and no one watching." He hauled Gareth's head back cruelly and drew his own knife. In a vicious movement he laid it not to Gareth's throat but the corner of his left eye.

"I could do it, you know—pluck your pretty eyes from your head, easy as spitting. Then how would you ride to the lists again? 'Tis what you are, is it not? A Norman knight—as vile a creature as ever trod the blessed soil of Sherwood."

Gareth said nothing. He scarcely dared breathe.

"It is your kind killed my wife—may the Green Man rest her sweet soul—and my young daughter whose life had barely begun. It is your kind slew the very justice of England, and who ruin everything they touch. Do you think a day of reckoning will not come? Do you think it cannot come for you now?"

Gareth shuddered, an involuntary movement. "Go ahead and do it," he said against his better judgment. He did not want to die and he did not want to live blind. But defiance was his only weapon.

He felt the point of the knife bite into the corner of his eye. In one vicious movement, Scarface dragged it downward, scoring a line on Gareth's cheek. Still holding Gareth's hair, the man grinned.

"How does that feel, eh?" He gestured with the

knife. "I know well how it feels. Who do you think gave me these?"

He waved the knife at his own scarred face. He looked so terrible at that moment—so like a demon—Gareth found it hard to believe he had ever possessed a wife or daughter.

But as if to emphasize the truth of it, the tall, fair-haired young man reentered the shed carrying Gareth's own dagger.

His quick eyes moved from his father's face to Gareth's, down which now ran a thin line of blood.

"Pa? I have the knife. It bears some sort of crest. Surely de Vavasour will recognize it."

Scarface let go of Gareth's hair and turned to his son. One of his brown thumbs rubbed across the insignia of Gareth's house.

"I have seen this symbol before." He asked Gareth, "What is it?"

Gareth, fighting down waves of rage, loathing and—were he truthful—the aftermath of powerful fear, said nothing.

"Answer me. Or must I cut you again?"

"Do as you will," Gareth replied.

"Pa, it was on the bridle of his horse, this same sign. And I think I have seen it on de Vavasour's banners when he rides out."

"Aye, to be sure—I remember now. We shall send this to de Vavasour, let him know we hold his fine pup of a nephew."

He swung round and looked Gareth in the eye. "It seems you will not die after all, Champion—at least not today."

Chapter Six

"I hear word has been sent to Nottingham. You will be released soon." Linnet spoke the words softly as she stepped once more into the tiny shed. Twice this day had she asked Martin Scarlet for permission to tend the prisoner. Twice had he refused until now, as night gathered, he had bidden her to fetch her supplies and go.

"I suppose we cannot let him die before we get full value out of him," he said in a hard tone, and eyed her sternly. "Be sure and not go in there alone."

"I will take Falcon."

But Fal was nowhere to be found, and Lark, still restless and apparently bored, volunteered to come. She stood in the doorway behind Linnet now, her knife in hand, and wrinkled her nose.

"Stinks in here. Smells of Norman swine."

In truth, it stank of the bucket that had been provided for the captive's needs. He had been forced to use it and, due to his tether and the size of the place, could not get far from it.

Linnet could barely see him in the deepening gloom. He stirred when she stepped closer to him, but he did not speak.

"Lark, get this out of here." Linnet snatched the bucket by its handle and thrust it at her sister, who recoiled.

"I am no servant to any Norman."

"Just empty it, pray. And bring a light."

Lark grunted and went. Linnet and the Norman were alone save for the guard outside, and the quiet gloom.

"How do you feel?" she asked.

"I have rarely been better." His voice sounded thin, worn with strain and probably pain, as well. Linnet told herself not to feel sympathetic. He was, after all, her enemy.

Still softly, she went on, "I am told your name is Gareth de Vavasour." Enemy, indeed. "And that you will soon be offered in exchange."

"For what, do you know? Will they ask ransom?"

"Perhaps." Linnet set her bundle on the floor. "And, I believe, the release of some folk who are being held unjustly."

"And if my uncle refuses to make the trade?"

"Surely that will not happen." Linnet could not imagine it. Who would leave his blood kin in enemy hands? And how desperately she wanted him gone, for he played havoc with her good sense. In his proximity, she found herself wanting all sorts of things she should not.

A flare of light erupted behind her and Lark came in carrying a torch and the empty bucket, which she tossed into the corner.

"Still stinks in here," she said. "Must be the occupant."

Linnet barely heard her sister. She was busy examining the patient with dismay. He looked much the worse for wear, his long limbs obviously cramped and the bandages at his shoulder once more stained. But it was not that which made her catch her breath. A thin, oozing cut marred his left cheek from the corner of his eye nearly to the corner of his mouth.

"Who did this to you?" Linnet felt her anger ignite and with it protectiveness, so strong it frightened her. No wound taken fairly in battle, this had been inflicted on a man already injured and tied and, as such, qualified in her eyes as base torture.

He did not answer, merely looked at her with those clear, gray eyes now flooded by light.

"Hold that torch steady, Lark." Linnet reached for her bundle and unrolled it with suddenly tense hands. She did not lose herself to anger often. When she did, it burned bright.

Lark swore and thrust the torch through a bracket just inside the door. "If you mean to mother him, I will not stay."

"I care not whether you stay or go."

Lark leaned against the doorpost. "On the other hand, I should remain on hand to make sure he does not wring your neck."

Gareth de Vavasour shot Lark a glare that indicated he would rather throttle her.

"Stop with your bluster," Linnet told her sister. "Cut him loose so I can see to that shoulder."

Lark did not argue it. She stepped forward and cut the tether with a slash of her knife.

"Looks like someone has already been at him with a blade."

"Hush, and let me think." Linnet found that curiously hard to do within reach of the Norman. Being near him worked to scatter her thoughts, like a spell of bad magic. Her fingers began to tingle; she found herself focusing not on his shoulder wound but that at his thigh, and the rent in his leggings that offered such an excellent view of what lay beneath.

She had seen naked men before. To be sure, she had seen Falcon Scarlet naked, which was naught to scoff at. During the heady days of other Midsummers, when the lads went skinny dipping in the village pond, she and the other maids spied, shameless, on all they had to offer. It had been impossible not to admire Fal's long, lean body with all its fascinating appendages.

But not so fascinating as the reactions stirred by this man now under her hands, nor the spear of titillation, almost like pain, that stabbed through her at the sight of his male perfection.

Nay, not so perfect, now—even as she peeled the dressing away from his shoulder, her eyes returned to his face. She supposed many a knight bore such scars—some, like the village men, probably even wore them like badges of courage.

So why did this anger her so?

Her hands shook as she poured unguent onto a soft cloth. "This will hurt," she told him.

Behind her, Lark snorted. "Better pour salt into it," she advised. "Pain him all you can."

Gareth drew a hard breath when she applied the unguent but made no other sound. Linnet's heightened senses seemed able to feel him, though—so intensely she fancied she could guess his thoughts. He held on hard to his few remaining shreds of dignity, one of which came of silence. He detested Lark and no doubt Linnet, as well. And he was not about to lower his guard before them.

She redressed the shoulder as carefully as she

could. Despite his ill-treatment, it showed some signs of scabbing.

"Lie down," she bade him then.

He questioned her with those incredible eyes.

"'Twill be easier for me to see to your leg if you are stretched out."

Lark snorted again, in derision. Linnet, who lost her temper but rarely, and with her sister more than anyone else, rounded on her. "If you mean to jeer at me, you can take yourself off."

"Need you coddle him like a week-old infant? He is a demon, like all his kind, lest you forget."

"I forget nothing, including the fact that I am a healer. How I practice my craft is dictated only by myself and the one who gives the skill to my hands."

"No need to make a great mystery of it. Just do the work and get away out of this reek."

Linnet resisted the urge to hurl the bucket at her sister. She turned her shoulder. "Run and bring me more bandaging, will you? I did not bring enough."

Lark flicked her gaze over the supplies, and did not unprop herself from the doorway. "It looks sufficient."

"Just go." Difficult enough to tend her patient without the added burden of Lark's discerning gaze. Linnet felt as if the walls of the tiny place closed in on her. She shot Lark another look and added more gently, "Please."

Lark went. Gareth de Vavasour stretched his long limbs in the limited space allowed. Linnet, focusing on the wound at his thigh, told herself he might be anyone: the smith with yet another nasty burn, a child with a skinned knee, not this man with his beautiful body. But her unsteady hands proved she did not believe it.

"This will hurt," she said again, and pulled off the dressing.

The wound looked angrier than the one at his shoulder and showed red and swollen in the torch light. She spoke a small prayer under her breath for guidance and felt his eyes return to her face. The muscles of his thigh quivered under her hands.

Did he feel what she felt? Was he, too, touched by this wild, unaccountable attraction? Or was she just a peasant to him, a Saxon and beneath his notice?

She had once seen a troop of Norman knights ride over a flock of Saxon children who did not move out of their way quickly enough, scattering and crushing them like leaves, and with as little regard. Of course this man, a Norman champion, held no regard for her. Why should he?

Yet her thoughts leaped like flames as she cleaned and dressed this wound, her fingers working at the rent in his leggings, the back of her hand actually brushing up against his manhood at one point. He caught his breath then and she told herself it was against the pain. But when the dressing had been placed, they were both breathing hard.

Lark was taking an unaccountably long time fetching that bandaging. Linnet found herself glad. She slid up beside Gareth de Vavasour's shoulder and touched his cheek with one finger.

"Who did this to you?"

"Does it matter?" His voice sounded hoarse. She must have hurt him much, even though she had tried to be gentle.

She said nothing, merely poured more unguent onto a pad and pressed it to his face. The motion brought her close above where he lay. They might almost be lovers, she thought, he sprawled upon a cot and she bending in to bestow a long and luxuriant kiss. How she would delight in the chance to taste him, trace those lips with her tongue and test the flavor of his skin.

By the Green Man's horns! She never entertained such thoughts. Anyway, there was no bed, only this filthy dirt floor, and his pain.

His free hand, untethered, came up and caught her wrist. It made the first time he had touched her voluntarily, and the impact of it made her eyes fly to his.

Did he mean to harm her? But no, for his touch was gentle, and rather than fear she felt— Best not put a name to that surge of emotion.

"What did she mean," he whispered, "the woman with the fierce eyes? What, when she said you need not make a mystery out of healing me? And you—who is this 'one' you say gives healing to your hands?"

Linnet gazed into his eyes and answered simply, "The giver of all life, the power, the magic that dwells in Sherwood. The Green Man."

"I do not understand."

"She speaks of the living being that is Sherwood itself," said Lark's voice from the doorway, "that we guard so well from your ruinous kind. Now leave go of my sister, if you would live to breathe another day."

Chapter Seven

"Haul him out here into the daylight. There is someone who wishes to take a look at him."

Hard hands seized Gareth de Vavasour from where he leaned against the wattle wall. A blade cut his tether and he was dragged, for the first time since his capture, from the foul-smelling enclosure.

How many days had he been here? He thought it must be three, but he might be mistaken. Time blurred when he slipped in and out of consciousness. Almost no food and precious little water had been provided during that time. But the woman with the beautiful dark eyes had come to tend him thrice.

He had dreamed of her last night, a disturbing dream that came in pieces and then refused to release him. She had bent over him, her dark hair loosed from its cap, flowing down. The front of her bodice had been loosened also, an offering of the soft temptations within. She had laid her lips upon his, fused her mouth to his, called up something within him so powerful it scorched his soul. She had summoned his spirit to her bidding with magical ease.

From this vision had the cruel hands torn him. Now he stumbled out into the summer dawning and confronted a ring of faces. Mist rose all around, nearly obscuring the huts that clustered beneath the trees. It seemed as if the forest breathed visibly, and all else wavered amidst it.

Gareth shook his head. The dream had addled his wits. Clearly, this was no fit time for fancy. He scanned the circle for danger and for a single face among the many—Linnet's face—and found only the danger. Scarface was there, and he wore an odd expression that resembled gloating. His accursed and ever-present son stood at his side, and there was the lass with the fierce, yellow eyes, the one who was the healer's sister, though they did not look much alike.

They had the same, rich dark brown hair, aye, but there all similarity ended. No one could ever mistake Linnet for anything other than a woman. Her narrow, gentle hands, her graceful form, even the scent of her, all declared it.

The sister clad herself like a boy and went about bedecked with enough weapons to stock a small arsenal. Tiny and with that fearsome gaze, she seemed to harbor enough hate for both sisters.

Gareth dismissed her now with an arrogant lift of his chin. His head might well swim with weakness, he might ache to his toes, his injured leg might threaten to go out from under him, but he would be damned if he would let these dogs see any of it.

"He looks young for a proven knight," a man said. Something about the voice, deep and husky, made Gareth's eyes fly to him. He stood front and center beside a tall woman, the mist curling around them both like the vestiges of enchantment.

Ah, but Gareth did not believe in enchantment. At least, he never had.

The speaker had height and breadth of shoulders both, a head of brown hair liberally streaked with silver and what, in other circumstances, might be termed a kind face. He must have made a daunting opponent in his youth. He wore rough leathers covered over with what looked like a ram's skin for a cloak. The woman at his side...

Gareth met her gaze and received a jolt. Her fierce, yellow eyes marked her as kin of that other, the one called Lark. As if Gareth needed further proof, this one went clad like a male also, her long legs encased in leggings and with a tunic disguising her femininity. She carried a tall staff, headed by a curious, twisted form, and she emanated an aura of power.

Scarface replied to her companion's comment. "They start them young, these Norman bastards. They breed hate into their whelps from the cradle. Never doubt it."

The woman with the golden eyes spoke. "Ah, but you have done a foolish thing, Martin. I do not see how you can send him back. He will know us—he will lead his uncle back to this village. De Vavasour will retaliate and we shall be at war again."

Scarface smiled slowly. "Let it come. We have been too long betraying ourselves for the sake of peace."

The crowd stirred uneasily and the woman shot Scarface a hard look. "Have you forgotten the cost? Would you have others die as did Sally and Thrush?"

"They will slaughter us by any road, the accursed Sheriff and his ilk—that much we have learned. What if we alter him before we send him back, so he cannot speak? Cut the tongue from his head, for starters."

Gareth caught movement from the corner of his eye. Someone pushed to the front of the crowd: Linnet, disheveled and out of breath. Her gaze fixed on Gareth and did not waver.

"Aye, so you would return de Vavasour's blood kin maimed and thus further anger him," said the woman with the staff.

"I care nothing for his anger," Scarface spat. "Get him on his knees," he added to the men holding Gareth. "You, Norman, will kneel before your betters."

Rage unfurled inside Gareth, red hot. He would be damned before he bowed to these savages. But the two men holding his arms were joined by a third. They grappled with him viciously and he felt the bones in his broken arm grind together. One of them kicked his bad leg and it went out from under him so he fell rather than knelt.

Scarface's expression of satisfaction argued he cared little for the means, so long as Gareth was on the ground before him. "Do you not know you are in the presence of royalty?" he barked fiercely. "The royalty of Sherwood! Aye, you would abase yourself before your damned liege lord, Henry, would you not? You are on our ground, now."

"He knows naught of who we are," said the man with the ram's skin, "or of the powers of Sherwood."

"He will learn. Aye, Sparrow, he will be sent back to Nottingham in pieces or whole—it matters not to me. But while here, he will learn a thing or two."

Gareth, suffused with pain, fought to keep his head up and his gaze level. Surrounded by wolves he might be, and his strength in shreds, but he would be damned if he would surrender the last remnants of his dignity.

He turned his head, defying the staring crowd, until his eyes met Linnet's. There alone did he see any measure of compassion. He straightened his spine.

"Come," said Scarface to the other two. "We will discuss the terms of his exchange." He tossed additional orders at the men who held Gareth. "Peg him there where everyone can get a gander at just how a Norman may be forced to crawl."

The three moved off in the direction of one of the larger huts. Gareth found himself booted to the ground. He fell hard and his broken arm shrieked with pain. For an instant his surroundings—people, mist, and buildings—swam around him. Hard hands fastened a rope to his neck. The other end of the short line was fixed to a metal stake in the ground. His handlers, chuckling among themselves, moved away.

The onlookers, most of them, did not. They stood in a rough circle gaping at Gareth like the dolts they were, as if they had never before seen a man tied up like a hound.

Gareth struggled up, hampered by his broken arm. He could not move far, so short was his tether. He was barely able to sit upright without straining at it. A deep shudder seized him, and he tasted hate.

A few souls abandoned the crowd. A parcel of children, ragged and solemn eyed, pressed forward. One threw a stone that hit Gareth in the side of the head. A second tossed a half-bitten turnip. A third picked up a still larger stone.

"Away! Away out of this," a soft voice scolded. A hand shooed the children and a face appeared in Gareth's line of vision: oval, lovely, and troubled. Linnet.

"Here," she said. She held a cup of water, which she raised to his lips. He drank greedily, though he hated being forced to accept charity before all those watching eyes, even from her. He shot one look into her face and turned away.

She knelt down in the dirt beside him, which partially shielded him from the gazes of the onlookers. "Have faith," she whispered. "My parents will speak sense to Martin. You will be sent back to your uncle whole."

"Your parents?" He realized she spoke of the couple wreathed in magic. Aye, for the tall woman had her sister's fierce eyes.

"They have arrived unexpectedly to celebrate Midsummer with us. Just as well—they will argue it out, the three of them." Earnestly she added, "There is great power in the number three."

"Linnet!" A hard hand came down, seized her shoulder, and pulled her to her feet. "Leave him to his ordeal." The wild-headed young man, son to Scarface, shot Gareth a look of pure loathing.

Linnet freed herself from his grip with alacrity. "He is under my care."

"And you have provided that care. You will not coddle him here for all to see—better try to coddle a rabid hound. Do not be so soft."

"And you, Falcon," she glared into his eyes, "do not be so harsh. Where is your compassion?"

"For that?" Falcon flicked Gareth with another look. "It burned to death with Ma and Thrush. Or have you forgotten all his kind have done? Dead or sent to Nottingham, I care not. I only want him gone."

Chapter Eight

"We have much for which to be thankful this Midsummer: no illness in the villages, a good crop in the fields, and firm weapons to our hands. We should, and will, celebrate."

Linnet shot a look into her mother's face and tried to gauge her mood. One could not always do so from her words. Wren Little—wife of Sparrow Little, son to Robin Hood's companion, John Little, or Little John—lived her days surrounded by magic. No less might be expected of the guardian of Sherwood, keeper of its secrets and its strength.

From the time Linnet could remember, she had been taught that Sherwood was less a place than a living entity, a deeply magical being. Spirits dwelt there, ancient and powerful, including that of Linnet's grandfather, Robin Hood. Her mother had met and spoken with him. She had even carried his spirit with her at times.

When Linnet and Lark were very young, they lived with their parents deep in the forest, raised on a curious blend of their father's deep love, their mother's practical wisdom, and the presence of Sherwood itself. Linnet recalled strange things from that time, companions who came and went and played with her, including a diminutive woman called Lil and a great bear of a man with a bristly beard who wished her to call him Grandpa.

Wren Little was a shaman and a priestess, purveyor of magic. She could speak to Linnet's father without moving her lips, mind to mind. She taught her small daughters reverence for the forest and the healing arts. But by the time they reached the age of six years, she began to entertain the possibility that isolation made no fit life for them.

So they had left the forest hermitage for the village of Oakham. For a time they had all lived there together, and Linnet's parents had striven to fit the life. But the forest and their roles as guardians called them too strongly. At last, after much discussion with the third member of the triad that guarded Sherwood—Martin Scarlet—and his wife, Sally, it had been decided the twin girls would reside with the Scarlets and Wren and Sparrow would once more retire to their hermitage.

At first Linnet and Lark had seen their parents often, either journeying into the forest or receiving them at Oakham. But as the years passed, those visits grew less frequent. The girls had a life in Oakham; their parents did not. Simple, Linnet thought, eyeing the well-loved faces, and so terribly complex.

They sat all together now in the home Linnet thought of as her own, sharing a meal prepared by her hands. Outside, night fell softly. A party bearing an ultimatum for the Sheriff of Nottingham had departed for the castle some time ago. The prisoner still remained pegged out like an animal—a sacrificial goat, perhaps—at the center of the village.

Linnet strove mightily not to think of him hurting, thirsty, hungry—but she failed.

"So," said Lark, who invariably became voluble

when in the presence of her parents, "why have you come? We did not expect you here for Midsummer. Indeed, I thought we should have to venture into the forest to see you."

Wren and Sparrow exchanged glances. Linnet wondered if they were communicating between their minds. Sometimes, when younger, she could catch the echo of their thoughts, but never the words themselves.

"I was given warning," Wren said, "that something was afoot."

Lark's golden eyes, so like her mother's, glowed. "Was it a vision?" For time out of mind, Lark had been fascinated with the flashes of knowing and images that came to her mother. She often lamented that she could not, herself, see visions. "How am I to be a guardian of Sherwood someday," she sometimes complained, "if I have not the Sight?"

Now Wren shook her head. "A message was delivered to me by your grandfather."

"Which grandfather?" Lark asked eagerly. Both were dead.

Wren smiled. When she did, her normally grave face glowed and became beautiful. "My father, Robin."

"Ah." Lark propped her chin on her hand and gazed at her parents; she thrived on talk of magic and mystery. It sometimes made Linnet wonder if Lark were not the one, of the three of them, destined to live at Sherwood's heart, channeling its magic into strength with which to fight.

Which would leave Linnet to wed Falcon. Her thoughts darted again to the man tied out in the center of the village, suffering. Barely understood longing pierced her heart.

Wren turned her head toward Linnet sharply, almost as if she could sense Linnet's thoughts. "There is danger at hand," Wren said, "wide and deep."

"Danger?" Linnet repeated. "To whom?"

Again her parents exchanged glances. Her father, usually so calm and serene, looked uneasy. His eyes—nearly identical to Linnet's—caressed her.

But it was her mother who spoke. "Death, and peril to the circle."

Lark's lips parted. She looked the way she had long ago when Pa told her tales of the old ones who dwelt in the forest.

"But," Lark protested, "that cannot be. The triad stands strong; the magic of Sherwood is safer than ever. We have years yet before we three need worry about taking your places."

"So we thought." Wren shook her head. "Yet I cannot doubt the message, nor the messenger."

Real fear stirred in Linnet's heart. She could not bear the thought of losing any of them—not her father with his deep gentleness that was somehow also deep strength, not her mother with her quick-changing fierceness, and not Martin with his undefeatable will for justice. They meant the world to her and, like the power of Sherwood which she breathed, had made her the woman she was.

To be sure, Linnet had heard tales of the last two triads. The first had been comprised of Robin Hood himself, his wife, Marian—Wren's parents—and the Green Man, spirit of Sherwood. When Robin fell, Marian succumbed to her grief and withdrew to a nunnery. Three others had stepped up to hold the triad and keep Sherwood strong: the healer, Lil, who had raised Wren after Marian abandoned her, Geoffrey, then headman of Oakham, and the holy hermit, Alric, who had taken the Green Man's part.

Aye, Linnet knew the tale, how Geoffrey, Lil, and Alric had died one by one and been replaced by Martin Scarlet, Wren, and Sparrow Little who, bonded together, had gone to ground at Sherwood's heart.

Someday Linnet, Lark, and Falcon would, in turn, take their places. Two of them would bond even as Linnet's parents and grandparents, as Lil and Geoffrey had. The other would in essence wed with the forest itself. Such was the tradition, though Wren had altered it some. Linnet knew her fate, but...

"Not yet," she said aloud. "It is much too soon."

"It is always too soon." Wren spoke with her customary alacrity. "But the truth remains—two of us cannot stand without the third. We can try." Her hand reached for that of her husband and clutched it tight. "We have seen it attempted in the past. We will fail. The power lies in three. It will take only one of us to fall."

The blood drained from Linnet's face. "Which—?"

"Which of us?" Wren, unsparing, took up the question Linnet could not bring herself to voice. "We have not been given that knowledge."

Lark, stricken silent by dismay, looked at her sister.

And Linnet, spurred by sudden terror, said, "But you should not have come. You should have stayed safe in Sherwood, where nothing can touch you."

"That is just it, Lin," her father said in his deep voice, like the rumble of thunder through the trees. "When something touches one of us, it touches all, wherever we be. We cannot hide from this. And your mother thought it important to bring warning."

Lark cursed and then asked, "Have you told Martin?"

"Of course." Wren spoke evenly, though Linnet could now feel her agitation, like a ripple on water.

"Yet," Linnet said softly, "he has gone off with the party to deliver the ransom demand in Nottingham." Martin and Falcon both had gone, with a party of four other men.

"I could not dissuade him," Wren said. "No one ever dissuaded Martin Scarlet from anything."

"Does Fal know?" Lark asked.

Wren shook her head. "Martin refused to tell him." Her expression grew troubled. "I cannot but think that a mistake. We never kept anything from you."

Fiercely, Lark told her parents, "You should go at once back into Sherwood."

"So," Wren lifted a brow, "you would sacrifice Fal's father, would you?"

Lark's eyes burned fiercely. "Martin is like a second father to us. I would defend any of you with my life." She said it so simply Linnet could not doubt its truth. "But the two of you, Ma and Pa, guard Sherwood's heart."

"So do we all," said Sparrow gravely. "And the three of you must stand ready to take your places after us, however this thing comes to pass." He fixed his daughters with his dark, compelling stare. "For whatever happens, Sherwood's magic cannot be allowed to fail."

Chapter Nine

"Here, quickly! Here, to me!"

The cry, sharp as the blade of a honed knife, broke the stillness of early morning. Even before Linnet opened her eyes, her heart leaped into her throat and began to pound like a crazed blacksmith.

Around her the other occupants of the cottage stirred. She had given her parents the pallets by the fire, a place of honor, and they slept twined together, nearly one. Lark, eternally on guard, had stationed herself near the door. Linnet saw her lift her head and then scramble up and reach for her bow in one movement.

Linnet followed; her parents rose as she passed them. In the doorway, which Lark had left open, she paused.

The air outside was still gray; dawn had barely come, but she had no need to see who had called out to identify him. Falcon, it was—and now she heard other voices raised, and a scream of anguish that closed her throat.

Someone roared like an animal in pain.

She hurried in Lark's wake, stumbling over the hem of her sleeping gown. She saw figures at the center of the village not far from where the prisoner was tied, and still more gathering.

"Martin," said her father, just behind her, and her mother pushed past. Sparrow took Linnet's arm and they went forward also. By the time they reached the place, Wren was already on her knees at the side of a figure stretched hard on the ground. Falcon knelt across from her.

Another roar came from the fallen man: Martin Scarlet, indeed. He lived, then. Linnet's breath came again. It was not so bad as it might be.

She paused at her mother's shoulder. Fal looked up into her eyes and raised both hands, red with blood. "Save him. You must save him."

Linnet did not move. Her mother possessed far greater ability as a healer than she. Linnet had skill, true, but Wren's hands held magic.

"What is it?" Lark voiced the question in the mind of everyone gathered. "What has happened to him?"

"We met with a party of soldiers on our way to Nottingham," Falcon said bitterly. "They gave us fight, and it went badly. We spent all night dodging them in the forest and never got the ransom demand to the castle."

Martin roared again. Linnet had heard a hart make that kind of bellow in its death throes. The agony of it froze her where she stood.

"It is grave." Already Wren's hands were upon him, and stained red. "Be still, Martin. You do yourself no good."

He groaned and then quieted.

Wren's head snapped round to Linnet. "Run get supplies—all you can carry."

"What—?"

"It is a sword thrust. I think it touched his heart."

Dismay drove all the breath from Linnet again.

Lark barked at her, "Go!"

She ran. Not until she reached her own hearthside did she realize her father had come with her.

"Tell me what," he said, "and I will carry."

"Naught can mend a strike to the heart."

"Do not say that. Your mother can do remarkable things. I have seen her bring men back to life."

"But the warning—"

"It brought her here, where she is needed."

"You think that is all?" Desperate, Linnet reached for any reassurance. Martin Scarlet had been there all her life. And, the next triad was not ready to take this one's place. She was not ready.

She thrust items into her father's hands and caught up more herself. When they returned outside, the dawn had strengthened enough that she could see...

Martin lay sprawled on the ground like a man already slain, but she knew his heart still beat. For one thing, his eyes were wide open, too wide. For another, the blood pumped out of him, making a black pool of his chest.

Linnet went to her knees beside her mother with a sob.

"Steady, lass," Wren said. She—or perhaps Fal—had already cut Martin's tunic away, exposing the terrible wound. Wren's hands, like Fal's, were now red past the wrists.

Folk stood silent and still as the trees. Only a child whimpered somewhere in the distance.

"Bandaging, a thick pad of it," Wren requested. Linnet placed it in her mother's slimy hand. Her stomach heaved.

"More."

They all watched as Wren packed the wound in an

attempt to stanch the bleeding. The blood welled up around the cloth, persistent as the life still in Martin Scarlet's eyes.

Beneath her breath, Wren muttered a prayer, or more likely an invocation.

Linnet felt the power come.

It rose up out of the soil at her mother's bidding, materialized from the air of the dawning, streamed down from the trees, and poured through Wren the way water pours through a funnel, into her hands and into Martin.

He groaned again. He gritted his teeth as against pain of great intensity. Light flickered around Wren's hands, pinpricks of shed gold. Martin's body arched and his head strained back. Wren continued to speak under her breath, low and steady.

On his father's other side Falcon still knelt, anguish in his eyes. His hands covered his father's and gripped tight.

Wren cast a look at Sparrow. "Help me. I cannot hold him."

Sparrow placed his hands on her shoulders. The gold fire streaming from her fingers grew stronger and then, a moment later, streamed green.

The color of fresh grass, the color of leaves at the height of summer, of the Green Man's holy eyes...

Linnet felt the backlash of that power in the pit of her stomach. She trembled and thought that, for an instant, the whole world paused.

Or perhaps that was Sherwood.

Wren gasped. Her head drooped abruptly, like that of a woman who has heard an answer.

To Fal she said, "I am sorry, Falcon, lad, I cannot

hold him."

Fal's face crumpled like that of a child.

Wren laid both her red-stained hands on Martin's forehead and gazed into his eyes. "You know I love you."

"Wren—" He gasped.

"Go to your Sally now. She waits for you. We shall see you anon."

"No!" The word came not from Martin, but his son. Falcon's face was now devoid of color, and his eyes burned dark. All the compassion inside Linnet reached out to him.

But it was Lark who provided comfort. She wrapped both her arms about his shoulders from behind and held on.

"Son," Martin gasped, "do your part well."

They proved his last words. His body eased as his spirit left it, and the green fire lessened under Wren's hands, then faded away.

For one long moment, trembling silence held. Then someone wailed. A child cried in response. A woman keened. Those gathered round the man who had led them a score of years mourned him fully, as a mother mourns a dearly loved son.

Wren raised both bloodstained hands and buried her face in them. Grief tore through Linnet, another backlash of what her parents and Falcon felt.

"I failed him," Wren mourned.

"No, I failed him," Falcon cried. "I was there when the fight came upon us. I should have defended him."

"No one ever defended Martin Scarlet," Sparrow said, in grief. "He fought always for himself." He drew a breath and asked Fal intently, "Will they be coming, lad?"

"Who?"

"The soldiers who engaged you. Will they follow here?"

Falcon lifted his shattered face. Linnet could feel him struggle to think. "Aye. Perhaps. We lost them for a time in the forest, but they will come searching."

"You cannot stay here. If you are found in this place, the village will pay." He glanced toward the tethered prisoner. "He cannot be found here, either."

Falcon leaped to his feet. The folk gathered round parted for him as he whirled and flew at the prisoner in a fury. "This is your fault, you and your accursed kind." His first blow took Gareth de Vavasour in the head; the second knocked him sideways to the ground and was followed by a boot to the ribs. A number of village men converged upon Fal. Sparrow reached him first.

"Nay, lad," he said, and wrapped Falcon in his arms. "Do not."

Falcon twisted in Sparrow's grip and stared into Gareth de Vavasour's face. "You will pay," he spat. "I promise! You and all your kind will pay."

Chapter Ten

"Get up."

The words, spoken by the big man in the sheepskin cloak, roused Gareth from his day-long stupor. He looked up into the dark eyes of the speaker and wondered whether he could obey.

He hurt all over and his head swam. No one had been near him since whatever happened earlier had happened and the wild-haired young man called Falcon flew at him. From all the shouting, wailing, and cries of mourning, Gareth suspected there had been a death, but he had been unable to see much with so many backs in the way. After the Saxon knocked him down, he thought someone had been borne away. He had not so much as glimpsed the healer, Linnet—daughter, so he recalled, of this man now standing over him.

They had the same dark eyes, steady and sane. This did not look an angry man like the other, Falcon's sire. Gareth's mind struggled with it; could it be Falcon's sire, Scarface, who had died?

"Up with you," the man said again. "I have cut your tether."

Gareth scrambled up, unable to suppress a grimace of agony. "What has happened?" he asked. Clearly, if Scarface was dead, his son blamed Gareth. Was he now to be slain in retaliation?

But Linnet's father merely said, "You cannot stay

here. Come with me."

To Gareth's humiliation, he staggered, almost too weak to walk. He could not remember the last time food had passed his lips. The day had been a warm one, and he had been afforded no water. His tongue felt swollen, and his mouth full of grit.

Yet he straightened his spine. He was a Norman knight, a champion. Could he let these Saxon dogs see him falter?

The big man led him toward one of the village huts, the same from which Gareth had seen Linnet emerge when she tended him.

Before they entered, Gareth heard a voice from within. "I will not! I travel nowhere in his company. Slit his accursed throat and send his corpse back to his uncle, I say." Raw grief and rage colored the words.

A woman's voice, not quite calm, replied, "You cannot stay here, Fal. I know you hurt. Do you think I do not hurt also? I have had a third of my life torn away this day. But we must think what is best for the future. You, Lark, and Linnet are now doubly precious, and must be kept safe."

The big man—Sparrow—planted his hand between Gareth's shoulder blades and shoved him through the doorway.

Everyone inside the hut turned and stared. So small was the space, it seemed crowded with the four inside—the woman with the fierce, golden eyes who had just spoken, her daughters, Linnet and Lark, and Scarface's son.

The latter looked distraught with grief, and that answered Gareth's wondering. Aye, Scarface must be dead. He felt a surge of satisfaction at that; the man had been a brutal savage. Yet his death undoubtedly changed the game, and not for the better, so far as Gareth was concerned.

"Do not bring that varmint in here." Scarface's son leaped to his feet. "I will not breathe the same air as he."

"Steady," said Sparrow. "None of us will be here long. Linnet, have you packed up all you need? Lark, you have your weapons?"

"I always have my weapons." The small fury leaped to her feet, a knife appearing in her hand as if by magic. Before Gareth could draw breath she was upon him and had the blade at his throat. "Fal, would you have me end it now—blood for blood?"

The big man at Gareth's shoulder spoke in a rumble. "He is too valuable for that. Come now, I want to be away into the forest by nightfall."

The forest? Surely they did not mean to drag Gareth away with them into Sherwood? To be sure, he knew that was where outlaws and peasants alike disappeared when they did not want to face justice—the Sheriff's or the King's. But would they take a Norman captive with them?

Apparently so, for the girl withdrew her knife with a scowl, they gathered up their packs, and Scarface's son spoke, his face twisted by grief.

"Aye, Norman swine, we shall take you to Sherwood, and maybe abandon you there—see how the forest deals with you then."

****

"Come along."

Yet another yank on the rope around Gareth's neck, and he stumbled forward into the darkness. He could not guess how these people could see where they were going. All around was blackness, whispering tree boughs and shadows, and silence that steadily deepened.

But the silence was not truly silent—it rustled with the movement of small animals, fluttered with the stirring of leaves, and bristled with a sensation that felt like someone touching Gareth's bare skin.

His companions moved with barely a sound. The woman—Wren—led the way faultlessly and without pause. The smaller of her daughters, Lark, followed her, with Fal behind, then Linnet and, keeping Gareth on a short rein, her father. Gareth could not see them but knew they were there.

The curious thing was it felt as if someone came behind him, as well. So real was the conviction, Gareth turned his head a few times, but glimpsed only more darkness.

"Sit," the man Sparrow told him, and pushed him down where he stood. Gareth tried to feel offended at being treated like a trained hound, but all his indignation had disappeared into exhaustion. His broken arm ached incessantly, and the wounds at shoulder and thigh burned like fire.

Light flared suddenly in a shower of golden sparks, and a torch was lit. A face swam above Gareth—Sparrow again. "We will stay here the night. I will hobble you, but should you get free, 'twould be foolish to hare away into the trees. Do you understand?"

Gareth gave a nod, his only possible response. The others began talking softly among themselves while Sparrow fashioned a line between Gareth's ankles and two trees.

Above him the wind rose; he could hear the swaying of branches. It sounded like other voices whispering.

He closed his eyes and tried to pray for strength. He struggled to remember the prayers his mother had taught him. That had been so long ago, so far away. He remembered only her smile, and the softness of her eyes.

Light flickered against his closed eyelids. He opened his eyes and looked up.

Linnet stood there, a torch in one hand, a flask in the other. "Here." She sank to her knees beside him. "Water."

Thank God. He reached his good hand for it. His fingers brushed hers and she looked away.

He drank greedily, drained half the flask's contents, and then made as if to hand it back to her.

"Drink all you wish. There is a stream close by." She hesitated. "You must be hungry."

He shook his head. He ached too much for hunger. He had not hurt so since he first began training, the butt of all the older lads' cruelty.

"There will be something to eat soon." She arose and left him, never once having looked him in the eyes.

Gareth tried not to feel a sense of loss. She meant nothing to him. A Saxon peasant. He could allow her to mean nothing. And the sense of connection he thought he had felt between them had been sheer fancy. A beautiful woman touching him, tending him, should stir his interest and his manhood. That was only to be expected.

He closed his eyes again and wondered if he would ever be sent to his uncle. He wondered if he wanted to be. Aye, anything was better than this situation in which he now found himself.

He must have fallen into a pain-wracked doze, for the next thing he knew he roused to a touch on his arm. Linnet knelt beside him once more, with her mother, straight and tall, standing over her.

"Tend his hurts," Wren said, "and then get away from him." In the harsh torch light, Wren's face bore the signs of grief. Gareth wondered just what Scarface had meant to her—something dear, plainly, for she had aged in a day.

She added to her daughter, "Do you need my help?"

"Nay, Mother." Linnet gazed up at the woman. Gareth tried not to notice the graceful line of her neck or the beauty of her bosom. "You must be sorely depleted after…after—" Linnet's voice broke. "You go rest."

Wren ran a disparaging look over Gareth. "You, whelp—do not give me reason to end your miserable life. Do not lay a finger on my daughter." To Linnet she added, "I suppose you had better feed him when you are done."

Throw a scrap or two to the hound, Gareth could not help but think, and struggled to straighten his spine again. The woman stepped away, not far, and Gareth turned his eyes on the healer. He could not be sure what had taken place back in the village. But Linnet's face showed the marks of tears, and her emotions pulled at him unaccountably, almost as if he could sense all she felt.

She busied herself with her salves and bandages, her eyes upon her hands and not on him.

He could hear the others talking—Fal on a rant, encouraged by the small sister, Lark. And he could still hear the trees whispering.

"This will hurt," Linnet told him. It must be what she said to everyone she tended. He shook his head; he could hardly hurt more.

But he was wrong. The pain, when she peeled the blood-caked bandages from his shoulder, left him sweating. Her hands shook when she cleaned the raw, angry wound.

"This looks worse than it was yesterday. It has not had a fair chance to heal. Perhaps I should consult with my mother."

"No."

"But she is far more skilled at healing than I, with powers I do not possess."

"She has no reason to aid me." A foolish thing to say. Did he think Linnet had? Clearly, Scarface had meant something to her and clearly, like the others, she had translated her grief into a fiercer hatred for him, Gareth. She could not even bear to meet his gaze.

A shadow moved behind her. The other lass, Lark, stood there, an ugly look on her face, the ever-present knife in her hands. "Trouble, sister?"

"Nay, Lark. I wonder only how to keep him alive until his use to us is done."

Lark spat. "To my mind, he has no use. Let Fal kill him slowly, to ease his grief."

"Nothing can ease his grief." The corners of Linnet's mouth tightened.

"I do not know how you can bear to touch that reeking pile of offal that calls itself a man."

Linnet shot one look into Gareth's face and averted

her gaze again.

He lifted his chin. "I did not kill your friend's father. That is what has happened, has it not? Your headman is dead?"

Lark leaned down and snarled directly into his face, "Aye. And you did kill him—that's what you do not see. 'Tis plain enough to the rest of us, who are forced to live under you: you Norman bastards are all the same, every one of you—all evil to the bone."

Chapter Eleven

"Kiss me."

The demand curled through Linnet's mind and senses, soft and persuasive as a sigh. It called to something inside her and caused her to part her lips receptively.

Supple, long-fingered hands captured her face. A mouth descended on hers and all life narrowed to one sensation: the heat and delight of it, the flooding need and the answered yearning. His weight came down on her body and with it more heat. She felt her spirit expand and then open to accept him and take him in.

She wound her arms about his neck in order to draw him closer. Her fingertips found delight in the smooth muscle of his shoulders and the softness of his hair. He tasted like warm, summer mead, and her flesh leaped for him. She could feel every part of his body now, vital and strong.

"Linnet, wake up."

Her eyes flew open but the dream did not fade. She was used to waking all of a piece with no confusion, but now the vision lingered and clung to her, made unreality of the morning light that drifted down through green leaves, and her sister's face that hovered above her.

Oh, by all that was holy, it had been nothing but a dream.

Lark scowled at her. "What is amiss with you? You never sleep so long. We are nearly ready to leave. Pa says tend the swine before we get to moving."

"Must you call him that?" Long-fingered hands, lithe strength... The heady taste of him still lingered on Linnet's lips. Why would she dream thus of a virtual stranger? She so rarely dreamt at all.

"What else should I call him? And why do you care?"

A fine question, that. "He is injured, and alone."

"Harness your sympathies, sister. I know you are a compassionate creature—it is one of your strengths, and also your greatest weakness."

"So you say." Linnet struggled to her feet as the last remnants of the powerful dream dissipated. Gareth de Vavasour sat some twenty paces distant, still hobbled between his trees. *De Vavasour,* she reminded herself—a hated name and that of her enemy, not her lover.

"If anyone deserves your compassion it is Falcon." Lark's gaze stabbed at Linnet. "He has lost his father, all the family that remained to him."

"We are his family," Linnet replied truthfully.

"The triad is broken with Martin gone. Our parents are in danger. Try thinking on that."

"What makes you suppose I am not?"

Lark gave an odd shake, a quiver of her shoulders. "Instinct. I do not like the way you look at him." She nodded at the captive. "It is the same way Fal looks at you."

"Do not be daft. He will soon be sent back to Nottingham, and that will end it."

"Aye, perhaps, given one of us does not murder

him first."

Lark stalked away, and Linnet followed to where her parents and Falcon stood talking. She laid a hand on Fal's arm.

"How are you?"

He turned ravaged eyes on her. "I will be all right. I must be strong—it is what Pa would want."

True. There had been no weakness in Martin Scarlet, and he had despised others who displayed it. Fal knew that better than anyone.

Linnet tightened her fingers on his forearm. "If there is aught I can do—"

A faraway look came to his eyes. "We are called to service now, Lin, with the circle of three broken. We were born for this, you, Lark, and I."

Linnet looked to her parents, who watched quietly. "Where are we bound? Surely not to your hermitage."

Wren shook her head. "I will not take him there." She nodded in the direction of Gareth de Vavasour. "But we will stay deep in Sherwood until we decide what to do next." She fixed Linnet with a golden stare. "Go, take some food to him. I do not want him lagging behind and slowing our pace."

So, Linnet thought as she gathered up food last prepared at her own hearth, Gareth was to be treated like a herded animal, kept alive for his value on the hoof. Aye, and what more did he deserve?

She closed her mind firmly to the memory of her dream and approached the hobbled man, well aware that everyone else watched them closely. When she reached Gareth he looked up, and she caught her breath at what she saw in his eyes.

Defiance, anger, and a hint of arrogance, still. Aye,

he was Norman to the bone.

"You had best eat something," she told him. "We will move on very soon."

He looked at the food and she could very nearly tell his thoughts: it gagged him to take charity, yet he knew he needed his strength. He accepted a heel of bread and his fingers touched the palm of her hand. *Strong, tapered fingers capturing her face, silver eyes gazing into hers, and his mouth—*

Linnet swayed where she stood. She strove to beat back the tangled emotions.

"How are your wounds? Better after being tended last night?"

"I am well enough." A rampant lie; his fine eyes looked bloodshot, the seam Martin had opened on the side of his face appeared ugly and tender, and lines of pain rode the skin beneath the new-grown, golden beard.

"It is just as well. My mother means to set a hard pace today." She turned to leave.

"Wait, please." He abandoned the bread and reached for her hand. She shrank from the memory of his touch, the intensity of feeling it had prompted in her dream. He saw her reaction and dropped his fingers abruptly.

"When will they decide what is to be done with me?"

"I do not know," she told him honestly. "There are more important things, now, on everyone's mind."

****

"Amazing what a scrap of bread can do," Lark said. "He is keeping up better than I dared imagine." Walking at Linnet's side, she glanced back to where

Gareth de Vavasour once more brought up the rear of their party, still led by his rope harness.

"Likely his dignity will not let him falter," Linnet said. Somehow she kept herself from looking back.

"Dignity?" Lark snorted. "He does not make such a fine figure of a champion now, does he? Costly clothes in tatters, and walking on our ground—sacred ground." She appeared to reflect. "Have you thought about what this means, Lin, the significance of Martin's death, to us?"

"Of course I have." Always the threat of taking up responsibility for the triad had hung above Linnet's head. "But Ma and Pa are still here, and Ma is not one to surrender the reins easily."

"True. But the old triad is shattered. The way I understand it, the woven magic will hold a short while. Last night, whilst you tended that swine, I asked Ma how long. She would not say."

"Do you think Fal will take up the place of headman in Oakham?"

Lark scowled. "I am worried about him." She lowered her voice and shot a look at the back of Fal's fair head. "All his life he has tried to live up to what his father expected of him, even when it went against his nature."

Linnet blinked at her sister, surprised by the astute observation.

"Do not look at me that way, Lin. I know him." Lark added simply, "I have always known him, here, inside." She tapped her breast above her heart. "He is not like Martin, not really, though he tries hard to be. There is perhaps too much of his mother in him."

Linnet nodded. Sally Scarlet had been a gentle

woman who loved fiercely. Her devotion to her family had been complete. Linnet saw much of that in Falcon.

"Now," Lark continued, "I fear he will break himself in his father's memory, trying to live up to Martin. And possibly deny his own heart." She turned a burning look on Linnet. "You are his heart, Lin. I would rather lose him to you than see him ruin himself over it."

"Oh, Lark."

"I love him," Lark whispered, barely above a breath. "And he loves you."

"Or he thinks he does. His heart is so torn now, who knows what he truly wants? I care for him—I always have—only not in that way."

"Is life not a cruel mistress?" Lark's voice sounded husky with emotion. "You will have to have him now—or soon, for the sake of the triad."

"Aye." Linnet touched her sister's arm softly. "At least, one of us will."

Chapter Twelve

"How much longer will we stay here?" Gareth directed a look into the face of the woman who bent over him, and caught his breath. By heaven, she was lovely with her dark hair only half braided and streaming around her and the front of her bodice loosened against the warmth of the day.

When she stooped to tend his shoulder, he could see—well, far more than she likely dreamed. She had perfect breasts, paler than her arms and throat, and tipped with tantalizing, rosy points. When she moved, the weight of them pressed against the fabric of her bodice, and Gareth's groin tightened in response.

But he could not let himself think about that, could not allow for the distraction. By his reckoning, they had been at this place nearly a seven-night. Linnet and her family had built a simple shelter for their needs here in what he could only term a forest bower. Trees taller than any he had ever seen towered above, and made a leafy roof. At night it was darker than the pit of hell, but by day Gareth had followed the path of the sun by its shed light and gleaned his direction.

He thought he knew which way to run, should he get free from his infernal tether. The others, who shared their shelter while he lay pegged outside like the hound they likely thought him, had performed a pagan rite several days ago and spoken words of farewell to

Falcon's sire. They ignored Gareth most of the time, but Linnet still tended his wounds, and either she or her hoyden of a sister brought his food. Falcon had stayed away from him, except to glare his hate.

He watched Linnet now, as he could not help but do whenever she was near him. She gave him a thoughtful look before she shifted her basket and sank gracefully to her knees.

"Thirsty?" She offered the flask at her side.

He accepted it thankfully. Water from this place tasted like none Gareth had ever had—cold, peaty, and refreshing. He had been living on it and on one of the King's deer brought down by the big man—Sparrow—and Falcon, who seemed to enjoy equal prowess with the bow.

No man ate the King's deer, save nobles. That much had been beaten into Gareth's head. But here it seemed right, natural, like the words the leaves whispered.

"My parents will decide, soon, whether we will move on. Does the broken arm still pain you terribly?"

Without waiting for his answer, she leaned forward and gently touched the limb, affording Gareth still another glimpse inside her bodice. He caught her scent, too—warm and beguiling.

He managed one word. "Nay." Despite the hardships he had experienced, he could feel his body mending and his strength returning. But he could not tell her that, not if he meant to attempt an escape. Ah, and if he needed proof of his recovery, surely it lay in his response to this woman's nearness.

"Good. And the face?" She ran a fingertip down his cheek and he quivered involuntarily. "It looks well.

See, all this is new skin." She hesitated. "How about the leg?"

If by "leg" she meant the area of his thigh, it was currently in fine fettle, embarrassingly so.

Her eyes dropped and then flew to his. Warm color flooded upward from the direction of those delectable breasts to fill her face.

"It is well." He dared not allow her slender hands to touch him there. He could not endure it.

He wondered what it would be like to kiss her, to touch with his mouth those lips like berries, to taste the inside of her mouth and touch her tongue with his. He itched for it, by God. Nay, that was too mild a word—he ached for it the way a man in the throes of suffocation starved for air.

She had gone breathless, and studied her hands intently with lowered eyes. Sheer impulse made him ask, "What is between you and Scarface's son?" He jerked his head toward where Falcon stood even now watching them.

Linnet sighed. Her dark eyes met his at last, and held. "It is commonly believed we are to wed."

It hit Gareth like a blow to the gut. Everything within him rejected the idea, and he was forced to swallow words he dared not speak. He wondered if Falcon had bedded her yet, cupped those breasts in his hands as Gareth longed to do.

"He has spoken for you?"

"Not yet. But he will. 'Tis a thing of need."

"How so?"

"That is complicated. You would not understand."

"Explain it to me."

"Why?" Again her eyes touched with his, tangible

as a caress. "It matters not to you, does it?"

It should not. Gareth found that it did, very much. "Please."

"Here, take and eat this, so they do not wonder why I linger so long."

Obedient, Gareth accepted the food she handed him. This time he let his fingers linger on hers.

"The three of us—Falcon, Lark and I—have a duty we must assume. It has to do with the guardianship of Sherwood and the ability of our people to stand against oppression and continue our fight for justice, for all Englishmen." She shrugged slightly. "The three of us must stand together; two of us will ultimately wed. 'Tis the way it has been, time out of mind."

Gareth stared. What madness was this? Talk of guardianships and duties—was not the Sheriff the King's guardian of Sherwood? But he saw by the serious light in Linnet's eyes she spoke in earnest, and he dared not scoff. She, at least, believed what she said. "Well, but can your sister not wed with him?" he asked with some desperation. "I should think she would wish it. I have seen the way she looks at him."

Linnet's brows lifted. "Indeed? Aye, and she could wed with him. I believe he prefers me."

As what sane man would not? Gareth reflected upon it. The small fury did have something about her—no doubt that diminutive body housed a veritable arsenal of passion. But Linnet was grace walking.

"Should the elder of you not wed with him?" It was how such things worked in his world. He added swiftly, "You are not the elder, are you?"

"I am, but not by much. We are twins."

Again, he stared.

She allowed herself a thin smile. "I know we do not look it, but 'tis true enough. Lark takes after Mother, I more after Pa."

Gareth tried to reconcile this slender creature with that mountain of a man—only their eyes were alike. He said nothing.

"Have you family other than your uncle waiting for you in Nottingham?"

He shook his head. "I have a brother who oversees my father's lands, north of York, and a sister long wed and gone from home." He thought once more of his mother, that beautiful child bride who had survived barely ten years of his life.

Linnet asked, a bit too casually, "Have you, perhaps, a betrothed who awaits you?"

Their eyes met. Gareth's heart began to beat high and hard, which fairly well matched his condition below. Had things been different, he would have traded his life for one night in this woman's bed. But things were not different. He shook his head again and changed the direction of their words.

"How deep are we in the forest?"

"This place lies, nearly, at its heart."

"But Nottingham lies south?" He turned his eyes that way.

"Aye." She laid her fingertips on his arm. "I pray you will not do anything foolish." Could she tell what lay in his mind? He widened his eyes and strove to appear guileless.

"Because," she went on, "the forest, and this part of it in particular, is no place for you to be on your own. It is very ancient, and inhabited."

"By what? Other outlaws?"

Her eyes met his once more. "By spirits. They live here among the trees and in the earth itself. The magic here is very deep."

"Magic?" He could not help but scoff. "That is pagan nonsense. With proper burial, are spirits not laid to rest?"

"Proper burial under the auspices of your church, you mean? What is that to these spirits? They walked here long before Christ was born."

"So you may believe." The girl knew only what she had been taught. Her ignorance was not her fault.

She gathered up her supplies and rose. "So it is," she told him implacably before she walked away.

****

Carefully and deliberately, Gareth worked the hobble free of his right ankle and began work on his left—no mean feat, using but one hand, and in the near total dark. A thin moon rode high in the branches of the trees and cast what he deemed the perfect amount of light—enough to let him see his way, hopefully, but not enough for him to be easily followed. He must act now; he might not have another opportunity. Desperation swamped him, and he broke out all over in a sweat.

His left ankle came free.

He stretched his legs and tried to evaluate his position. His captors had become careless these last two days. And he felt as fit as he was likely to be. Now was the time for flight.

He stood and glanced toward the shelter. Did they all sleep? He looked at the moon again, which had risen some time ago out of the east. He would travel with it on his left shoulder. Surely he could then find his way to Nottingham. After all, he was a proven champion and this was but a stretch of forest.

He wished he had a weapon and could move as swiftly as his captors. He wished he might have kissed Linnet but once.

On that thought he moved off out of the clearing, into the thick of the trees and the increased darkness. He went carefully, knowing he could not withstand a fall. The trees closed around him and the whispering, high among them, returned. Pure fancy, surely, but he almost thought he could catch a word here or there.

Follow.

Ours.

Champion.

Moonlight flickered about and above him. A wind came, stirring the leaves and making the pale radiance flicker. He began to sweat again, and confusion pricked his senses. No more than a hundred paces from the clearing, he was no longer sure of his direction.

He felt someone behind him.

So strong was the conviction, he whirled about and almost fell. He expected to see one of his captors— perhaps Linnet herself—but found only the trees closing in. He suddenly remembered how he had felt on the way into the forest, as if someone strode at his back.

His skin pricked all over and he whirled again. The moon had risen high enough that he could no longer be sure of east from west, north from south.

"Do not be a fool," he told himself, and heard his father's harsh voice in the words. "Are you a child? Will you weep for your mother still? Get hold of yourself or I will take the strap to you."

And so he had, many times. Gareth bore the stripes on his back and buttocks to prove it. The same cruelty that had killed his mother had failed to break Gareth. It had shaped him, perhaps, but...

"Champion."

He spun once more. A man stood behind him, wreathed in white mist pure as the moonlight—a man Gareth did not recognize. Gareth reached for a weapon he no longer wore.

"Peace," the man said.

"Who are you? How come you here?" And was he real? Gareth dared not ask that. He almost thought he could see through the man. A vision then, or a dream.

His mother, daughter of Celts, had believed in visions. Gareth assured himself he did not.

"I am the spirit of this place. Some call me the Green Man. Others call me Robin Hood."

"Robin Hood is long dead." Gareth had heard the tales. Who had not?

"Aye, long dead," the man agreed, "as are many here. This is our bastion, our refuge, a place of faith and strength."

"You mean like heaven?" Gareth's voice sounded hoarse to his own ears.

The man smiled. His narrow, clever face changed and warmed into something intensely attractive. "Far better than any heaven."

"What do you want with me?" Surely and surely, he was back asleep on his tether and dreaming all this.

"Nay, lad, you are not dreaming."

"Can you hear my thoughts?" What madness was this?

"Not madness, either. Listen to me. We have not long—they will soon be coming."

No need to question who. Already Gareth thought

he caught sounds of pursuit, raised voices and movement through the trees behind him.

"Let me go," he said, still hoarsely.

The man lifted his hands, palms upward. "Do I hold you?"

"I know not. Do you?" Gareth felt tethered as surely as back on his hobble.

"I ask of you, young man, only one thing, one boon, one favor if you would survive this night."

"Of course I will survive. How not? This is but darkness, and trees, and moonlight."

The man waved one of his hands. A creature appeared beside him, a pure white wolf with its hackles raised. Another subtle movement and he was suddenly flanked on the other side by a great white hart, its sides streaming mist. The trees overhead tossed their branches and Gareth felt the power gather, sharp and vital, around this being who faced him.

Fear such as he had never known—not even when awaiting the arrival of his father with the strap—engulfed him. "What do you seek of me? What boon, what bidding?"

"I ask of you but one promise, that you should follow what is in your heart." The man smiled again. "Does not a champion, a true champion, always follow his heart?"

Gareth had no answer for that either. His father had insisted a champion strove for perfection, to be faultless in all things and above reproach.

"My heart has been dead a long while." He did not know why he said that—it felt drawn from him.

"Nay, not dead," the specter told him. "Merely closed tight." Before Gareth's eyes his form wavered like a reflection in water, as did those of the creatures on either side. As Gareth stared, they shimmered and blended together until all that faced him was a brown hart, head high and rack displayed.

The spirit's final words floated to him even as the hart bolted. "Now run, my son. Flee!"

Chapter Thirteen

"Halt, or I swear I shall spit you where you stand."

The words, shouted up ahead of Linnet, could only be directed at the fugitive. Falcon's voice—it would have to be Fal...

All around her, moonlight danced among the trees like mist. Somewhere nearby her parents must search, along with Lark. But for the moment it seemed she, Falcon, and Gareth were alone. She caught her breath and hurried forward.

Not more than twenty paces on, Fal held Gareth de Vavasour at bay. De Vavasour had been caught with his back to a tree, and his chest rose and fell desperately, though his gaze held steady.

Falcon, posed in the classic archer's stance, had his longbow up and an arrow notched. Foolish to think Fal could not hit his mark in the uncanny light. Fal could hit almost any mark, always, and especially at such a paltry distance.

All at once, Linnet felt sure she was about to see Gareth de Vavasour die. The arrow would fly, as it must, and take him through the heart.

The heart that should belong to me.

Ah, by all that was holy, why had that thought come to mind?

She moved forward, and Gareth's gaze flicked toward her once before returning to Fal.

Falcon did not look at her—he did not need to; he could sense her most times even as she could sense him. At the moment she felt his anger running rampant, all the excuse he needed for loosing his shot.

"Fal—" she said.

"Go get your father."

"Do not spill his blood, Fal, not here. This is sacred ground."

"Then I shall make of him a holy sacrifice. The fool thought he could escape, but he only ran deeper into Sherwood." Falcon smiled. His smiles, usually sunny, tended to light up his face, but this was reminiscent of his father and bespoke his desire for revenge.

"What is this?" Lark broke through the trees and slid to a halt at Linnet's side. She caught her breath, and Linnet felt her surge of satisfaction. "Ah, fine work, Fal! You have him now. End it. Slay the dog!"

"Go find Pa," Linnet told her. So far, Fal's arrow point had not wavered. Despite the emotions raging through him, it remained steady as rock.

Lark glared at her. "I will not. You go."

Linnet stayed where she stood, convinced the instant her eyes moved from the point of the arrow Fal would loose the shot. Instead, she raised her voice. "Pa! Here!"

All around her, the trees rustled. Spirits gathered here, so near Sherwood's magical heart. They came now to watch and listen. Awareness of them flowed over Linnet's skin like the aftermath of summer lightning.

Her parents could not be far; surely they would come. Meanwhile—

She moved as if called, or driven, and took herself forward to stand between Gareth de Vavasour and the arrow, facing Falcon.

"Linnet, what are you doing?" Falcon's voice revealed his tension. "Get out of the way."

"No."

With a cry, Lark flew forward and struck Linnet in the chest with the impact of a boulder. They both went down. Linnet heard the twang of Fal's bowstring and the arrow passed above her head.

She wailed. The protest came from her heart, and with it came strength that gave her the power to overthrow Lark for once in her life. She pushed her sister from her and reared up, desperate.

Gareth de Vavasour lay at the base of the tree. Dead? It took Linnet an instant to realize Fal's arrow quivered in the trunk of the tree and not in de Vavasour's flesh.

"Curse it, Lin, get out of the way!"

Before she could blink, Fal notched another arrow. Linnet evaded her sister's grasping hands and threw her body over Gareth's.

And, oh! She could feel him, alive and vital, just as it had been in her dream when his body covered hers. She could feel his blood rushing and sense his thoughts.

"Ugh!" Her sister fell upon her and dragged her bodily from the Norman. Lark's hands were not kind; they pulled Linnet's hair and clawed at her arms.

Lark crowed, "Now! Now, Fal—shoot!"

For the first time, Fal's arrow wavered. Linnet, peering up through her hair, saw that he shook where he stood.

"Shoot!" Lark screeched again.

86

"It is an act of cowardice to fire upon a fallen man." Anguish filled Falcon's voice.

"That is no man. It is a Norman knight." Lark and Gareth scrambled up at the same moment. Before they were on their feet, Lark snatched the bow and arrow from Fal's hands.

"He lies no more. What are you made of, Falcon Scarlet?" She notched the arrow and drew the bow. Fal's bow should be too heavy for her small stature and weight, but anger let her accomplish the deed.

Before she could loose the bolt, light flared. It came in a shiver of sparks white as the heart of flame, and erupted into brightness almost too intense to behold.

When it faded, a hart stood between Lark and her target, its head high and its flanks steaming.

Linnet felt Gareth's hand seize hers, hard. She clutched at him and stared, knowing she witnessed pure magic.

Lark lowered the bow. For one timeless instant the five of them stood unmoving. Then the hart leaped away into the forest.

Linnet heard her parents approaching, and her mother call out, "Lark? Linnet? Falcon?"

"Here, mother." Linnet raised her eyes to Gareth's face. "We are all here."

****

"Do not ever do that to me again," Fal shouted at Lark, enraged.

"What?" Lark snarled in return. "Show you how to act the man?"

Linnet knew Lark had been shaken to her core by what had taken place among the trees, but it was Lark's way to cover uncertainty with bluster.

"Snatch my bow from my hands when I am set to make a shot!" Falcon bellowed at her. "I accept such use from no man," he sneered at her, "nor lad, either."

Linnet felt that blow pierce Lark to the heart. She alone knew how her sister felt toward Fal. That he should call her a boy had to strike deep.

For once, Lark remained silent. Falcon, dismissing her, stalked to where Gareth stood, still breathing hard and once more hobbled. "As for you—"

The blow had all Fal's anger behind it and knocked Gareth de Vavasour off his feet. Falcon stood over him, his hands fisted, visibly aching to strike again.

Gareth, now sprawled on the ground, glared up at Fal with equal anger. "Courageous, Saxon, to strike a hobbled man. Someday I will be free to face you fairly, with a sword in my hand!"

It sounded like a vowed challenge. And Falcon accepted it as such. He nodded his wild head at his promised opponent. "See you do."

"Here," Linnet's father intervened. "What happened out there?"

For an instant, the four young people looked at one another, anger forgotten.

"Naught," said Falcon then.

Linnet's mother stepped forward. Her eyes glowed bright, and Linnet could feel the surge of her emotions. "Do not lie to me, Falcon Scarlet. I felt magic, powerful magic—that of the Green Man himself."

Angrily, Lark said, "Ask Lin. She defended that piece of offal. Fal blames me for spoiling his shot, but 'twas she got between the arrow and its mark."

"As did the hart." Fal spoke in a low voice that

trembled, and Wren's head came round toward him.

"You are mistaken," Lark exploded. "You did not see what you thought you saw. You are a fool, Falcon Scarlet, who does not recognize what is before his eyes."

Fal raised a glowing gaze to hers. "If that is so, why did you fail to shoot?"

"And risk hitting my sister?"

"Sherwood wants him alive." Linnet's own words surprised her. "I do not know why."

Wren stepped to Gareth de Vavasour where he stood, having once more dragged himself up on his tether. "Are you all right?"

He gave her a stiff nod. Linnet wondered what he thought he had seen out beneath the trees. She remembered the feel of him under her, a power that surged and called.

"'Twas foolish of you to run," Wren told Gareth. "There exist in this place safeguards you cannot hope to evade. You will never escape Sherwood on your own."

He nodded again.

"As for you..." Wren switched her bright gaze to Linnet. "Come, Daughter. We need to speak together alone."

Chapter Fourteen

"He will have to be returned to Nottingham. You know he must."

Wren stated the words softly, yet they were unbending. She and Linnet sat apart from the others beside the stream, and all around them daylight strengthened. This endless night, Linnet thought, had at last flown.

She made no reply to her mother and kept her gaze fixed on her hands.

Wren spoke again. "It is understandable that you should find him desirable, I suppose. He is young and not ill-favored. And you have been tending him this while. It is a potent combination."

Linnet did look up then, startled. She saw a rueful light in her mother's eyes.

Wren shrugged. "Do you think I do not remember such feelings, nor comprehend the power of attraction? When you did not give yourself to any man, all this time, I thought you saved yourself for Falcon."

"You hoped I did." Linnet's voice sounded rusty to her own ears. "But Fal is like a brother to me."

"He loves you."

"As a brother should."

"Not like a brother, Lin. Do not act the fool, for you are not a stupid lass."

"Be that as it may, I do not want Falcon."

"Still, the triad is the triad, and cannot be gainsaid—more than ever, now. With Martin gone—"

Her voice broke and Linnet wondered, not for the first time, what lay between her mother and Martin Scarlet. Wren had once needed to choose between Martin and Linnet's father, Sparrow. The connections still ran deep. Linnet could feel, even now, the weight of Wren's loss.

"I say only"—Wren strove to sound calm—"you cannot let this young man come between you and what must be."

But, Linnet protested inwardly, what about that which Sherwood decreed? Sherwood was the unspoken fourth in the magical circle and it had, this night, come out in defense of Gareth de Vavasour. Why?

"Let Lark have Falcon," she said implacably. "For she wants him."

"Lark? Surely not. They fight like two cats in a sack."

"That is because he refuses to see her the way she desires."

"Aye, well, I will speak with her also. For now, I am concerned with you. Do not break your heart over him, Lin. It cannot be."

Linnet bowed her head, but her spirit was far from compliant. Why could it not be?

As if her mother heard her thoughts, Wren said, "He is a world removed from you, from us, from our cause."

When Linnet failed to reply, Wren drew a breath and said, "I think it best if I tend him, henceforth."

That made Linnet's gaze fly up. "You do not trust me? Not even for that?"

"I am trying to do you a kindness."

"So," Linnet mourned, "I am allowed to choose nothing. Not my role in life nor the man in my bed. I am merely to accept Falcon and a future as a guardian."

"I am sorry, Daughter." Wren covered Linnet's hand with her own. "Sometimes sacrifices must be made. The triad comes first. Sherwood must always come first."

****

"What happened out there?" Gareth de Vavasour posed the query as Linnet passed him, tied on his tether. She paused involuntarily and felt his good hand snag her wrist. Startled, she looked from his fingers that encircled her flesh, burning, to his wide, gray gaze.

Behind her the others, caught in discussion, debated their immediate course of action. For an instant, their attention remained diverted, but Linnet knew it would not be long before someone recalled her from this forbidden patch of ground.

Resentment flared inside her. Long had she been mistress of her own hearth, used to living apart from her parents. Was she to lose that independence now? Must she listen to the instructions of her family, or worse, Falcon?

Nay, for Fal would never be husband to her.

She sank to the ground beside Gareth de Vavasour. Only let them come and drag her away.

He no longer looked the part of the fine young Norman first captured. His clothing torn, his glossy hair mussed, with the jagged cut down his cheek and with scratches and abrasions everywhere, he looked more the outlaw than she did.

His fingers, warm and brown, still held her wrist,

and his eyes refused to release hers. "I saw—that man turned into a hart."

"There was no man." A flash of white light, the herald of powerful magic, and then the hart standing, making of itself a barrier protecting Gareth de Vavasour. *Why?*

"I saw the man and I saw the hart twice." Gareth sounded desperate.

"Twice?"

"Once whilst I fled. He spoke to me. He said he was—" Gareth's throat closed and then worked mightily. "He said he was Robin Hood."

Everything around them became very still. Even the summer sunlight, drifting down through the trees, seemed to freeze and every leaf quieted, as did the breath in Linnet's lungs.

"Tell me it was a dream," Gareth beseeched her, "or imagining."

"I cannot."

"But Robin Hood is long dead."

"He is, aye, and he is not. He lives here yet, in Sherwood. He is my grandfather. He is lord of this place."

Gareth's eyes widened.

"He," Linnet told him softly, "was one of the foremost guardians of Sherwood, though there have been many over the centuries since people first came here and discovered the magic of this place."

"Centuries?"

"He was the first of my blood to hold the magic, so far as I know. He established the first triad, the first circle meant to guard Sherwood's power—he, together with my grandmother, called Marian, and the Spirit of this place. Others have served since, and kept the circle. Always three."

"That man with the scarred face?"

"Martin Scarlet. He was one of the three who held it during my lifetime. Now, with his death, the circle is broken. Soon, three others will need to take the places of Martin, my mother, and my father."

"Aye, so you said before. It is to be you." Quick as silver light, Gareth's eyes leaped to Lark and Falcon. "And those two."

"Aye."

"But, what of that which the man—Robin Hood—said to me?"

"What said he?"

"He bade me follow what is in my heart." Suddenly Gareth's eyes glowed. He released Linnet's wrist and raised his fingers to touch her cheek very gently, almost as if he feared she might shatter.

"And," Linnet barely whispered the words, "what is in your heart?"

"I scarcely know, except—" He leaned toward her. For an instant, Linnet was so sure he would kiss her, her lips tingled. Her entire soul ached for his kiss and reached to bond with him, yearning wildly.

He withdrew his fingers and Linnet felt the loss like the coming of winter cold.

"It cannot be," he whispered.

"I do not believe in 'cannot,' " Linnet told him, and felt startled to realize how strongly she meant it.

"But you are part of this magical three, and I am destined for service at Nottingham."

"And yet my grandfather stood to defend you from harm. A very great mystery."

"Linnet!" Fal called from across the clearing.

Gareth de Vavasour lifted his gaze. "He wants you." Envy filled his voice. "Will you consider his suit?"

"No, not yet."

"Good, for I do not wish you to wed with him."

Impossible that he should care, and yet Linnet's heart bounded. "I know."

"I ask you to keep from giving yourself to him, despite this preordained bond of which you speak."

Emotion rose to Linnet's head, wild and staggering. She did not understand this powerful thing between them. She merely knew what she felt.

"Lin!"

Gareth's eyes sought and held hers persistently. "Promise me you will not accept him."

"I cannot so promise." Linnet struggled with her wild emotions and then gave him the only promise she could. "But I will wait as long as ever I can, as long as events allow."

Some of the tension went out of him. "It is well. Because, you see, you are meant to be mine."

Inexplicable as they were, the words sounded like a vow. Conviction blossomed with them, raw and bright, and took up residence in Linnet's heart. Her eyes filled with tears, she who so rarely wept. She nodded once and got quickly to her feet, knowing she had to walk away from him now.

But she would not be apart from him, not truly—never again.

****

I must be mad, Gareth thought, stark raving, to make of her such a demand. Yet his words had been called forth from him by her beauty, by the expression in her eyes when she looked at him, more by the forest itself, the trees all around and the light that sifted down. They were called by the hunger of his flesh for her, a rampant thing all wrapped up in tenderness, breathless and waiting.

And impossible, all of it. How could he ask of her any kind of promise when he remained a prisoner, and beyond that a Norman knight? And she, a part of this blood-sworn resistance against his kind and, beyond that, part of the very enchantment breathed by this place.

"Follow your heart." He heard again the words of the man with the narrow, clever face and the transformative smile—Robin Hood. Nay, but it must have been delusion, some aberration brought on by the desperation of flight, and the moonlight.

And he had forged a vow on the strength of it. He had no doubt that was what his words to Linnet had been—a vow of intent.

"De Vavasour." The big man called Sparrow stood over him. "We must speak together of my daughter, Linnet."

Gareth struggled to his feet. He did not feel wary of this man, not as he did of Linnet's mother with her sharp gaze and her tangible command of magic. Gareth suspected Sparrow possessed magic also; it virtually clothed him. Yet something about him spoke to and calmed Gareth.

"Sit." Sparrow waved him back down and took the place beside him.

At some distance across the clearing, it appeared the others busied themselves packing up camp. "Are we leaving this place?" he asked.

"Aye. Falcon, Lark, and Linnet go back to Oakham. Fal wishes to see his father buried, or at least mark his passing, as he is no doubt already in the ground."

"And I?"

"You will stay here for the time, with myself and Wren. When it is safe for a ransom demand to be taken to Nottingham, Lark or Lin will send word and let us know."

"My uncle will never ransom me."

"Why not?" Sparrow studied him with eyes as dark and deep as Linnet's. "You are his kin, his blood."

"Yet he barely knows me. I have seen him rarely since I was small." And if Robert de Vavasour proved anything like his brother, Gareth's father Maurice, he must be a hard man indeed, devoid of both sentiment and familial feeling. Had he not patronized the final part of Gareth's training and demanded his service in return, Gareth would not be here now.

"Still, I cannot see him leaving you in our hands."

Gareth shrugged and Sparrow gave a tight smile. "It remains to be seen. Until that time, you will stay with my wife and me, in Sherwood. Wren will see to your healing."

"And Linnet? You said you wished to speak of her."

Sparrow drew a breath that expanded his great chest. His eyes examined Gareth almost kindly. "You will not see her again."

Gareth turned his head sharply. His eyes found Linnet across the clearing where she bent gracefully over a bundle she assembled, her dark hair streaming down.

"Life is long," he told Sparrow. "You cannot make such a declaration. If she and I are meant to meet again, we shall so meet."

Sparrow's expression turned wry. "Leave her alone, if you would do her any service. She has her place in this world as you have yours. You are a Norman knight. Linnet is even more vitally important."

Gareth did not speak, but everything inside him cried his resistance.

Sparrow went on, still in his calm rumble. "You could do for her one thing else, if you will."

"What is that?"

"Forget her. Forget, also, the location of her village and the names of those dear to her. Your uncle we know for a vengeful man, devoid of mercy. Protect her as you can."

Gareth gave a hard nod. That he could do. But see her go from him... It made a harder prospect.

Sparrow met his gaze and gave a tight smile. "I do not know all of what happened in the forest last night. Like my wife, I sensed great magic. The wheel of our lives turns mightily just now. It does not go easily for me to trust a Norman. But it seems I must trust you to protect my daughter, Gareth de Vavasour."

Chapter Fifteen

"Smell that—'tis the scent of burning on the wind." Falcon's head reared up like that of a wild creature sensing danger.

Lark, coming up next to him, paused with her whole body aquiver.

Linnet, who brought up the rear in their return to Oakham, struggled to gather her thoughts. Too much had happened back in the forest; she felt torn, as if the better part of her had been ripped away and left behind with Gareth de Vavasour.

That it should be so terrified her. He was the very last man upon whom she should settle her heart: Norman knight, nephew to her mortal enemy, sworn opponent to all she held dear. She barely knew him, had not yet kissed him, for all her longing. Yet her heart had leaped to him without her leave. And now she carried a part of him with her, even as she had left a measure of her soul in his hands.

"Come, hurry." Lark, ever indefatigable, took off at a run. Falcon quickly followed. They were not far from Oakham—home—now, but the journey had been a long one, and Linnet felt a sudden weight of dread mingle with her weariness to hold her back. She suddenly knew she did not want to see. Yet she forced herself to follow her companions.

The reek of burning intensified as they went. When

they burst from the trees that sheltered the village, they dragged to a halt, one by one.

Most of Oakham lay in a still-smoking heap, even though the disaster was clearly not new. Air heavy with ash hung beneath the sheltering boughs of the trees, along with a suffocating aura of oppression. Somewhere a dog barked and a child wailed, sounding tired and hungry.

Linnet stared in disbelief, unable to make sense of what she saw. The west side of the village, where her own hut had stood, lay mostly ruined. On the east side, beyond the communal gardens, some buildings still stood.

"Oh, God," Falcon breathed: an invocation.

Lark seized his arm with both hands. "Retaliation," she seethed, "for the robbery and capture of that accursed Norman. It must be!"

Gone, thought Linnet, stunned. All gone. Her wee hut and everything she owned inside it—precious little it might seem to some, but to her it meant independence. Herbs gathered and blended over weeks and months, her few treasures—the wooden stag her father had carved for her when she was ten, the silk charm bag Ma had passed down from the wise woman, Lil—irreplaceable keepsakes of her life.

She struggled to pick out the particular pile of rubble that was her own, and her heart ached.

Folk wandered the grounds looking as lost as Linnet suddenly felt. Catching sight of the new arrivals, they began to gather.

Linnet glanced into Falcon's face; he looked anguished, and he breathed but one word. "Pa."

"Surely he was safe in the ground before this

happened," Lark told him. "Surely. And if not, Fal, 'tis a hero's funeral, as he deserved."

"I should have been here, not off haring about the forest." Falcon's voice sounded rough with pain. Linnet knew him to the heart and knew that, despite his habitual easy demeanor, he felt things deeply, and never more so than now.

"What happened?" Lark addressed those who gathered to meet them. "When?"

The smith, Yancy, spoke. "Two days past, now. They came with torches at daybreak."

"Who?"

"Soldiers from Nottingham. Said they wanted those outlaws who held up the party on the York road and took the King's taxes."

Lark and Falcon exchanged looks. Falcon spoke. "Did they ask after the captive?"

"Nay. And they refused to believe us when we denied all knowledge of their lost riches. We found out yesterday they burned Held as well, and most of Elderdale."

"That means they do not know whence came the men who held them up on the road," Lark murmured.

"And so everyone pays," cried a woman whose shocked eyes burned in her pale face. "My home is gone."

"We have three dead," Yancy said gravely, "one a child who perished from the smoke, and many injured." He looked at Linnet. "We need the skill in your hands, lass."

She gestured helplessly. "I have lost all." The few healing supplies she had taken with her had been left with her mother, for Gareth. "Of course I will do what I can."

"My father," Fal said brokenly, "had he already been buried?"

Another of the men answered, "Aye, lad. But the things of his we had saved for you, his hood and his quiver, those arrows he kept for remembrances, are all gone. The shelter where they lay is burnt to cinders. Only his sword remains, and that badly damaged."

Grief twisted Falcon's features. "I should have been here, to stand and fight."

Yancy's eyes flashed. "You think we did not stand? The worst wounded are those who tried. Well do you know, young Falcon, a man on foot is no match for one mounted, and with a sword." He reached out and clasped Fal's arm. "But we need you now. Oakham needs the leadership of a strong headman, more than ever with your father gone."

Falcon seemed to shrink. "Can you not take the place, Yancy? I am not the man my father was."

"Nor am I, lad. I daresay there will never be another like him. Come, though. You must have known the place would be yours one day. And folk are anxious to look to someone. They feel lost, and there is much work to be done."

It seemed to Linnet the whole village stood holding its breath for Falcon's answer. But he did not make it. Instead his face crumpled and his eyes went wide.

Lark, still holding his arm, spoke steadily. "Of course he will step into the breach. We shall all pull together as we always do. What have those without roofs been doing these two nights past?"

A woman spoke. "Sleeping outside, or with neighbors."

"At least the weather is kind," Lark said briskly. "We shall begin with rebuilding as suits the need. Gather all those who have lost their homes here, beside me, and those sore hurt in another group, for Linnet. We shall see to everyone. Aye, Fal?"

He nodded brokenly. The village folk, given something to do, seemed satisfied and hurried off.

Linnet, staggering emotionally under the weight of all to be done, looked at her companions. "Someone should tell Ma and Pa. Or do you think they know?"

"I think they suspected what we would find here," Lark returned. "It is likely why they sent us." Her golden eyes met Linnet's. "They mean for the three of us to work together. And so we shall. Is that not right, Fal?"

He had covered his face with his hands. "All lost, gone the same way as my mother and poor wee Thrush."

"I know how you are hurting." Lark's voice softened.

"I failed him."

"If that is truly how you feel, then resolve you will not fail him again. Step up and take the place he held for you all these years."

"You are wrong." Fal raised an anguished face. "He held it not for me but because he was a leader to the bone. As I am not! How can I act as these folk expect? Better you take the place of headman, Lark, than I."

"Never mind." Lark hooked an arm about his neck and drew his head down to hers. "We shall hold the place together, eh?"

They went off and left Linnet alone, save for one

child who lingered, large-eyed, with his thumb in his mouth. "Go home to your mother, Roger," Linnet told him kindly. "She will be missing you." Not until she had spoken the words did she realize his home, close by her own, stood no longer. "Here." She held out her hand to him. Best she find his mother, amid all this madness, and see him safe.

She came upon the child's mother standing with a knot of other women, gossiping, and stood to speak with them. The children, they said, were sore frightened, tired, and hungry. Linnet set them to organizing a communal cook pot and bade them bring their little ones to a cleared place where she could tend their injuries.

She could see Lark and Falcon across the way, still in tandem and giving similar directions. That was, Lark appeared to be giving instructions while Fal stood at her side, shocked and silent.

Linnet stole a moment to walk back to the rubble that had once been her home, where she looked to see what could be salvaged. Nothing. The thatch must have burned and come down, engulfing everything inside. The rubble still gave off heat. Perhaps when it cooled she would be able to search, but she could not imagine finding anything intact.

Tears flooded her eyes and she had to catch herself up, hard. No one ever said life was not difficult or that things would be just. But following so swiftly on the loss of Martin, this seemed a cruel blow indeed.

And now what? With her parents still deep in Sherwood, must she, Lark, and Falcon take the reins in their hands in order to move forward? Was that what her parents intended, to set the new triad in motion and force them to accept their places?

And would Ma and Pa now disappear into Sherwood like all those spirits who inhabited it, lose themselves in the magic that held the ancient forest? Better that, Linnet acknowledged, than to lose them as Falcon had lost Martin. Even though she did not see her parents often, they were the bedrock of her life, and her heart ached at the idea of going on without them. The prospect of trying to exist without her Pa's smile, the steady wisdom in his eyes, the comfort he emitted, or Ma's lightning humor and sharp wit, and the strength of her knowing, seemed impossible. How did Fal endure it?

And what of Lark? She seemed as strong and undefeatable as Ma, but in many ways Martin Scarlet had been her hero, and that part of her world had been destroyed.

How could Linnet be so selfish as to think about herself at such a time? How wonder at being able to go on in the absence of Gareth de Vavasour when others had lost so much? How let herself pine for a pair of clear, gray eyes, when Fal's eyes were full of pain? How hunger for the taste of someone she had never even kissed...

Get hold of yourself, girl. A short while ago, you did not know he existed. But you have always known the path that lay before you. Time to set your foot upon it and forget him.

"But I cannot forget," she said aloud into the ashes of her past life. "I cannot hope to forget."

Chapter Sixteen

"Drink this."

The demand roused Gareth de Vavasour from his sleep. The dawn sun was just rising, and all around him the forest lay in a deep hush. Light had begun to seep between the mighty boles of the trees and through the high canopy of leaves.

Linnet's mother stood above him with a wooden cup in her hands.

He blinked at her and sat up. His bed had been the moss of Sherwood and he had slept surprisingly well. He remembered—and did not remember—dreaming; the remnants of sweet visions still wrapped round him. *Linnet.* Surely he had loved her, in his dreams.

And surely this woman offering him the cup knew it. She seemed so aware of everything. Three days they had been together at this new place, Gareth, Wren, and Sparrow. And Gareth had begun to develop a strange, inexplicable affinity for the magic here that he breathed like air.

Sometimes it all seemed too real, painfully vital— the light, the sounds the trees made whispering among themselves, and the twining threads of power. Sometimes nothing at all seemed real or substantial, not even the people with whom he found himself. It might all be illusion, like his vivid dreams.

He looked into Wren Little's eyes and wondered

what he saw there, besides impatience. He did not reach to take the cup from her but instead asked, "What is that?"

"A draught to make you stronger."

So it might well be; she had dosed him with many vile potions these days past. Most tasted of dirt and sticks. But something about this offering pricked his senses.

"What have you put in it?" He always asked. Usually she did not tell; she just insisted he drink. He found the woman relentless.

"Herbs."

Cautiously, he accepted the cup in his right hand. The contents steamed a bit, the way the trees did when the morning sun first hit them. He sniffed and the contents smelled bitter; the vessel might contain poison, or pure enchantment.

He stirred and stretched his limbs on the end of his tether. Secured to a young ash tree that persistently rattled its leaves at him, he had watched Wren each day while she secured the bond with a murmured spell.

"Drink it," Wren repeated inexorably and folded her legs beneath her, so to sit beside him. He knew from experience she would stay until he ingested every drop.

He could not doubt her skill as a healer or that she employed some measure of magic when she treated him. He could feel that much whenever she laid her hands on him, a bright tingle that penetrated his flesh and seemed to heal his wounds from within. He found it an altogether disconcerting sensation and hoped she would not touch him now, even though her care had lent him immeasurable strength.

"We have been given signs," she announced, "telling us you will soon be able to go home."

"Home?" But he had none. Any such claim had been buried with the whimsical creature he had called Mother.

"To Nottingham. What place shall you hold in de Vavasour's company?"

Gareth shook his head. "I know naught beyond that he has summoned me."

"To be his wolfhound and chase us to ground here in the forest? If so, you have been given a great advantage, having seen how and where we live."

"He patronized the last of my training and demands my service in return."

"Ah, perhaps you are meant to replace the vile Monteith as Captain of the Guard, since that man has not had great success in curtailing our activities." She smiled a dangerous smile that made her look very like the man, or spirit, Gareth had encountered in the forest—Robin Hood.

"I am unable to hold any place at all, what with my arm broken."

"We shall see to that. Drink."

Gareth raised the cup to his lips. The contents tasted sharp and smelled intensely aromatic. The bitterness stung his throat on the way down. Aye, poison, no doubt. He wondered that he did not feel more upset about it.

When he could speak again, for the taste, he said, "It is not possible to merely re-knit the bone in my arm. Such an injury takes many weeks' recovery."

"We shall see. When you are finished with drinking that—to the last drop, mind—strip yourself down. You are going into the water."

Gareth felt heat sweep over him. "I think not."

She raked him with her gaze. "Do not flatter yourself, lad. I am scarce interested in what you have beneath those rags. They are in such tatters you have few secrets anyway. But do not concern yourself; my husband will tend you in this."

"Why should either of you care to tend me, by any road?"

She smiled again. "I have my reasons, and my reasons are Sparrow's. Only do your part. You will feel better for it."

With that, she got to her feet and moved off. Gareth, rueful, had to admit he already felt better. He downed the last of the cup's bitter contents and tried not to shudder. After that he merely sat and let the strengthening light come find him, settle on his hair, and sift through him from the head down. Each morning had it been thus; magic rode on the light.

And since when had he begun believing in magic? His eyes flew open wide at the question. He was a Norman knight, trained in practical things, a proven champion and product of a man who sneered at anything other than control and physical prowess. His father had permitted no talk of fancy, nor vision. He had tried to knock such nonsense out of his young wife.

But Gareth's mother, with her Celtic blood, had refused to yield her instinctual belief. Indeed, she had died before ever doing so.

A flare of hate raced through Gareth's veins, his consistent reaction when he thought of his father and the way that man had treated his mother.

"All right, lad?" Sparrow's deep voice rumbled

over him. "Up on your feet. Good thing 'tis a warm morning, eh?"

Sparrow's big hands made short work of the tether and the magic that secured it. Gareth stripped off his clothes, able to feel the difference in his body when he moved. Many of his scratches were healed and almost all the aches and bruises gone. He could wiggle the fingers of his left hand with almost no pain.

"The bandages, as well," Sparrow told him.

Gareth peeled them off and scrutinized the wounds. Mottled with new, pink skin, they appeared far less inflamed. He raised his fingers to the long cut Scarface had given him on his cheek. Not nearly so tender.

"Come along to the stream."

It felt good to move free of the hated restraint. Gareth stretched his body as he went. The stream ran deep here, and clear, between clean-cut banks. Where two trees leaned together across it, a pool had formed.

Sparrow gestured. "In with you."

Gareth shot him a look. It might well be a warm morning, but he knew from experience how cold that water ran. He had already been sluiced in it and told to wash himself from the bank.

He slid down into the water and promptly lost his breath. Moving quickly, he submerged himself to the neck.

It felt—wonderful. The water, clattering over stones, streamed across his shoulders and pooled around his body. After a moment he stretched out his arms and laid his head back. When he raised it again, the hair slapped wet against his back.

Sparrow seated himself on the bank and placed his staff across his knees. Gareth could not help but wonder about that staff. A great, mighty thing, it had a twisted trunk and looked something more than a weapon. Surely it wielded magic.

He curved his lips in a wry smile. There was that word again: *magic*. How absurdly often it now came to his mind.

"Funny thing," Sparrow rumbled, as if having a casual conversation, "how men are all the same when you strip them down to the skin. Take you, for instance. At the moment 'tis hard to tell whether to figure you for a fine Norman lord, a peasant's son, or someone who simply does every daft thing he is told—like sit in a pool of cold water."

"The latter, without question."

"Where are you from, lad? Oh, I do not mean your blood lines, though I suppose those are relevant enough. I mean where are you from—you, the man inside? For we all come from a place molded by our experiences and those who have loved us."

An image flashed across Gareth's mind of a slender woman, honey-haired and with fey, knowing eyes. He dismissed it quickly and thought instead of his father. "My sire owned a large estate north of Leeds. It belongs to my brother now, since his death."

"Any other siblings?"

"A sister, long wed and gone." She had been traded for her value, and Gareth had scarcely seen her since.

"Were you raised in the Church?"

The question seemed so strange, Gareth raised his eyes to meet Sparrow's. They were dark and wild and held wisdom so potent it sent a chill up Gareth's spine.

"Of course," he replied. Could it be otherwise? A man accepted the Church's teachings if he did not want to spend eternity in hell when this life was done. And for a Norman knight, life could end at any time. Youth lent no guarantee.

Gareth knew men who had bought favor and had tried to purchase absolution. His own brother, Bernard, had made a rich donation on his father's behalf after he died. Much good it might do, Gareth thought bitterly. The man deserved to writhe in endless torment.

"Some men who take to the sword," Sparrow said thoughtfully, "do so for the sake of righteousness, some for pure gain—that is true of your kind and mine as well. I just wondered what sort you were."

"Neither," Gareth replied wryly, and not untruthfully. "As you said, I do as bidden and go where told."

The big man leaned over the bank toward him. "Some day, Gareth de Vavasour, you will have to make a choice. You will need to decide whether to follow your head or your heart. So much is true of all men. And so much, for you, is told by the stars."

"What have the heavens to do with it?" Gareth asked, taken aback.

"The heavens, the earth, the fire, and the water." Sparrow gestured with the staff to the pool where Gareth lay. "All things conspire, lad, to bring us to our destiny."

Chapter Seventeen

"Where is your headman?" The cry broke the morning stillness the way an axe blade might shatter a skull. "On your feet when you face your betters, you lazy vermin. Do you not know who I am?"

Robert de Vavasour. Linnet's mind supplied the name even before she poked her nose from the temporary shelter she, Lark, and Falcon shared. She had heard that haughty voice before and could not mistake it now. Her heart stuttered and then leaped in terror.

Dawn had just come to Oakham; the gentle light of summer sifted through the trees and into the ruined village. But all hope of peace was scattered by the stout company of mounted men milling not far from where Gareth de Vavasour had once been pegged out like a sacrificial goat: soldiers and two knights, all wearing the insignia of Nottingham Castle—a pair of foresters flanking a castle—and a man with a thin, severe face and an air of absolute superiority.

Aye, she remembered him. Rich brown hair, high-bridged nose, haughty demeanor, and fine clothing. The Sheriff of Nottingham, himself, here.

Almost before she could grasp the fact, she found herself elbowed aside by Lark, who took one look out the doorway of the shelter and called, "Fal!"

Falcon unfolded himself from the pallet upon which he had spent much of the past three days. Linnet

113

was not sure how she felt about Fal's response to the call of leadership. She loved him like a brother and she knew how badly he hurt, how lost he felt. But he had retreated to a place inside his head and seemed reluctant to emerge again. Whatever she had expected of him, it had not been that.

It could not be denied that Lark had been leading them all since their return from the forest. A small fury, she had been everywhere, speaking encouragement, organizing for the needs of the villagers, and deciding what should be rebuilt and when. Folk turned to her readily, simply because she was accessible as Fal was not. True enough, she carried Falcon's banner, prefacing most of her words with "Fal says," or "Falcon thinks."

No question, Lark was—and should be—the new headman of Oakham. But she could not step forward now, when the Sheriff of Nottingham called the village leader to appear before him. Falcon knew that as well. Linnet saw as much in his eyes when he stepped to the doorway and laid his hand on Lark's shoulder.

Lark responded to the gesture instinctively and wrapped her arms about his waist. The two of them had bonded in some curious way Linnet could not completely understand. She knew she could rightfully attribute the connection to love on the part of Lark. But she feared on Fal's it came mostly of need.

She heard her sister speak to him now, low and urgent. "You must show yourself and put a brave face on it."

Fal nodded. Linnet felt rather than saw him pull himself up precisely as if he donned a coat that had belonged to another, likely his father. He stepped out into the morning light with Lark half a step behind him.

Robert de Vavasour's gaze found him at once. He pulled his horse around, no doubt bent on using his superior position to good advantage. The Sheriff had light-colored eyes beneath brows of reddish brown, and a cruel, impatient slant to his mouth.

"What is your name, serf?" he demanded of Falcon.

"Scarlet."

"Are you headman here?"

"I am."

Linnet had to hand it to Falcon; his voice sounded steady and sure. He seemed to have donned some of Martin's confidence along with his manner.

"We are searching for a knight seized some days ago on the road south from York." No mention of the others taken captive with Gareth. Being mere soldiers, they did not matter much to de Vavasour, she supposed.

"He is not here." Falcon shook his head and added, deliberately late, "My lord." He waved a hand. "Your men already searched the village before they burned it. Naught is hidden."

"I am aware they have already searched. They will continue to do so until the man in question is turned over to us."

"I am sure we would give him to you at once, my lord, if we could."

"Are you? I am afraid I lack any such conviction. But I come here myself this day, as to every other village under my domain, to assure it. The man I seek is my nephew, Gareth de Vavasour. And I tell you there will not be a village left standing in all Nottinghamshire if he is not returned in good health to me."

Falcon, like those around him, stood mute, a stubborn look in his eyes.

De Vavasour gave him a hard glare and turned to his men. "Seize him."

"What? Nay!" The cry burst from Lark's throat and was echoed by a half score of others.

The Sheriff raised his voice. "We are taking the headman of each and every village to Nottingham, where I will hold them as security against my nephew's return." He smiled thinly. "Think of it as a mercy, for this ransom you can pay."

"You cannot do this! How dare—" Lark got no further. One of the two knights leaned down from the back of his mount and struck her with a gauntleted fist. She flew sideways and lay as if broken. Falcon roared and hurled himself at her attacker. Violence erupted everywhere at once.

Linnet ducked a drawn sword in an effort to reach her sister's side, but before she got there Lark sprang up and leaped into the fray. The two mounted knights shifted their horses, using them like weapons, and Linnet had to move her feet quickly to keep from being trampled under the chargers' hooves.

Amid the screaming, blows, and confusion, she saw a flame ignite as a torch was lit.

"No!" she shouted but no one heard her or, if they heard, heeded. A knight spurred his horse to one of the few standing houses and put flame to thatch. Three soldiers now had hold of Falcon, whom they had beaten down mercilessly. As Linnet watched, they bore him to the ground, with Lark, once more on her feet, attacking all the while.

One put his sword to Fal's throat.

"Now, then," said Robert de Vavasour, calmly, "let us try this again. Have you knowledge, serf, of my nephew's whereabouts, or must we question you further at Nottingham?"

Falcon bared his teeth in a grimace. It was Lark who again screamed, "No!" She threw herself at Fal in a wild attempt to free him from the grasp of his captors, nearly disarming the soldier who leveled the weapon at Falcon's throat. Almost casually, Robert de Vavasour leaned down and struck her with the blunt of his sword.

"Troublesome wench." He looked round at the stunned faces of the villagers. "You have a fortnight, which I call a generous allowance. After that we will begin putting our captives to the death." He gestured at Fal, bloodied and snarling. "Your headman will die first."

One of the soldiers hauled Fal up across his saddle bow, like a felled hart. With a great clanking and jingling of harness, the party gathered themselves and moved off, Fal straining back for one last look at the place where Lark lay.

Linnet fell to her knees at her sister's side. Lark's eyes stared, wide open, and blood covered the side of her face.

Her lips formed but one word. "Falcon."

****

"I shall kill them all slowly and painfully, every carrier of vile Norman blood! I will save him for last—the accursed Sheriff, Robert de Vavasour—and let him see the spike on which I mean to impale his ugly head."

Linnet eyed her sister with misgiving but said nothing. She could feel Lark's terror and disquiet and knew she had been shaken to the core by Falcon's

117

seizure. No doubt she found some relief in her bold declarations. In Linnet's opinion, Lark should not even be up on her feet, but so far Linnet had been unsuccessful in keeping her down.

Most of the fires had been put out. A few piles of thatch still smoldered, and village folk milled about wearing devastated expressions. Some of them, elders who had been Martin Scarlet's cronies, along with friends of Falcon, as well as Lark and Linnet, had gathered to discuss what should next be done.

"We must get Falcon back," Lark declared, unswerving.

"But how best to answer the Sheriff's demand?" wondered Adam Wright. "The young prisoner he wants is here no longer."

"Your parents have him?" asked Yancy, the smith, of Linnet.

"Aye," Linnet confirmed unhappily.

"I say we fetch the bastard out of Sherwood and send him to Nottingham in pieces," Lark growled.

"A message will need to be sent," said Eldwin, who was Fal's friend. "The lord Sparrow and the lady Wren must be told what has happened. We were hoping to use the Norman lordlet to ransom Derek and the other prisoners. Instead, now the Sheriff has still more of our men."

"I will go into Sherwood," Lark declared, "bring the cur out, as I say, and prepare his stinking hide for Nottingham."

"You are fit to go nowhere," Linnet told her sister. She lifted her eyes to the smoke-heavy air. "But Ma and Pa must be told, aye. I will go."

"You are needed here, young Linnet," said Yancy,

"for tending the wounded."

"I will see to everyone's hurts before I go, including yours, Lark." Linnet looked at the men. "The rest of you try and organize shelter for the wounded, if you can, and bury our dead." Three had perished in the skirmish, one a small child trampled beneath the hooves of the horses.

Lark drew herself up and spoke fiercely. "I want to go."

"Nay, it should be me." Linnet did not wish to admit to herself that, much as she needed to see her parents, she hoped as well for the sight of Gareth de Vavasour, maybe even for the touch of his hand.

Ah, and how could she even think of him with favor when his kind had done this to her village, her people?

Lark glared at her. "You must act swiftly, Lin. What if that bastard Sheriff does not keep his word? What if he decides to kill Fal at once, as an example, today or tomorrow? Promise me you will do all you can to save him."

Linnet looked into her sister's eyes, wild with terror and defiance, and answered the only way she could. "Aye, Lark, and I do so promise."

Chapter Eighteen

"Falcon has been taken prisoner. So far as we know, he is being held in the dungeons at Nottingham. We have been given a fortnight to ransom him, and the headmen of the other villages with him, before he is put to the death."

Breathless, Linnet spilled the words into her parents' ears. She spared but one glance for Gareth de Vavasour, tethered to his tree at some distance, even though his presence pulled at her the way the sea pulls at a shore. Even the expression in her mother's eyes failed to distract her completely.

"I knew 'twas something dire." Wren threw her hands in the air and exchanged looks with her husband. "We knew. It has been like a cloud hanging over us. When did this happen?"

"Early this morning, at first light." Refusing to look again at the captive, Linnet added, "The Sheriff himself came with soldiers and two mounted knights. De Vavasour demands the return of his nephew in exchange for Fal's life."

Her mother scowled. "It is ill news—the new triad at risk before it is even fairly founded! We must think carefully about what is to be done."

"There seems but one thing can be done," Linnet's father put in. "De Vavasour must be returned. We cannot wager Falcon's life."

Pain bit deep into Linnet's heart at hearing the words, even though she had more than half expected them. Falcon, the triad, and the protection of Sherwood were far more important than her feelings for a man she barely knew.

Gravely, she said, "Oakham is burned to the ground. Folk will need all the help we can muster. They may well need you to return out of the forest. Lark is acting as headman now," Linnet added fairly, "and doing a fine job of it, I must say. But following so soon on Martin's death this is a hard loss to bear, and folk look for a guiding star."

"Then you must be that for them." Wren reached out and touched Linnet's hair in an uncharacteristic gesture of tenderness. "Your father and I must step back now and give the three of you a chance to find your feet. In truth, we cannot carry the leadership much longer, with our circle broken." Her eyes filled with unexpected tears. "You, Lark, and Falcon need to forge your own bonds and follow your own light."

"But I am not ready." Again, Linnet cast a look towards Gareth. Too distant to hear their conversation, he nevertheless turned his head precisely as if he sensed her attention upon him. Their eyes met and Linnet's pulse sped.

Kindly, Sparrow said, "Aye, Daughter, but events will not wait for you. You must take up your places now."

"I know." Linnet had always understood this day must come, but had supposed it would be far in the future, at a time distant and unseen.

"Come." Without waiting for her to follow, Wren stalked to the prisoner, who huddled staked to a young ash tree. He got to his feet as they approached, his tether not so cruelly short as to prohibit ample movement, and Linnet lost all the breath in her lungs.

Gareth de Vavasour no longer looked even remotely like a Norman noble. Clothed in the leather garments of a woodsman or peasant, he stood quietly, most of his cuts and bruises faded and nearly healed. Wounds at shoulder and thigh lay hidden beneath the clothing, but the cut on his cheek now made no more than a thin, red line.

He had not shaved since Linnet had last seen him, and his beard had grown in golden brown, like the hair Linnet had glimpsed on his chest when she tended him.

How could he be altered so greatly in but a few short days?

Wren spoke to him before Linnet could. "You told us your uncle would not stir himself to ransom you."

"So I did believe." Gareth's eyes lingered on Linnet's face before moving to Wren's. "Has he done?"

"My daughter brings word that he has burnt the village and taken our Falcon prisoner in an effort to force your return. What say you to that?"

Gareth's surprise appeared genuine. "It can only be a matter of pride with him."

"Of course it is a matter of pride," Wren tossed back. "His sort are all about pride, and very little sense or mercy."

"I doubt much he knows anything of mercy," Gareth agreed.

A curious thing to say, yet Wren allowed him no time to expand on it. "We need Falcon back. Thus something will have to be done. My question to you is can we trust Robert de Vavasour? Will he keep his word and hold to the bargain should we send you to him?"

"I cannot fairly say; I barely know him. From what I do know, I would suppose he might believe that any means are justified in pursuit of the end he seeks. I doubt he will find much need to deal honorably with folk he considers traitors in their own right."

"My estimation, as well." Wren glanced at Sparrow. "We shall need to study on this, seek wisdom from a higher source." She touched Sparrow's arm and they walked off together, leaving Linnet staring into Gareth's eyes.

"You look well," she told him, knowing it for a vast understatement. Without his torn and filthy clothing, clear-eyed and hale, he made a dangerous temptation. Oh, why could he not have been a wright's son, a farmer's or a fletcher's son, born in some neighboring village? And why could she not be just some ordinary lass without a heavy claim on her future?

"Your mother has been busy healing me," he replied. "Look, she has removed your splint, and already I can move my fingers." He wiggled his left hand and then raised rueful eyes to Linnet's. "I believe she used magic. A month ago I would have scoffed at such a suggestion. But this was like naught I have ever experienced, and I mended very quickly indeed."

Linnet nodded.

"Can you tell me why she would do such a thing?" he pressed. "Why would she heal me, only to send me off to Nottingham?"

"She will have her reasons. She always does, though they are rarely easy to understand. I dare say she did not expect to have to trade you away for Falcon.

But we must get him back at any cost."

Gareth eyed his tether, only loosely secured to the ash tree, and then shot a look after Linnet's parents who had disappeared into the trees as completely as if they had never existed. Did he weigh his chances, even now, of escape?

But no, for he gave another wry smile and gestured to the bond.

"It is secured with a spell of words as well as a knot. Believe me, I have tried to break it."

What must this be like for him, Linnet wondered suddenly, this privileged lord, young champion, now bidden to go or come and subjected to disciplines he did not comprehend?

The nobles she had encountered in the past would have raged at it, but Gareth de Vavasour stood before her calm and composed. In some curious way, he appeared to have accepted the edicts of this strange world into which he had been thrown.

And everything about him called to her: he drew her with his eyes, with the promised touch of his hands, with his every breath. Even his thoughts seemed to speak to her, as if they vibrated in harmony with her own.

Unable to help herself, she stepped nearer.

"With whom will they consult in order to seek this wisdom?" he asked.

"The spirits of this place, those who dwell here and who have passed from this life, as well as the one who is lord of this wood."

"Has that lord a name?"

"He has many names, and many guises. The villagers call him the Green Man, Herne, the Old One,

Cernunnos—or simply God. He can appear as a stag." Watching his reaction carefully, she added, "Or as my grandfather, Robin Hood."

Gareth caught his breath. "He whom I saw the night I tried to escape."

Linnet lifted a brow. "You do not sneer and call it superstition, you who were raised in the tenets of the high Church?"

"How can I? I know what I saw that night. Yet to my understanding, Robin Hood was a real man who died. How can he then be a god?"

"My grandfather may have died in a hail of arrows rather than on a cross, yet in so doing he became holy, as did the Church's Christ. Who can explain the boundaries of faith, Master de Vavasour, or the ultimate godliness of men?"

"Do not call me that." Emotion flashed in his eyes. "I pray you will call me Gareth."

She lifted her chin. "Gareth, then, do you find no reason to scoff at our beliefs?"

"Have you seen me do so? I would be a fool if I denied there exists something here, when I have felt—and seen—it." He reached out and touched her arm softly. His warm fingers started a tingle that raced through her body like summer lightning. "Please, while you await your parents' decision, will you sit and talk with me, before I must away to Nottingham? I am hungry to learn everything about you, Linnet. I would carry what you know with me."

Aye, and this might well be their last chance to talk together of anything at all.

His hand brushed her arm in a deliberate caress before he captured her fingers and tugged her down onto the moss.

"Pray, can you tell me of these beliefs that mean so much to you?"

Amazed, she searched his eyes but saw there no deception. "If you wish. How best to begin? Our faith is all about life," she told him softly. "That which stirs in the rabbit's heart in spring, that which causes the sapling to bud, and which quickens in a new mother's womb with her child." She laid her hand lightly against his scarred cheek. "It is what makes the flesh knit anew and what sleeps beneath the winter snow. It is about everything always and always coming again, an eternal circle with no end in death. It is about claiming, and belonging." She drew a breath and her eyes met his. "It is about love."

His fingers came up and covered hers, which rested still against his face. "And all that is founded here, in Sherwood?"

"Sherwood is a haven for it. Since the first folk came here, long ago, when all of England was forest, strong magic has gathered at this place, born of their belief. It gave them identity and worth, as it does us, still. So long as the forest is protected, so is our strength and our freedom." She added deliberately, "Freedom even in the face of Norman tyranny, for there are things that cannot reach here—at least so long as the guardianship holds and endures."

"Guardianship," he repeated doubtfully, and his clear eyes met hers. "Aye, you spoke of that before. And you say you are one of these guardians—you, with your sister and Falcon."

"We are the next three—four, if you count the forest itself, for it is a living being—to take up the burden and the privilege. It cannot be denied, you see, not for any cost." Her eyes filled with tears. "No matter how I might wish."

"And do you so wish?" He bent his head towards hers. For an instant she was sure he would kiss her and all her being strained toward him. But instead he spoke, his warm breath coursing across her lips. "Am I to leave you here to your privilege and your duty? You expect me to walk away?"

"Surely you always knew you must. There is no other hope for it." Despite appearances, he was still a Norman knight. "Do you not long to be away out of your captivity?"

"Aye, so a part of me does. But part of me—" He closed his eyes and turned his face into her hand. "Part of me longs even so to stay, if that be my only means, ever, of seeing you."

Linnet's heart—treacherous heart!—bounded in perilous victory. Overhead, the trees swayed softly. High up in a bough, a bird sang a song so sweet it fell on her ear like pain. Life was all pain, it suddenly seemed, and all impossible beauty.

"You will soon forget about me, in Nottingham," she proposed softly. "No doubt your stay here will seem no more than a dream."

"You are a dream," he whispered. "But...I to forget you? Never!" Gently, he took her hand from his face and pressed a kiss into her palm. An act of devotion it might have been, did she not know better. She shivered with longing.

Huskily, she said, "Once back in your world, it will be easy for you to use all you have learned against us. I do not doubt the Sheriff would be eager to know of the power he might gain by destroying the triad. I am a fool—I have made us vulnerable."

"You think I could ever do aught to bring harm to you?" He reached out, swiftly now, and his fingers tangled in her hair. Strong and warm, they cupped the back of her head, and desire speared through her like a bolt of fire. She leaned toward him, lips and soul both questing.

Their mouths met almost tentatively and then fused avidly, with sudden, consuming need. Reality came apart at the seams, torn asunder with an inevitability that rivaled that of life itself. The fire leaped, and wild desire, once unleashed, promised never to be contained again.

I am a practical woman, Linnet thought even as her spirit surged up through her body to reach for his. *I like my house orderly and my life tidy, but there is no order or sanity in this, and no holding it, either. Better try to hold a spark ignited in dry straw. For, from the first moment I saw him, I had no hope of preventing this.*

A sigh came from him and he drew her hard into his arms, even as all Linnet's senses took flight. He tasted of the first wild berries of summer, warm and sweet, and he affected her like a draught of strong mead. Surely all her life she had been living for this.

Aye, and never had she lain with any man, though many had tried—Falcon in particular. But she knew instinctively how it would be with this man.

Even as his tongue caressed hers, wooing, and then plunged into her mouth, so would his body pierce hers in glorious claiming, demanding nothing more than she longed to give.

Kiss me once more, Linnet—please, kiss me again, he begged, and the words curled into her, a whisper not of speech but of knowing, spirit to spirit, that she heard only in her mind.

Chapter Nineteen

Linnet, Linnet. Gareth's entire body sang her name. Had there ever been a more beautiful word? So dazed was he, so drunk with the glorious pleasure of touching her at last, it took him precious moments to realize that, his mouth being so sweetly engaged, he spoke the words only in his mind. *Kiss me.*

And she heard. What kind of miracle was this? He could not tell, only that she responded, wound her arms about his neck and pressed her mouth to his again. *Aye, Gareth, kiss me. Oh, please, touch me.*

Her voice—or an echo of it—fluttered in his mind like the soft rustle of birds' wings. It vibrated there the way desire for her vibrated through the rest of him. He could sense all of her in every part of his body, admittedly some more than others.

He knew just where she wanted him to touch her, and his hand moved to her breast as if she guided it. Ah, God, that he might always obey her so! For she was the sweetest thing ever he had tasted, better even than he had dreamed. He might lose himself in her completely, and never rue the loss.

Her bodice made only a thin covering over her breasts. Her flesh burned beneath it and the softness scorched his hand. He explored with wondering fingers, half wild with delight, found the hard nub of a nipple and teased it with his thumb.

Her pleasure exploded in his mind, wild and exalting, and further inflamed him. He knew not what this was, how came this intense connection, but it went straight to his head. *Ah, and does that bring you pleasure?* Since his mouth remained fused to hers, his tongue yearning to fill her, he must have asked that in his head also.

She wiggled in response and, catching the essence of her desire, he pushed the thin fabric of her bodice down so that one perfect breast spilled into his hand. Her delight blossomed still more strongly in his mind and traveled through his flesh. It pooled between his legs and turned him hard instantly.

More, she sobbed into his mind.

He did not hesitate nor even stop to wonder where her parents were, or what they might do to him if they arrived now. Instead he stopped kissing her long enough to gaze into the fathomless darkness of her eyes, and then freed her other breast and bent his head to run his lips over it.

Her entire body jerked in response. His followed, as the demand of the flesh screamed through him. He spent one dazed moment admiring her perfection—rosy ripe and now bared to the light—before he caught her between his lips and traced her deliciously with his tongue.

Sweet merciful savior, had he ever held anything more intoxicating in his mouth? Greed and desire flooded him in equal measures. He could never get enough of her, but, aye, he would gladly give his life to try.

Her hands, warm and still carrying that tingle of healing, left his neck to cup his face. She arched into him and sang to his mind even as he suckled her.

Oh, please, please, do not stop.

Nothing loathe, he made a wet trail with his mouth from the first to her second breast and felt her pleasure spike again. Her pulse raced, and his kept time with it. He did not know what madness this was that let him feel her emotions along with his own, fair strong enough to kill him. Nor had he ever known he could play a woman's body like a beautiful instrument, but he knew now he would gladly die in her arms.

Take me, she begged in his mind.

I cannot. A lie, for he knew he could as easily as breathing. *Not here. Not now.*

She drew his head up from her breast and looked again into his eyes. What he saw in her gaze stole all the breath in his body. *You must. I must.* Nearly incoherent, the words tumbled into his mind even though her lips, ruby red from his kisses, did not move. *I cannot live if I do not have you.*

I know. Desire of the flesh was one thing and, he believed, could be denied. This was not mere desire of the flesh—it reached to the depth of his soul with its demand. *But your parents—*

As if conjured by his mention of them, he heard a call.

"Linnet!" Her mother's voice, surely—the last Gareth wished to hear at this moment, though he suspected her father could break him apart with his bare hands. Wren's all-seeing gaze intimidated him, and he could not imagine trying to explain away this scene.

Linnet gasped and freed herself from his grasp. Her naked breasts hung like two tantalizing treasures, still wet from the ministrations of his mouth. Gareth once more lost all immediate hope of sanity.

"By the Green Man's horns, I must go." She tucked herself back into her bodice, looking all at once flustered, and bit her reddened lips. These words were the first to issue from her lips since first their mouths had met.

She scrambled to her feet and then took a breathless moment to lean down and kiss him once more full on the mouth. His blood leaped wildly, but before he could reach for her, she slipped away. He sat with his head bent, fighting the pain in his groin and the hole in his soul, wondering what, by all the holy saints, had just happened to him.

Before he could begin to make sense of it, the echo of her voice floated back into his mind. *I will return to you tonight. Await me.*

And how could this be, this wonderful, silent communication? What magic that let him hear her thoughts, and let her catch his? Was it part of the wild claiming that had passed between them when their lips met, or something far more? And how could it feel so natural for him to accept her into his head, and his spirit?

Was this thing born of the magic of this place, that had knit his bones together, and had let him see a man long dead transform into a hart? And, oh, would she truly return to him this night?

By God, could he survive that long without her?

****

"How does that arm feel? Move those fingers for me." The abrupt demand, issued above Gareth's head, came from Wren and jerked Gareth's head up.

The afternoon had passed in a warm lull of droning

insects. No one had come near him until now; he figured their conference and decision-making had stretched long, but he heard a curt decisiveness now in Wren's tone.

She did not look happy, and when he met her eyes they were sharp as flint.

Where was Linnet? His heart sped at the very thought of her. He hoped they had not already sent her back to the village and away from him. But no, even as he asked the question he saw her enter the clearing with her father.

"Is there pain?"

With a grimace he wiggled his fingers. "Not as much as before." Pain he could endure. It was the inexplicable occurrences that bothered him.

Far from being pleased, Wren scowled. "'Twill have to do."

He ventured a question. "Has a decision been made?"

"Aye." She raked him with those curious, golden eyes, the way she might look at a rodent she found in her stewpot. "I have heard more advice concerning you, this day, than I care to recount."

"Concerning me?" Surprise touched him. But how could he continue to feel surprised? This place was, all in all, like a mad dream.

She bent down and wagged a finger in his face. He sensed, then, just how angry she was, furious. "I do not like it one bit. But the spirits are insistent. Me, I would be happier slitting your throat."

Startled, Gareth held her gaze; he believed her completely.

"But," she added bitterly, "there are and always

have been matters far greater than my desires. Destiny is destiny. We need to get Falcon back, so you will be sent to Nottingham."

"When?"

She closed her eyes a moment as if listening to an inner voice—a thing he could no longer doubt. "On the morrow."

And Linnet? He wondered, but dared not ask. Would she be sent back to the village at once? He looked past Wren to where he could now see both Linnet and her father moving about the camp.

Would she, as promised, be free to come to him tonight? How could he even contemplate such madness with her mother glowering over him and her father nearly within reach? Ah, but the fire in his blood assured he could.

Almost as if she, too, could hear his thoughts, Wren reached down and grasped him by the chin.

"Listen to me, young man. I know not what you are, and I like not your presence in our lives. I have been assured of your importance and I must let this thing play out. But if you ever hurt my daughter or bring to her any harm, deliberate or otherwise, it shall be that much the worse for you. Understand?"

Gently, he drew back from her cruel grip and looked once more into her eyes. "Mistress, I understand very little of what has happened since I came to this place," he told her truthfully. "But you can believe of me one thing—I will never seek to harm Linnet."

Wren straightened. "Aye, Norman, just see you do not."

Chapter Twenty

Beautiful Linnet, I have no wish to hurt you.

Did Gareth de Vavasour say those words aloud or whisper them only to Linnet's mind? She could not tell, and she was not willing to hold back long enough to find out.

The night surrounded them, warm and quiet but for a restless wind that tossed the high branches of the trees, deep and dark. Linnet had waited, with impatience dancing through her like fever, until she believed her parents slept. Only then had she spoken a prayer and tiptoed across the clearing to the place where Gareth lay.

Now she could barely see him but, oh, she could feel him. It seemed as if every part of him called to her, spirit and flesh. She had never wanted anything as she wanted this man.

You cannot hurt me, she told him, *save by denying me.*

He made a curious sound deep in his throat, and she felt his desire come at her out of the darkness, tangible as fire. *I have strength for many things, but not to deny you.*

Still she could not tell if he spoke aloud or not. She barely cared. Standing above him, she began to shed her clothes and the warm night air caressed her flesh as they fell away, and heightened her desire. When nothing but her hair clothed her, she dropped, eager, into his arms.

He gasped. His hands came up and he touched her like a man in a dream, first the hair streaming loose down her back, then the skin of her back itself, and around to breast and thigh. With fingers that trembled, she touched him in return, her hand splayed against the warmth that lay inside his opened tunic.

When he caught his breath again and began to speak, she bade him, *Hush.* Her mouth, on his, stopped his words effectively even though she still did not know if they sounded only in her mind.

Linnet.

Nay, of course they did not speak aloud. But she knew her name possessed his every thought, and its utterance sang through her, even though their mouths fused with heat.

Wait, he begged.

She was not sure she could. How wait for air? For water, when dying? She needed his touch, needed him inside her where no other man had ever been.

Why do you hesitate? she asked, and bit his lip.

He sobbed in response. She could feel him shaking with need and put her hands to work on his clothing while never leaving go contact with his mouth.

What is it? Do you not want me?

His only reply came as an incredulous laugh. His hands explored her naked flesh, serving as his eyes in the dark. But he said into her mind, *I do not understand. How is this? How can we speak without uttering words? Tell me.*

Magic. She breathed the word into him. *It is all magic. Everything about Sherwood and those it chooses.*

So we are able to hear each other, mind to mind?

And heart to heart. Think of it as a gift given in love.

And I am able to feel you, all of you—

She could feel him too, in a way that both daunted her and inflamed her senses. She could barely wait to complete the connection between them. *So, my fine champion,* she whispered on a note of daring, *are you fit for the task before you?*

Linnet, are you certain? She felt what it cost him to ask, and loved him for it. Aye, she loved him, loved him, *loved him.*

Gareth, I have been given very few choices in my life—almost none. My course was laid before ever I was born. Let me at least choose this.

You have never yet lain with any man?

Never.

And he repeated, *I have no wish to hurt you.*

She laughed. *The forest conspires to this, Gareth. The very trees do, and the breath of the air. The night's darkness assures it. Do you think I will let so small a thing as an instant's pain keep us apart?*

Her fingers succeeded—at last!—in loosening the front of his leggings. He surged out at her, strong and proud, and she curled her fingers around him in delight.

His entire body jerked. *Ah, sweet heaven!*

Kiss me, she bade, but they were already kissing. Linnet wound her arms about his neck and shifted herself closer in his arms. Even as she felt his tongue invade her mouth, yearning, she wrapped her naked legs about his waist and lowered herself down upon him, a willing and joyful sacrifice. And, oh, he filled her as she had never thought to be filled, seared into her with welcome heat, taking up a space it seemed she had always kept for him and answering an emptiness she had not even suspected she harbored.

I love you.

She twined her legs more tightly around him and shouted victoriously in her mind. Aye, and perhaps this was the real reason she had been born. And he, despite the fire she could feel rising inside him, hesitated one moment more before he flexed his strong back and surged more fully into her. The pain came then, in one blinding flash, and flew away into the night.

Like music building and burgeoning, they began to move together without question, she rocking in his lap and he hollering with wonder into her mind. Overhead, the wind rose and the trees tossed more wildly. Magic seemed to flare in the darkness, but Linnet cared for nothing save the man she held so fast to her heart.

No longer could she tell where her body ended and his began, no longer separate his thoughts from her own. His strength was her strength and her will his will. She could not distinguish whose pleasure it was that built into a wild storm, as elevated as the night itself and as powerful as a conflagration. But when the storm broke with an intensity that racked both of them, when he flooded her with his essence, she knew she had been wanting this all her life without knowing and was, at last, complete.

Then, still joined, he laid her down on the moss, in his arms, and they held to each other like two near-drowned souls returned miraculously to life. Above and all around them the night continued to sing its beautiful song. Leaves rustled and insects buzzed and fluttered as if eager to witness a miracle.

But Linnet knew the true miracle had occurred inside her.

Breathless and nearly thoughtless, she ran her hands over the beauty of him, smooth muscle under supple skin. All sense seemed seared from her. She knew only that she could not let him go.

He stirred in her arms, stroked her hair and her cheek, and kissed her softly. He whispered into her mind, *Did I hurt you?*

She laughed again, in joy. *A small price.*

I do not want this to end.

Please, let it never end.

The silence around them deepened, the wind began to calm as if it had been called up by their stirred passion. Linnet concentrated on the sensation of him, still inside her—a blessed claiming.

Moments passed, and their heartbeats slowed in unison.

He marveled, *You said you loved me.*

Aye.

Yet you barely know me. And I am enemy to all you hold dear.

I know you. Part of me has always known you.

I must leave you and go to Nottingham.

Do not speak of that now. The pain that convulsed Linnet at the thought of parting hurt far more than any that had come before. *How can we be parted, in truth, when so surely joined?*

I cherish this gift you have given me. He brushed his lips across her lips in a gentle caress. His fingers slid up her side and once more cupped her breast. *Know that even in Nottingham, I swear I will never do aught to bring you harm. I know how your life is set.* In her mind, his voice broke with emotion. *I know what duty calls you. But I confess I cannot bear the thought of you bonding, as you may, with Falcon.*

Linnet drew a breath. *Falcon and I are already bonded, aye. It cannot be otherwise. But 'twill never be like this.* Light exploded again in her mind. *Never like this. The guardianship is a duty laid upon me. You, I choose.* She brushed her lips across his in turn, for the sheer wonder of it. *You are all I choose.*

Will you have to wed with him, lie with him—like this? Linnet felt protest race through him, and realized how acutely she could now sense all his emotions.

Nothing could ever be like this.

That is no answer.

One of us, either Lark or I, will wed with him and bear his child, Sherwood's child.

Let it be Lark!

He wants me. He always has. It seemed Linnet could hide nothing from Gareth now. Her mind, like her body, lay utterly open to him.

You are mine, beautiful Linnet. Possession flared within him. *Promise me he shall not have you, not like this.*

A sigh breathed through her as she considered the impossibility of it. *I wish I could make that promise. How can I?* Her fingers caressed his face. *But I will make you another: you alone will hold my spirit, and you alone will hold my heart. Is it enough?*

Aye. Nay. An instant with you keeps me from starving. An instant with you only makes me want more.

If we are to have but this one night, I pray Sherwood makes it a long one. Endless.

She wrapped her arms tight around him, marveling at the depth of their connection. He was hers for this moment and for all time—no matter if they became separated physically.

His hand tensed on her breast and she felt him quicken inside her. Instantly she came alight, her passion igniting from his without resistance. It felt as if the blood that pounded through his veins flowed also to hers. She imagined his lips at her breast and, instantly, he bent his head to suckle her. The fire flared into a conflagration bright enough to consume her soul.

Delight taking hold in every part of her, she began to move her body beneath his. And she could feel his pleasure as intensely as her own, the way he lost all his breath when her inner muscles clenched around the hard length of him. She felt the softness of her own flesh within his mouth, the hard nub of her peaked nipple against his tongue, and knew even how the scent of her affected him.

I want all of you, she sang into his mind. *Enough to last the rest of my life, if need be.*

I give all of myself to you. And there, in the singing darkness, he did, again and again.

Chapter Twenty-One

Linnet. Gareth awoke with the taste of her still on his lips and her name still in his mind. *Do not leave me.*

Ardently, he spoke to the woman he held in his arms, she who had now become the center of his life. Only, when he opened his eyes to the morning light, his arms were empty. Like the bird after which she was called, she had flown.

Protest swamped him, closely followed by dismay and regret so strong it flared like pain. Before he opened his eyes, he would have sworn he could still feel her lying against him, her hand curled in his and her breath brushing his face. Now the memory faded like an echo, leaving only his rumpled clothing and the cold light seeping in.

Aye, and the woman who stood over him, glaring: Wren.

"Get up," she ordered, and prodded him—not gently—with her toe.

Speared by the look in her eyes, he moved quickly while his thoughts struggled to decipher what had and had not happened during the night. Might he have dreamed it all? If so, sweet, merciful saints, what a dream! But no, for his leggings gaped open and his chest was bare. He distinctly remembered Linnet's hands splayed against his chest, and the feel of them sliding around to caress his back even as he came into her sweet warmth.

Still more vividly did he remember her fingers at work on the laces that tied the front of his leggings. She had freed him and wrapped her fingers around him. The lingering, wild pleasure of it still made him tingle.

Now her mother loomed above him like an angry, vengeful goddess with murder on her mind. Did she suspect what had taken place here last night under cover of the darkness? They had kept very silent, saving all words to exchange only between their minds.

He struggled up and then tied his fly shut with deliberate fingers. Those of his left hand felt stiff and sore, but they did the job. To be truthful, his whole body felt the effects of his exertions last night—some more than others.

He looked Wren in the eye. "Where is Linnet?"

"Gone."

His heart sank sickeningly, and he bent his head so his hair partially shielded his face. Could he bear it?

Viciously, Wren added, "She is away where you will see her no more. You are to set out for Nottingham Castle this day."

Desperately, he reached for some measure of hope. She might be gone, and without a word, but she had become part of him last night, taken up residence in his heart, vital to him as his own breath. Surely he would see her somewhere along the journey.

"Has she returned to that village where I was held, Oakham?" He could get there somehow. He would crawl there if he must.

"You listen to me." Wren stepped up to him. A tall woman, she met him nearly eye to eye, her anger palpable. "What happened here last night had to happen—I have not been told why, though I can guess. But it was bidden and I had to let it occur. That does not mean I must like it."

"Bidden? By whom?"

She made a gesture that encompassed the trees, the light, and the forest itself. "Those who dwell here and whom I follow. But, having had her, do not suppose you shall possess her. She is destined for higher things. She has her place in a guardianship you cannot begin to understand."

Gareth, too, glanced around briefly before meeting Wren's gaze. "Guardianship of the forest, you mean? It is possible others may also become such guardians."

The disparagement in her eyes flared. "Do not flatter yourself, Norman whelp. You have no part in this, save for what you played last night."

"I love her." The words burst from him, all truth and defiance. He could no more hold them than halt the blood in his veins.

She laughed. When she did, she looked very much like the man he had seen among the trees, the one who had bidden him to follow his heart. And he had, oh, he had as never before.

"Scoff at me as you will. You do not know the future," he said, still defiant. "You cannot say what will or will not happen."

The hard mirth died from her eyes. "I know enough of it. I know what must be. It requires courage and sacrifice." Completely sober now, she told him, "If you do care for her, let her do as she needs to do, and be what she must be."

"And wed Scarface's son, you mean," Gareth returned with mounting anger of his own. "Bear his children."

For an instant, Wren's expression became distant, as if she contemplated something she liked not at all. "Whoever's children she bears, she belongs to Sherwood and not to you. Remember that, de Vavasour."

He wetted his lips and thought furiously. Perhaps Sherwood could be persuaded, even if this woman could not. "What if I were to dedicate myself to Sherwood?"

"For her sake? It requires a calling, complete devotion, a demand bred in the bone. You have not the blood."

"So? Even if I was meant to be with her last night?" For it had happened. Now, up on his feet, he felt sure of it. He had bonded with Linnet in a night filled with passion and blessed by the trees around them.

But, his heart cried, Linnet knew that as well as he, yet she had left his arms, risen, and gone from him.

How could you? He hollered in his mind.

And the response came to him, faint and distant, barely heard: *Oh my love, my love, my love.*

So stunned was he, so bent on listening, he did not realize Wren had dismissed him. She made a furious gesture that severed the magical bond that tethered him.

"We leave at once for Oakham, and thence you go to Nottingham."

****

"Come along." Sparrow rumbled the command and tugged on the lead once more fastened around Gareth's neck. His tone, less unkind than Wren's, nevertheless made it clear he was no happier with Gareth than was his wife.

Did he, too, know what had taken place last night on the moss bed? As they moved off through the forest, Sparrow balanced the great, twisted staff on his shoulder. Gareth figured one powerful blow from it could smash his skull like an overripe turnip.

What he could not glean was the measure of Sparrow's emotion. Unlike his wife's, his anger did not show in his guarded eyes and calm face. But Gareth could sense some potent feeling simmering below his surface. One thing he did know—he would not wish to sample this man's ire once he became truly roused.

They walked out of the forest by trails Gareth could neither see nor apprehend. Wren led the way and Sparrow followed, dragging Gareth's halter, while the morning strengthened around them, birds fluttered and glinted like jewels among the branches of the ancient trees, and the remnants of last night's music flitted through Gareth's mind.

He had been offered neither food nor water, and he barely cared. He thought only of the fact that Wren had said they were bound to Oakham and thence to Nottingham. Would he have a chance to see Linnet in the village? He could endure anything for hope of that.

Are you there? Deliberately, he formed the words in his mind and sent them forth, struggling with an ability that had seemed so natural just last night, had flowed between them effortlessly. All the while they lay together, they had communicated so. He might have believed the ability needed their touch to endure, had he not heard her voice, albeit faintly, this morning.

He shaped the thoughts, clarified them, and made another attempt. *Linnet, can you hear me?*

Sparrow, just ahead of him, twitched so the staff bounced on his shoulder, and Wren turned her head. Could they hear? By all that was holy, he hoped not.

Gareth, my dear love.

The breath caught inside him, and his heart clenched and then sped. Ah, but she sounded so far away, so impossibly distant. Beginning to sweat with the effort, he reached for her again. *Where are you, beloved?* There, he had said it: beloved, his love—the word that had held no meaning for him since his mother died, and that had been born in him again last night. Linnet was all about love, her touch and the warmth of her, her scent, and the tenderness of her spirit, which, like her body, he had embraced and held. He would follow that anywhere, no matter how far.

Oakham, I am in Oakham.

His joy surged. Wren's head jerked again, but she did not glare at him this time. Yet surely Linnet felt the intensity of his gladness? *Good. We come to Oakham.*

I will not see you.

What?

I cannot. I was sent ahead to prepare the party that will take you to Nottingham and ransom Falcon. But I will not see you here.

His dismay arose, strong as his previous joy. Still struggling and fumbling to reach her, he grieved, *Is it because you do not wish to see me?* Had she fled him? Had she realized, and been unable to accept, she had lain with an enemy? The thought turned him sick inside.

No, no, no, no— She came to him more strongly, almost like a wisp of music on the breeze. *I want naught more than to be with you.*

And I live only to be with you, he told her truthfully.

But it is best this way, Gareth, my love.

Best?

'Twould hurt more for us to see each other again.

Nothing could hurt more than this.

A clean break is best.

Why must we break at all?

Because, love, you go to Nottingham. My place is in Sherwood.

We can change that, I can change it. I can be—

You can be what? You are a Norman knight, proven and sworn. You are the King's champion.

I am sworn, now, to you.

What of your vows? What of mine? What is their worth if we do not hold to them?

I promised to be yours, always.

And you will be. For will we not always be able to touch each other in thought?

Gareth distinctly felt his heart seize in his chest and then break into jagged pieces. *It is not enough.*

It must be, my love. It is all I am able to offer you.

I will find a way—He screamed it to her, another vow. But she had slipped from his mind and he received no reply.

Chapter Twenty-Two

"I understand that you are unhappy, Daughter. But it is time to put childish things away from you and take up the burden of your life."

The harsh words caught Linnet and spun her around. She glared into her mother's eyes, for once wholly unbowed and defiant. She believed she had accepted her duties following her one precious night of passion with Gareth de Vavasour. Had she not already told him so along the sacred pathways between their minds? But watching the party intended to escort him to Nottingham leave Oakham this day without seeing the man at all—for he and Sparrow had waited off in the forest—had seared her soul.

Now she returned Wren's glare in full. "Do you speak to me of duty, and accuse me of childishness, Ma? When have I ever been a child? I was forced to grow up long ago. I half raised Lark, and Fal as well." She drew a breath. "You know what took place in the forest last night."

Wren gave a hard nod, not liking it.

"That had little of childhood about it either. I am a woman, and I know what lies before me despite—"

Despite the fact that if she closed her eyes she could still feel Gareth's hands upon her, the calluses on his palms abrading her flesh, setting her alight. If she let herself, she could feel him penetrating her, and catch his heady scent.

And she could feel him battering at her mind, steady and relentless. She had managed to close the door that shut him out, but the effort of keeping it closed cost her dear. She feared she would not succeed long.

"Have you, then, decided to accept Falcon upon his return?" her mother asked sharply.

"I did not say that. I am willing to take my place in the circle, since I understand the vital importance of it. Is that not enough? And have you considered what should happen if the Sheriff does not keep his word and Fal fails to return?"

Wren drew a sharp breath. "If that happens, Daughter, we are undone. It will be a slow death, aye, but sure. The magic that dwells in Sherwood will fade; the forest will shrink in upon itself and die, and our hope of freedom with it. We will lose all ability to fight, and we will become slaves indeed."

"Some of us are slaves already," Linnet retorted. "I do not feel free."

Her mother's glare softened a bit. "We are all ultimately free in Sherwood, which is why we must guard it and preserve all who dwell here in flesh or spirit. It is a holy trust."

"That I have always understood. I have said I am willing to act as I must." Linnet's gaze dropped as she listened to the pain in her heart. "Just do not expect me to rejoice in it."

****

"Lin!" The joy in Falcon's voice caught at her and caused her to reach for him, in response. A full day and a half had they waited for the return of the party from

Nottingham with the ransomed headmen. Now, at midafternoon on a day that wept rain like tears, they came at last.

She found herself gathered hard into Falcon's arms almost before she registered his presence. Always had she been able to sense his feelings, though never so acutely as Gareth's, and she felt in full his gladness now as he held her, and her own relief rose to meet it.

He squeezed her so hard she nearly smothered against his shoulder. Joyfully, she fought her way free.

"Thank goodness you are back! We half feared the Sheriff would not keep to the agreement. Let me look at you."

He appeared thinner, which did not seem possible after only three days, filthy and worn. His hair formed a wild tangle, tumbled around his face. And, along with the gladness, she saw hard determination in his eyes.

"I could scarcely be happier to be here," he admitted. "We were all released except for Godfrey of Linfield, who died of some sort of fit in the Sheriff's dungeon."

A crowd had begun to gather around them, folks eager to hear what Falcon had to tell. Lark, who had made one of the party that had taken Gareth to Nottingham, and who had undoubtedly already greeted Fal, nevertheless pushed through the onlookers to his side.

"And Gareth de Vavasour?" Linnet could not keep from asking. "Was his uncle glad to have him?"

It was Lark who answered. "That exalted man did not show himself then. His captain, Monteith, accepted the prize on his behalf, and had our folk fetched out from the bowels of hell."

The villagers mumbled. The dungeons at Nottingham, legendary pest holes, had cost the lives of many a good man and woman. Someone asked, "Was it as foul there as they say, young Falcon?"

Falcon's expression grew grim. "Aye, Macy. All shoved into one cell we were, a stinking pit with no light and very little air. After Godfrey died, we hollered for the guards, but they left him. And so we spent the rest of our confinement there with his corpse."

Linnet's stomach wobbled and turned over. She reached out and touched Fal's hand, and his fingers clutched hers.

"Any sight of our Derek?" asked someone else.

Falcon shook his head regretfully. "He may be there in still another cell, or he may be held elsewhere in Nottingham. We could not tell." He turned his eyes on a woman who stood wringing her hands—Derek's wife, Gert. "Sorry, Gertie. I wish I brought you more hopeful news."

Other questions came then, thick and fast, fired like arrows from all around: had Falcon or the other headmen gleaned any useful information? Had he got a good look at the castle fortifications? Would de Vavasour be satisfied with the return of his nephew, or would he move further against them?

All the while Lark stood at Falcon's elbow, quiet save for the fierce expression in her eyes. Her gaze moved from Falcon's hand, fast joined with Linnet's, to Linnet's eyes, where they held, revealing a virtual storm of anguish.

Linnet had never found it difficult to sense her sister's feelings. Since birth they had been together, for better or worse, joined also by the bonds of the triad, that often let them hear snatches of each other's thoughts. But she did not need to hear Lark's thoughts now. They shone from her eyes and screamed in the mutinous set of her mouth. Had this not been Linnet's sister, the person closest in the world to her, Linnet would have said Lark now declared open war for the love of Falcon.

I do not want him, she attempted to tell Lark in her mind.

And Lark's burning gaze returned to their linked hands. *Then, sister, leave go of him.*

Linnet attempted to free her fingers from Falcon's grasp, but he clasped them still more tightly even as he responded to those gathered.

"The Sheriff did have us hauled before his court when first we were taken in. Though he did not say so outright, he is desperate for the return of the money taken along with his nephew. He declared it a crime against the Crown and told us he will continue to burn our villages until it is returned."

Falcon let his eyes roam about the ruins of Oakham, the rubble that had once been these people's homes. "But those monies, my friends, are the coffers of war. We have hit him where it hurts, for he must make answer to his king. I say we stand strong and spit in his eye. Is it not summer? The forest will shelter us. If de Vavasour comes looking, we will vanish into its heart. Better we all fight together for justice than let him imprison and destroy us one by one for the sake of his bloody taxes."

Linnet's eyes widened. This sounded like a new Falcon. The grief still lingered beneath his words, and weariness with it, but he had donned a fierce certainty that carried a hint of his father's indomitable anger.

And those around him, used to Martin Scarlet's bold leadership, at once responded. The men nodded their heads; women tightened their holds upon their children. No strangers to want and subjugation, they understood the necessity of fighting back and what that fight might require.

The Normans always underestimated the common folk, Linnet reminded herself—those they called peasants, the farmers, craftsmen, and laborers. Men like de Vavasour forgot from whence these people had sprung—Saxon warriors at least as bloodthirsty as themselves, who had come to England behind swords and axes to claim this blessed land. Added to that was a good measure of Celtic blood, that of the mystical people whose warriors knew not the meaning of backing down and chose, so often, to fight to the death.

She felt her own blood stir, and her fingers tightened on Falcon's. Lying with Gareth de Vavasour, even gifting him her heart, did not make her less a woman of this place. Sherwood roosted in her bones, its song echoed in her soul.

"Never fear," Falcon declared, "we will stand strong against whatever de Vavasour throws at us." He turned and looked directly into Linnet's eyes. "Because we stand together, and that is all the strength we need."

Laura Strickland

Chapter Twenty-Three

"Fool! What good are you to me if I cannot rely upon you to see a simple transport safely to Nottingham?" The blow that accompanied the words took Gareth in the side of the face and rocked him where he stood. "Nephew, I am sorely disappointed."

The words—and no less the blow—were so reminiscent of Gareth's father he experienced a familiar rush of rebellious anger and shame. It had never been the blows that hurt so much as the accompanying accusations of worthlessness.

He raised burning eyes to his uncle's face now and, as ever, strove not to let his feelings show.

Robert de Vavasour, a big, powerful man, had the look of Gareth's father, Maurice, and even more the manner: haughty, disgruntled, and impatient, as if the world and everything in it had been created for his sole benefit.

Gareth told himself he was a lad no longer, doomed to stand quaking inwardly before the figure of absolute authority. He was a knight fully—if only just—proven, a champion. His worth rested not at all upon the opinions of this man.

Yet those words "I am sorely disappointed" might have come from his father's lips. How many times had he heard them, hurled at him like weapons?

He drew a breath to speak but, as if reading his

156

thoughts, his uncle ranted on. "Why did I invest in your training if you are to be of no benefit to me? Did de Breese teach you nothing up north? Does being proven no longer mean anything at all?"

Albert de Breese, an old friend of Gareth's father and the man who had fostered and schooled Gareth, had been a hard master, unsparing and rarely approving. Yet, Gareth reflected now, he had been also a just man who allowed always a chance for those in his service to defend themselves.

Nor had he possessed this streak of hard cruelty Gareth now saw in his uncle's eyes. That, too, had been common to Gareth's father, who had died in full rant while berating a serving girl who spilled compote on his sleeve.

"I regret you feel I failed in my duty, Uncle," he said stonily. "The party that attacked us did so swiftly and appeared out of the trees without warning. Almost before we knew what was happening, three of your soldiers lay dead."

Robert rounded on him. "Is that meant to be an excuse? There is no excuse. I am accountable to King Henry for that money. What am I to say to him? It was stolen by peasants—serfs—from under the nose of one of your knights, a man of my blood?"

He raised his hand to strike Gareth again, but Gareth, well prepared this time, seized his wrist before the blow connected. "Nay, Uncle, you will not. Whatever you think of me, I did not come into your service to stand your whipping boy."

Rage flared in Robert de Vavasour's eyes, and his lips skewed in a sneer. "Unhand me, cur! Why did you come into my service, if not to act the part of a Norman knight? You knew the situation here in Nottingham. Everyone from King Henry to the boy who totes the piss pots knows it. I am the laughing stock of northern England because I cannot keep the rabble in line."

He raged on. "You knew the road passed through the forest. You should have expected an attack, should have been on guard."

"We were on guard, Uncle." Gareth saw and felt it again—the green light slanting down through high branches, dappling the roadway, the flitting birds overhead and their songs, like a spell of peace. The attackers had materialized quite literally from nowhere, as if by magic.

"And could you not then fight them off?" Robert de Vavasour continued to roar. "A band of peasants?"

"As I have said, they shot the first of your men from cover before we knew they were there. They wounded two more who tried to flee." In mindless panic, though Gareth would not tell his uncle that. The soldiers had been nervous from the moment they entered Sherwood and when the arrows began to fly, their terror became palpable. Aye, Gareth had heard stories of Sherwood all the way south—strange things happened there, inexplicable things.

Like men who transformed into stags. *Follow your heart...*

Gareth leveled his gaze on the man who stood glaring at him. Most certainly, his heart did not lie here.

"And the rest of you, were you brought to answer by the sword? What kind of master swordsmen lurk in Sherwood, that can vanquish a trained knight?"

"You would be surprised." Gareth had been. "They hauled me off my mount and I broke my arm in the fall.

I fought hard—"

"More excuses. You mewling, craven coward! Your father would be ashamed." De Vavasour's sneer became still more pronounced. "I suppose it is your mother's weakness coming out in you. She was never worthy of his seed."

Gareth experienced a surge of rage so intense everything around him went white. He growled, "Do not speak of her so."

"What did you say to me? Mind your tongue, Nephew. You are sworn to my service, and I will speak to you as I choose. Aye, but you always were a mama's boy, were you not? Just as well she died early and Maurice got you out from under her skirts."

Anger stopped Gareth's throat. He felt it run through his blood like hot tar.

"And what of the King's tax collector, whom you were supposed to guard?" Robert renewed the attack.

"Dead."

"Aye, dead. And what am I to tell Henry? I am disgusted with you. Get from my sight!"

Gladly, Gareth thought, and turned to leave his uncle's presence, but Robert's voice caught him once more, like the sting of a whip.

"I hope you intend to prove yourself to me. I do not expect you to fail me again. As for these excuses with which you have presented me"—Robert's eyes raked Gareth—"your injuries do not look so grave. Where is evidence of this broken arm? And where the dire wounds?"

Gareth spoke through wooden lips. "Healed, Uncle."

"Healed, in a matter of days? How?"

"The villagers possess healers of some skill." *Her tongue, sliding over his skin, her fingers wooing him to come into her yet again...* "They considered me a valuable prize, so they troubled to have me tended." *Sweet, holy heaven, if only he could hold her again.*

"Well, there they erred," Robert spat. "For you are of no value at all. I would have done better having the tax money back rather than your worthless hide. For now you will make yourself busy training the younger men among my guard, understand? I trust you have the balls for that."

Gareth nodded stiffly.

"Oh, and Gareth—" De Vavasour called him back yet again. "I trust you have it well in your mind, the location of the village where dwelt these talented healers. For you and I together will go to root them out."

Chapter Twenty-Four

My love, hear me!

The words called Linnet from sleep, curled through her mind, and forced her eyes open. For days she had struggled to keep shut the door in her mind, closed against Gareth de Vavasour's wooing. His voice came to her day and night, early and late, sweet and distant. She knew she could not let herself listen, tempting as it might be. The comfort of touching with his thoughts became, in reverse, the sharp pain of longing for him, and more than she could bear.

But now he came to her in sleep, when all her defenses were down. And the endearment went straight to her heart.

So early was it the first light had only begun to sift through the trees and dance upon her eyelids. Linnet slept beneath the leafy roof in the open, with a knot of children around her. For the past fortnight, the men had worked hard to rebuild what they could, but they did so on the basis of need. The sick and elderly would receive new dwellings first. Linnet knew she would remain without a roof for some time.

Now she sat up, her eyes wide and her senses straining. Had she imagined the call? No, for she knew Gareth's inner voice as well as she knew her own heartbeat.

Ah, and she should force shut the door, slam it

shut. But had she the strength?

My love. Did she think or whisper the words? No matter, for Gareth fell upon them and his gladness spilled over into her, so strong and vital it made her want to weep.

Beautiful Linnet. The words seemed distant, and they came disjointedly, the way a fitful wind blows a far-off sound. But his emotions reached her clearly, the same warmth, the same intense tenderness she had experienced in his arms. *Why have you kept yourself closed to me? Why have you shut me out again and again?*

It hurts so much—too much, she admitted.

I regret. I would sooner die than hurt you. "I do not wish to hurt you"—the words he had breathed into her before he entered her the first time. All at once Linnet's body came alive with remembering. Longing blossomed inside her and, aye, it did ache unbearably.

I need to protect myself. You must understand.

But his voice in her mind strengthened as if it gained facility through his emotion. *You are my one comfort.*

Ah, and how could he say such a thing? Here she slept on the ground, roofless, homeless, her only clothing that on her back, while he doubtless lived in plenty at the castle, enjoying the benefit of his uncle's board and his privileged standing.

I need to see you.

Aye, and Linnet needed to see him too, yet she gathered all her will to do as she must. *No.*

Please. Meet me somewhere. Anywhere. In the forest—you choose the place.

Have you a death wish? Do not come here alone.

Promise me you will not.

I need to touch you, to hold you.

Linnet's fingers curled and her nails bit into the palms of her hands. She could feel all he left unsaid, and all he wished to do—touch her everywhere with his hands and his mouth, love her so sweetly and so long it made her forget all the pain of separation.

It feels, Linnet my love, as if I have left part of myself there with you in the forest, the better part. I ache for you.

She knew, aye, she knew.

And I, she agreed. She closed her eyes an instant. *But do not venture here. All the forest trails are closely watched.*

It is that I need to tell you. Sheriff de Vavasour is determined to regain the King's taxes stolen along with me. It is a matter of pride with him, and he will not rest. He wishes me to lead him to the village where I was held. He will apply what pressure he can. Our party— including him—leaves here at full light.

Aghast, Linnet remained silent.

You may be sure I will not lead him to you, love. But, indeed, I must lead him somewhere. I have thought to plead confusion and take him on some merry chase. He already despises me.

Despises you? How could anyone?

Now Gareth fell silent. And Linnet demanded, *Speak to me. Does he not value you?*

That is neither here nor there. I would not bring his wrath down upon some other village, Linnet. And he will spend his ire wherever I do lead him. He is that kind of man.

How soon do you leave Nottingham? Linnet

thought furiously; already the light grew stronger around her and the village folk began to stir. *There is little left to lose here in the village and we can disappear into the forest at need. I will convince our headman—*

Falcon. A world of emotion filled that one word. Linnet heard longing, jealousy, and regret.

What am I to tell him of how this knowledge came to me?

Tell him it came in a dream. Gareth bade her bitterly, *It is all we are to one another now. But, my love, do not close yourself away from me again, I do so beg.*

I must. I must. And, using all her will, struggling mightily, she shut the door against him. Not until she scrambled to her feet did she realize she had not even thanked him for the warning.

****

"Falcon?"

He turned his head at Linnet's call and gladness filled his eyes. Fal had been a different man since returning from Nottingham. It seemed he had summoned up a measure of his father's strength and headlong courage. The responsibilities they all bore clearly weighed upon him, yet Linnet still caught a hint of the old, gentle Fal in his smile.

"I was hoping for a moment with you," he told her. "It seems there has been time for naught." He cupped her cheek with one hand. "I have missed you sorely, Lin."

"Aye," she could only agree, "and I you." She longed for the carefree times and the laughter they had so often shared.

He hurried on before she could say more. "There is much to be settled between us. Matters seem to rush betimes." His hand remained warm against her face, the touch tender. "But it has come to me, you and I might be one another's comfort in all this madness, and this time that seems so bleak."

"We have always been that to one another," Linnet said, "the three of us." That had been especially true since the death of Fal's mother and sister. With Linnet's parents so often away and Martin Scarlet occupied with the fight against Nottingham, their bonds had steadily deepened.

Falcon shook his head slightly. "I speak not of games with Lark. Linnet, you know what you mean to me. When are we going to make a declaration of it, what lies between us?"

Without giving her a chance to answer he leaned forward and covered her mouth with his, quick and tender. Falcon had kissed her before, countless times, both brotherly kisses on the cheek and a young man's attempts at seduction. But his lips carried a new message this time: Linnet felt passion and intent. She felt what lay in his heart.

For an instant the sweetness of it held and realization crystallized in Linnet's mind. *He loves me. And I might have loved him after all, had another not already claimed my heart.*

She drew away and raised both hands to his chest. His eyes had grown dark and revealed the desire building inside him.

"No, Fal."

"What? Why not? Linnet, the time is now for us to sort out our places in the triad and firm up our bonds.

You and I were always meant to be together. Marry me now, and we will go into this thing doubly strong."

"What of Lark?"

"What of her?" Falcon tossed his head. "She has always known she is the odd one out. The circle requires three; there is no help for it. Two bond with each other, and the third with Sherwood. She knows that as well as we."

"I hardly think Lark well-suited to disappear meekly into the forest. Surely I am closer to the land when I take from it my herbs and use them to heal."

"Are you in earnest? I have never seen anyone more in tune with Sherwood than Lark. She asks permission every time she cuts wood to make an arrow and whispers a prayer before every shot. She can vanish into the trees like one of the Old Ones. Sometimes I think she is more than half spirit."

"Yet she has not the nature to make a hermit."

"Does it have to be that way?"

In the past, one of the three who made up the triad had gone to live in the forest, honing his or her knowledge and wisdom. That kept the magic of Sherwood bonded and available for the defense of its guardians. Linnet's own parents, along with Martin Scarlet, had changed the face of things somewhat; Wren and Sparrow had dwelled at the forest refuge together, affirming the power there. Martin Scarlet had presented the face of their defense with Falcon's mother, Sally, at his side.

The power had shifted but not failed—until now. Linnet knew she must do her part no matter what her heart might demand.

She closed her fingers on Falcon's arm. "We

cannot speak of this now. I came to tell you we must gather and move everyone out of the village. The Sheriff comes with a company of men."

Emotion kindled in Fal's eyes. "That bastard Gareth de Vavasour leads them to us, no doubt. I should have known he had no honor and would act against us even though we spared his life. Pa was right. We should have slit his throat and sent him back to his accursed uncle dead and cold."

Linnet drew a hard breath. "We do not know who leads them. And it does not matter now. We have naught left to lose in the village, save lives. If we scatter into the trees, we may at least protect the villagers."

"Aye. Find Lark and anyone else who can spread the word. Get everyone up and moving. I will organize the men. We will await them in the trees surrounding the village and slay de Vavasour's men when they come looking."

Linnet's heart plummeted but she strove to conceal her dismay. "Aye."

"Go swiftly. But Lin—" Now Falcon caught her arm. "How did you know? What magic brought this word to you?"

"No magic." Linnet smiled stiffly. "Only a dream." For as Gareth had said, that was all he could be to her now.

Chapter Twenty-Five

"This place looks deserted, not a soul here. Are you certain this is the right village?" Robert de Vavasour turned in his saddle to glare at Gareth. "Either they have abandoned the place or they were warned. Who has betrayed us?"

Gareth was spared answering by the arrow that cut the air beside his left ear, so close he heard the whoosh of its fletchings in passing. The shot was followed by a storm of others, two of which plucked two soldiers from their boots where they stood.

Gareth and his uncle—with the captain of the guard, Monteith, the only mounted men in the company—swiftly turned their horses and wheeled, only to be met by more arrows fired from their flank.

"Fall in!" Robert de Vavasour cried.

The village, a wasteland of burnt thatch and rubble, offered virtually no cover. But even the best longbows could only fling a shot so far. Gareth guessed the woodsmen would not expose themselves, and the center of the village must be safest.

The company shifted as one, soldiers dragging the two downed men. Gareth found himself very near the place where he had once been staked out like a sacrificial goat.

Enraged, Robert de Vavasour seethed, "How dare they! Peasants, to fire on their betters—I will have the skin off their backs, for starters." As if to emphasize the words, he drew his riding crop. "And which of you has betrayed us?" He struck at the soldiers gathered about his horse, which danced nervously. "Has one of you been bedding some slut in this village? Speak, if you know what is good for you."

Gareth shuddered inwardly at the uncanny accuracy of his uncle's surmise. He shifted his mount to cover the men. "It need not be any of our soldiers, my lord. Something could easily have been overheard at the castle."

"Out of my way." De Vavasour lashed at Gareth's shoulder. An arrow particularly well shot followed the movement and clove the air between them. It served to further whip Robert's anger. He glared away towards the trees.

At that moment he looked so like Gareth's father— the expression of haughty disdain, the severity of the features, the unreasoning cruelty in his eyes—it turned Gareth sick with hate. Gareth had hoped he had put that emotion away with his father beneath the cold soil of Yorkshire. Yet it dogged him still.

"They shall pay," Robert seethed, "for raising weapons against their betters. One way or another, they shall."

"Aye, my lord." Gareth bit the words hard. "But we have to get away out of here first."

The road that led from the fields, and on which their company had traveled, was surely blocked now. Any other route lay through the forest, which these folk knew far too well. Hampered with two wounded men, they might all be cut down.

By warning Linnet, had he assured the deaths of all

these men?

"What is the name of this village?" De Vavasour demanded, virtually foaming at the mouth. At least he showed no fear. Gareth had to give him that.

"Oakham, my lord," said Monteith.

"And is their headman one of those so lately released?"

"I believe so, my lord." Monteith's features pinched in disdain. "They are much like each other, these peasants."

"From this day forth, there is a price on his head. He will be cut down on sight. Understand?"

That still would not get them away out of here, Gareth thought sourly.

But Robert was in a full rage. "I will teach him and all his kind to raise a hand against their Sheriff and their King. Why, the very land upon which they subsist belongs to Henry. What is the name of this headman?"

"I do not know, my lord."

Robert glared at Gareth. "You were held here. Do you know?"

Again, Gareth was saved answering—and lying—by an accurate shot. The arrow skimmed the Sheriff's helmet, and he ducked indignantly. "Whatsoever his name may be," de Vavasour began, "he will die. I will make an example of—"

"Down!" Gareth shouted reflexively and shoved his uncle from his saddle. The arrow aimed at Robert's head grazed his arm and they both tumbled from their horses. Gareth fell heavily, and his mount shied. Robert, also winded, stopped shouting long enough that Gareth could hear the voice that sounded in his mind.

My love—are you hit?

Nay.

He felt Linnet's relief, like a shower of warmth breaking over him. *Where are you?* he asked desperately.

No reply. Gareth struggled to gather his scattered thoughts. By all that was holy, why had he saved his uncle's life? Why not let him take the arrow intended for him? Even as he leaped to his feet Gareth cursed himself for it. Had it been his father, Gareth would gladly have let the arrow take him.

Robert got to his feet even more furious than before. "Attack them! Seize them!" he yelled, waving his crop. "Do not let the bastards think they can best us!"

After one incredulous stare, Monteith rallied his men, all but the two fallen, and charged the nearest of the trees from whence issued the arrow fire.

To give Robert de Vavasour his due, he was at Monteith's side. An old campaigner, he seemed nothing loath to wet his blade.

Gareth found himself moving also, his training far too ingrained to let him stand while other men entered the fray, even though it repulsed him to the bone to face peasants with a sword.

He need not have worried; the villagers dispersed like smoke at the approach of the soldiers, leaving behind a hail of arrows. Another soldier went down, groaning, and the rest found themselves staring about with no opponents.

"Find them," Robert de Vavasour growled. "Spread out and search. Do your duty, curse you!"

"My lord…" Monteith began cautiously.

"It is suicide," Gareth put in when the captain

faltered. "They know the forest as we do not."

His uncle glared at him. "Are you a coward? What sort of man did my brother raise?"

Gareth forced himself to expressionlessness, a tactic he had always employed with his father. "They will pick us off one by one. It is what they want."

As if to emphasize his words, an arrow took another man.

"My lord," Monteith ventured again, "we have not a large enough company. If you wish for justice, I say withdraw now and come back with at least two score men."

Robert de Vavasour swore bitterly. "Do you recommend falling back before peasants?" he asked scathingly. "Saxons, who fight with bows and axes? By God, of what are you made? This is why outlaws infest Sherwood, and this is why they dare stand against their king."

An arrow, arced with exquisite precision, appeared from nowhere and found the seam in Robert de Vavasour's light armor, at his elbow. Gareth's eyes caught a movement among the near trees, a form he surely knew—small, swift, and fierce. Linnet's sister it was, though he could scarcely imagine a maid making such a shot.

Robert de Vavasour hollered again in rage and pain. He whipped at the men closest to him with his sword. "Will you stand and do nothing whilst your sworn lord is attacked and injured? After them, I say!"

Some of the men, more obedient than intelligent, moved off into the trees. Monteith appeared rooted to the spot, perhaps determined to defend his lord to the death.

When Gareth started forward, it was in response to no order at all, but rather a call he heard only within. *My love.*

She waited for him somewhere close by. To be sure, so did an arrow or a dagger—his death lay here. But far more urgently, so did his reason to live.

He stepped into the trees, his sword raised, and darkness closed about him like an embrace. Curiously, he could still hear the others moving around him as if his sense of hearing heightened even as his sight flew from him. He heard the villagers moving furtively; they made no more sound than might their animal counterparts in hiding. By comparison, the soldiers crashed about, easy prey.

He heard the twang of a bowstring near at hand and then the gurgling scream of a man going down. He heard—

Gareth. Here. Hands closed upon his wrists and his whole body tensed in response. He knew her by touch and by the scent of her, even before his vision cleared enough to allow him to see.

What magic is this? He asked not aloud but mind to mind.

Powerful magic, indeed, Linnet told him. *Come you with me.*

Aye, agreed Gareth, who would far sooner die than refuse her. *Wherever you go, so do I follow.*

Chapter Twenty-Six

"I needed to see you, to touch you," Linnet said, and tightened her hands on those of the man before her. Not a vision—he truly stood here, and the agony that had been with her since their parting eased for the first time. She did not understand this powerful wanting inside her, so much more than desire.

She gazed into his eyes and he into hers, and for an instant the rest of the world ceased to matter. The magic shield Linnet had called up hung among the trees and isolated them. The very essence of Sherwood conspired to give them these precious moments.

"I heard your voice. I came," he said simply, and raised both her hands to his lips. The gesture reflected the devotion Linnet saw in his eyes, and her spirit took wing and flew victoriously. The world might have gone mad around them, their situation might well be impossible, a future unimaginable. But he was hers still, and she his forever.

She leaned up and he down—their lips met delicately, almost tentatively, and clung. Hunger came surging then, swift as the rush of flame. Linnet's heart leaped within her, gladness tangled hopelessly with yearning.

She poured her words and her emotions into his mind. *I love you. You are the only one who will ever claim my heart.*

She felt his spirit leap in response. *I love you. This vow I give you before all others ever I have made: my loyalty and heart are yours alone.*

Joy flooded through Linnet, even stronger than the wanting. This, she knew, made the true measure of the man, and she could ask no more than this gift.

He kissed her again, and his thoughts tumbled through his mind in bright images: the two of them naked and twined together; his mouth hot at her breast; him entering her with searing pleasure; the fierce joy of their spirits merging as one.

Beyond impossible, she thought—a battle raged all around them. The Sheriff himself lingered so near she could hear his harsh voice calling orders to his men. Close by, her allies loosed death from longbows. Only the shadows gathered in the arms of the trees kept her and Gareth hidden from sight.

In truth, they stood on opposite sides of a wide chasm. Yet she knew to the root of her soul they stood as one.

Come with me, she said into his mind—just a thread of thought and yet it drew him as inexorably as had the rope tether her father once kept on his neck. Hands joined, they flew into the trees, and the obscuring darkness moved with them. Linnet led the way at the insistence of her heart, until at last the commotion died away behind and the darkness seeped back into the trees from whence it had come. Soon there was only the wind high in the branches, the songs of the birds, and the sense of protection that always found her here.

Though she had spent much of her life in the village, she was of the forest, both conceived and born here. It welcomed her now. And it welcomed the man at her side. Linnet could not understand it—born an enemy to this stronghold of magic, he should be treated like other men of the Sheriff's company who strayed too far, riddled with confusion, chewed by terror and spat out again, either alive or dead. Yet Linnet could not mistake the sense of acceptance that now met them both. Sherwood wanted Gareth here.

Not, by all that was holy, more than she did herself.

She stopped at last, breathless, and turned to face him. Once again their eyes met and the joy came flooding.

Love me, she begged. *It is meant.*

He raised his gaze to the trees, a man weighing the safety of his surroundings. He seemed to measure the light streaming through green leaves and to test the silence. When he spoke, his words surprised her. She might have expected some protest—he had just left a battle for her sake. But he said, mind to mind, *We are not alone here. Something watches.*

Linnet had never felt alone in Sherwood. Too many spirits dwelt here and too much magic. *Aye, but we are not so much watched as guarded.* She raised her hands and investigated the light armor he wore, all leather and iron. At her touch, all his resistance melted.

In the end, he helped her remove his clothing, and removed hers after. By then they were both breathless with wanting. Their hands began to explore even before their bodies met and they sank down into the shed leaves and moss.

Linnet came alive at his touch like the spring surging, and the intense pleasure of his mouth upon her chased away all other thought. There remained only this moment and the unbearable urge of their coupling, the consuming emotion of it, like a wild storm, when they claimed each other.

His seed filled her like light, far more vital than breath. As they took flight together, body to body and mind to mind, she experienced the full magic of it. No ordinary joining, this, but something perhaps ordained from her birth, and his.

Hold me.

Spent and yet not spent, they cradled one another, cherishing. Linnet raised her eyes to the leaves overhead; their song seemed to shimmer through her with the last notes of passion. Bemused, she allowed her gaze to drop to Gareth's face.

He lay with his eyes closed, savoring what she savored; she could feel that he did. And oh, he was wonderful to look upon, with the golden brown hair tousled on his brow, the deeper brown lashes spread on his cheeks, and his lean face perfect in repose.

Nearly perfect. With her finger she traced the remnants of the mark Martin Scarlet had left on him. It would lend a permanent scar, but that made him no less desirable in her sight.

His eyes flew open at her touch and met hers; in them she saw all she ever wished, for this moment and every moment to come.

"I already want you again," she confessed. "But not yet. I need to make this time last. Talk to me, my love."

Instead, he kissed her cheek and let his lips trail to her mouth. Heat followed in their wake and quickened desire close after.

Linnet marveled at herself. Never had she dreamed

of feeling such fierce, consuming emotion toward any man.

How long have we? He asked her mind, his lips still otherwise engaged. *When will the spell fade?*

It is not so much a spell as a gift. Sherwood wants you here, nearly as much as I.

Why?

That I cannot tell.

If Sherwood demanded my life in return for these moments, the price would not be too high.

He moved his mouth to her breast, naked, ripe, and warm in the summer air. She felt ripe withal, ready for something she could not even fathom. But she laughed unsteadily and caught his face between her hands.

"Wait, Gareth de Vavasour. I would know you."

Wicked light invaded his silver eyes. "I believe you just did—once again. Beautiful Linnet, you look like a goddess lying there, all part of the forest, your hair the color of those branches, and your eyes... By heaven, they are the most beautiful I have ever seen. I could sing a song of them, could I but sing."

"You can. I hear you singing when you touch me."

"You are the only song I will ever sing in all my life." His voice broke. "Let me love you again."

Aye, and he was up and ready for it, yet Linnet needed something else almost as urgently. "I would learn of you first, Gareth. I would understand the man I hold in my arms, and in my heart."

His body stilled, though she could still feel his thoughts running. "What would you learn?"

"All," she replied simply. She wanted to own him, to discover what it was that made Sherwood welcome him even as she did. "I have already felt much about you, your gentleness and the kindness that lies beneath your strength. But what made you the man you are?"

He eased down onto the moss and raised one arm to cover his eyes. Aye, and it hurt him to speak of his past, that much she could feel. An unhappy childhood?

"My father was a harsh man. Brother to Robert de Vavasour, he was very like him—cold and demanding, very sure of his place in this world. He took my mother to wife when she was little more than a child. The match bonded two great holdings, but she was little to his liking, a fey creature with a full measure of Celtic blood. She tried to suit him and to give him the heirs he desired, but after my brother, sister, and I were born, there were only stillbirths—one following another."

Gareth drew a breath. "Any sensible man who cared one jot for his wife would have left it there. Not Maurice de Vavasour. He destroyed her, body and soul. After the last miscarriage, when I was only nine, she bled to death."

"You loved her very much." Linnet could feel that. Did this account for the vein of gentleness inside him, as well as the vast gulf of pain?

"I did. She carried beauty with her—somewhat the way you do. She used to sing songs and tell me tales of heroes and dragons and beautiful, magical lands over the water. All that died even before she did. He killed it with his cruelty."

"And was he cruel to you, also?"

"Stern, he would have called it. The trouble was he had but two sons—and worse, a daughter—when he would have preferred ten. And as he despised my mother, he came to despise me. He could not wait to send me away to his companion at arms, Albert de

Breese, for training."

Perhaps better for the young man-child, Linnet reflected. "And was your foster father kind?"

Gareth laughed wryly. "No one could accuse Albert de Breese of kindness. But he was fair, and one way or another he saw me raised and trained."

He uncovered his eyes and gazed into Linnet's face again. "But such training costs money, and after my father died, Robert de Vavasour picked up the cost. He considers me under obligation to him, virtually in thrall."

She stirred and stretched her body against his, flesh to flesh. "You could throw all that over, break free of him. Come here to Sherwood and to me."

Desire flared in his eyes. "You think I do not want to? I confess, I have thought on it, though I doubt it would be much to your friend Falcon's liking. Be certain there is nothing I would not do for you. Yet you are engaged in a dangerous and unequal fight. What makes you think you can win?"

"Quite simply, we refuse to do otherwise. Back before I was born, my mother went to Nottingham Castle and sued for justice from King John. That was after he had signed the great charter to appease his barons. She challenged him with the notion that the same law should be afforded all Englishmen, Norman and Saxon alike."

"And she got away out of it with her life?"

"Only just. Any hope of achieving such justice was lost when King John died that next autumn—shat himself to death, as Martin Scarlet always said."

"Aye, a flux taken during a campaign, was it not?"

"Those here in Sherwood hoped for a better reign

under Henry. But it goes on as it did. The King and his nobles see us only as beasts of burden, and a source of revenue. Yet we fight for our identities. We fight for what lies here in Sherwood."

"It is a worthwhile fight." He touched her face almost reverently. "And that is why I cannot stay here with you, my love, but must return to Nottingham."

Protest rose within her. "Nay."

"Only consider, love—I am in a singular place to help you, close enough to my uncle to hear of his plans, and privileged enough to move about at will. I can warn you of his intentions, just as I did this time. I might even find ways to interfere with them. I am able to send you word in a way no one else can."

"Aye." Yet Linnet's whole being protested it. She now knew how desperately she wanted him here, not at some distance, even if he could whisper to her mind.

"Let me serve you as best I may." He kissed her again softly, a gesture of devotion. "But for that you will need to trust that I do serve you, only you. Can you?"

Could she? The scope for betrayal was wide. Yet could she fail to trust him when they had bonded so completely? Trusting him could cost all she held dear. Refusing to trust him would push away her very life's blood.

She gazed into his eyes and caught her breath at what she saw there. For better or worse, she must follow her heart. "I trust you," she breathed into him. "Now love me—well enough to make it last. Love me again."

Chapter Twenty-Seven

"It gratifies me, Nephew, to see you beginning to prove worth your keep. You conducted yourself bravely in giving chase to those wolfsheads in the forest last month, and now you make good progress with training these young whelps."

Robert de Vavasour meted out the words harshly. Stingy praise, yet Gareth felt a flash of satisfaction—not because he sought his uncle's approval, never that, but because Gareth had been working so hard to allay any suspicion and garner the man's trust.

And it seemed to be working. His uncle believed he had disappeared into the forest during the abortive battle at Oakham, some three weeks ago, merely in order to pursue those villagers who had fired upon them. In Gareth's absence, the remnants of the troop, including Monteith and de Vavasour himself, won their way to the road, as the villagers fell back. It cost them two more men, and by no means could the venture be considered a victory, but they had made it out of Sherwood alive. Gareth rejoined them at Nottingham after leaving Linnet, fully prepared to make an excuse about losing his way in the forest. But his uncle had clearly been ready to give him credit for helping put their attackers to flight.

Far more likely, Gareth thought ruefully now, Falcon, Lark, and their companions had merely run out of arrows. God knows, they had fired enough of them.

He stole a look at his uncle, standing in the sun at the edge of the practice field where Gareth was busy drilling the younger men. Since that day in the forest, Gareth had done everything he could to keep his promise to Linnet, though he ached to be with her and though his hatred for his uncle had grown into a terrible thing. It was fortunate Robert could not hear his thoughts as Linnet could.

Robert ran a discerning eye over the youths who sparred with sword and shield. The field lay in the open, and the day was a rare, warm one. Gareth, like the lads, had stripped down to his leggings, and he glistened with sweat. But the work felt good and served to distract him from the constant ache that occupied his heart and mind.

"They are coming along well," he answered, keeping all emotion from his voice. "One or two may make something of themselves, if they put in the effort."

"I am glad you learned something up north and that the coin I traded de Breese for your training has reaped at least a meager return."

Gareth nodded. He knew he must play the part of the dutiful young relation well enough to seduce his uncle into sharing any plans or information Linnet might need to know. Gareth despised Robert right well but dared not underestimate his intelligence. Like Gareth's father, the man was equal parts sharp wit, anger, and suspicion.

Gareth was well aware that Robert watched him, as he watched everyone. He had failed to include Gareth in the last two raids made on Saxon villages, and he must know Gareth had not been near Sherwood; Gareth had been busy keeping his head down and applying himself as bidden. Robert had no way of telling who had sent warnings ahead to those villagers—or how.

He said to his uncle, as if it were all that concerned him, "We shall be ready for the display at Lammastide, and do you proud."

Robert de Vavasour grunted and turned his gaze on Gareth. "See that you do. We have had word that Henry's agents, and perhaps the King himself, may be traveling north then." His lips twisted in a sour grimace. "To be sure, he will be after the quarter's taxes, which we hunt even now about the villages."

Gareth said nothing and let his attention rest on the lads still at work, as if they alone concerned him. "Aye, Uncle. How goes the hunt?"

"We burn another village at dawn tomorrow, and will keep doing until someone tells what he knows. I am sending a full troop, this time, with instructions to take prisoners. Torture may well loosen their tongues."

"You wish for me to accompany them?"

Robert fixed him with a cold, gray stare. Gareth met his gaze blandly, striving mightily to discern whether his uncle harbored any lingering suspicions towards him, above what he held toward everyone.

"Nay," Robert said, hard-bitten. "You keep to your work here."

"I will," Gareth returned. "Indeed, and I had given some thought to the display, and have an idea to propose that might raise an expectation here in Nottingham, both with the nobles and the peasantry."

Robert lifted an eyebrow. Gareth had learned he did not particularly appreciate initiative among his underlings. "An idea?"

"Something to motivate the lads as well as elevate your reputation—a contest, I thought, one such as my foster father held in York. Men combat against one another until there is but one ultimate champion."

The raised eyebrow quivered. "Are these lads ready for that?"

"I believe they are ready to compete amongst themselves. I further propose a similar contest among your knights, the winner to be declared Champion of Nottingham."

"Aye, Nephew, and would you think to participate in this contest?"

"I would hope to, my lord. I did take that title in a similar contest among Lord de Breese's men."

Rare approval flashed in Robert de Vavasour's eyes. His hand descended on Gareth's bare shoulder, more blow than mark of favor. Gareth tried not to flinch outwardly, remembering countless blows from his father's hand.

"It would be a feather in your cap, could you take such a title here, and would go far to elevate your position. Such a contest, would it be fought in the lists, or with the sword?"

"The sword, even as you see these lads at practice now—arm to arm and man to man, my lord. One does not fight peasant rabble in the lists."

"Do it." Robert's fingers clenched hard and fell away. "But make sure you can achieve the title, Nephew. Do not embarrass me."

"Aye, my lord, I shall do my best."

Spite glittered in Robert's cold eyes. "I have not been much impressed with your best so far—you will have to do better than that."

****

Dawn tomorrow, my love, another village burns. He did not say where. He does not yet trust me completely.

Linnet's distress fluttered in Gareth's mind. He sat atop the north tower of the castle as night came down, gazing toward the distant forest as if that could bring her closer. He found this a delicate, aching business, contacting her with his mind. He delighted in the wonder of it and at the same time longed so to be with her, to see and touch her, he had to summon all his endurance.

Soon there will be no villages left to burn. She nearly wept. *Would he drive all the folk into Sherwood, young and old, hale and sick?*

Across the distance, Gareth felt her worry and weariness as if they were his own. *He still hunts the monies taken from the King's coffers. It is saving face that matters to him.*

Those riches were spread among our needy, long since. The Sheriff will not have it back no matter how long he searches.

'Twill not keep him from trying. The King's agent comes soon, and my uncle will not want to admit his failures then.

Thank you for the warning. I will send word at once. Falcon will organize messengers and send them to every village that still stands.

Falcon again. Emotion blazed inside Gareth; to his dismay, he recognized it as jealousy. And if he felt it, so must Linnet, linked with his heart and mind.

Her voice whispered into his consciousness, soft

and gentle. *You need not worry, dearest one. I love no one but you.*

Gareth knew it. He even believed it. That availed him nothing when he burned to hold her.

Bitterly, he spoke into her mind, *Yet he is there with you. And your duty may eventually call you to accept him.*

He ached for her to deny that swiftly and completely. She did not, but fell so silent he feared she had deserted him.

Linnet, my love?

You work on my behalf. This I know. You need to trust me as I trust you.

He knew that also, but the feelings inside him did not answer to reason.

And the next words that reached him pierced him to the heart. *Even should the times and events press me to take a step that would strengthen and solidify the triad, it would indeed be at the bidding of duty. Whatever may happen in the future, be certain that my heart belongs only and ever to you.*

Gareth closed his eyes on a wave of pain. She did mean to accept Scarlet, to bond with him, lie with him, bear his children. Torture would be easier to endure.

Nay! He threw the protest at her through the gathering darkness. *Say you will wait for me.*

Wait for you? My love, my dear one, her regret poured into him, *we have no future for which to wait. The water between us runs too deep and is too wide.*

We will build a bridge.

Of what?

Of magic, if we must. In the forest that man, your grandfather—Robin Hood—bade me follow my heart.

So have I done! There must be some purpose.

There is, my love. A curious warmth curled through her and, thence, to him. But she pushed him away before he could identify it. *Stolen moments in Sherwood make wonderful memories that will stay with me always, but life and duty must be faced.*

You do mean to accept him—Scarlet. But nay, Linnet, you are meant to be mine and only mine. He drew a breath. *I will find a way. Do you hear me?*

But she had gone from him, withdrawn determinedly and shut the door in her mind.

He spoke aloud into the cold silence, "Whatever it may cost me, I will find a way."

Chapter Twenty-Eight

"What is amiss with you, Linnet?" Lark asked impatiently. "You mope about like a bird with a broken wing. Are you sickening for something?"

Linnet, startled from the fog that lately seemed to possess her, looked up at her sister. Nearly a month had passed since Gareth had left her in Sherwood and, save for his voice in her mind, he began to feel like a dream. She woke in the morning listening for him and stole away by herself at noonday so she might sit in stillness and catch his awareness.

At night, sometimes, he whispered her to sleep, allaying if not answering her torment. She thought she had concealed her ravaged state of mind, but it proved difficult to hide anything from Lark, so close were they.

What would Lark, unsympathetic at the best of times, say if Linnet confessed her love for the Norman, if she spoke of the conviction that haunted her—that she might even now carry his child? Linnet had no certainty of it, not yet. A month proved too soon. But her heart sang—and trembled—at the possibility.

She met her sister's implacable stare. "I think I need some time away from all this madness and strife. I thought to go stay with Ma and Pa a while, in Sherwood."

Lark eased herself down beside the fire, which burned on the bare hearth of what had once been their

189

home. "Do not bother. I have just been out searching for them. I wished to seek some wisdom from Ma, but they are not at the hermitage or anywhere I could find them."

That made Linnet stare. "They must be. Where else would they go?" Linnet and Lark had spent much of their lives away from their parents, but Linnet always knew how, and where, to reach them.

Lark's lips twisted in a wry smile. "Where, indeed? I spoke to the Old Ones about it." Lark delivered the statement, which might seem incredible coming from anyone else so matter-of-factly. By the Old Ones Linnet knew she meant certain of the ancient gods and spirits who dwelt in Sherwood.

"And what answer did you receive?" No need to question whether there had been an answer: those who sought with a faithful heart always found. And, above all else, Lark possessed a faithful heart.

"Ma and Pa have gone."

"Gone?" A spear of fear pierced Linnet through. "Gone where?"

Lark shrugged awkwardly, and Linnet felt her grief. "Withdrawn into the magic, into Sherwood itself, into the fire and the air, the water and the deep loam."

All the breath left Linnet's body. "No. They would not."

"Aye, that was my first reaction. But then I got to thinking on it. The hermitage was left all tidied, Lin. Ma's healing supplies were all put away or burned, some of them, for I sifted the ashes of their last fire. And Pa's supplies for making arrows—you know he always had ash wood and fletchings on hand."

Linnet felt the blood drain from her face. "Would

they take such a dire step without telling us?"

"I thought on that, as well. With Martin gone, I believe they think it best for the three of us to take up ownership of the triad in earnest. We would not do that with them still available to us. I do not know about you, Lin, but one of my first impulses is always to turn to Ma or Pa with any need or trouble. If they told us they meant to withdraw, we would have fought tooth and nail. This way, 'tis just a thing done, a fact with which we must deal."

"But," Linnet protested as panic flowed through her, "they must know how difficult this will be for us and how we will miss them. Ma can be brutal when needs must, aye, but Pa is never so unkind."

The rueful expression in Lark's eyes sharpened. "He will follow her anywhere. You know that."

Linnet acknowledged this also. Her thoughts raced over possibilities and eventualities. "Have you told Fal?"

"I just came from him."

"What did he say?"

"He took it hard. He has barely got over the loss of his father—now this." An unnamable expression flickered in Lark's eyes. "He wishes to speak with you. I do not doubt why."

Neither did Linnet. She reflected, with longing, on that last carefree day before Gareth de Vavasour had been captured and brought to Oakham—Lark and Fal playing together, tumbling like wolf pups and spoiling her morning's work. What would she not give to have that simple time back again?

"Fal knows his duty," Lark went on, not without bitterness, "as do you. Will you accept him now?"

Linnet lifted her hands, helpless. How could she, when her heart belonged so completely to another? When she might be carrying Gareth's child? And yet, how could she fail to take up the duty for which she had been bred and raised?

"You do not even want him." Lark said viciously. "Just as he does not want me, even though I would give my soul for him. By the Green Man's horns, Lin, could life be more unfair?"

****

"Lin? Have you a moment?" Falcon appeared out of the gathering darkness of early evening and, moving softly as a shadow, took the place at Linnet's side. All day long, ever since speaking with Lark, she had been awaiting and dreading this encounter. She and Fal had grown up together, yet she felt uncertain of him now.

"Lin." He spoke only her name. The two of them sat, looking out over what had once been Oakham. Much of the rubble had been cleared away and, like Linnet, folk now made their homes in the open air around their old hearths. Children ran and played until their mothers called them home to bed; hens pecked, and dogs slept with one eye open. Over it all the trees swayed and the breeze played its eternal song.

Linnet said into the deepening dark, "I wonder if this is what it was like when the ancients came here, the first folk who made the forest their home and found the magic."

"Found the magic"—Fal took it up—"and made it their god. The god has had so many names over the centuries, just as he has had many faces."

Linnet shot him a surprised look. This was a Fal of which she had seen little lately. While growing, the three of them had often mused over such things and spoken of their sacred bonds with Sherwood. She needed to remember the heart of that lad, now a man. Falcon had been ever a dreamer whom his father had called, innumerable times, to duty.

Linnet thought, again, she might have loved that lad, as a woman loves a man, had Gareth de Vavasour not entered her life. She wondered how much of Fal the gentle, the mischievous, remained.

"We need to speak together," she said softly.

He lifted his hands, broad-palmed but graceful. "Aye, and so I have come."

"The future, it seems, has rushed upon us."

"It has."

"Too sudden, Fal. I should have been prepared; I find I am not."

His hand stole over and clasped her fingers; his grasp felt warm and strong. "You are not alone. None of us is. The present may be unbearable and the future daunting, but the three of us must prevail. We have no choice."

From where had come this flint she sensed in him? Fal had ever been one to tease and play, to put things off, to tread the light path.

"So we journey on together. Wed with me, Lin. Let us take up our lives in earnest."

She squeezed his fingers. Sitting here with him as the night came down felt good. She might claim it as her future, would her heart but let her.

"There is something I must tell you, Fal." There were many things she should tell him—that she had lain down in the forest with Gareth de Vavasour, that she was not sure she could ever be the wife Fal deserved.

"It must be kept in strictest confidence between us, only you and me."

"Aye?" he looked at her and, through their linked hands, she felt his caution.

"I love you, Fal, but not in the way you might wish, as a woman loves a man." *Full and rushing, filling every breath and every heartbeat...* "I love you like a brother, nay, more than that. I love you like kin, to the bone."

His eyes searched hers. Through their fingers, she felt his emotions stir: regret, protest and longing. "That will do for now, Lin; it is enough."

"It is not." She knew now what love should be— bright and consuming. "You deserve someone who will give you her whole heart, love you, and breathe only for you. And there is such a one standing before you."

"Eh?"

"It is Lark who loves you, Fal, and desires you as a woman should."

"Lark?"

"I am not surprised you fail to see it. She hides her feelings well behind that fierce shield. But I know what is in her heart."

"Madness! She is like a brother to me, a companion."

"Then you have not looked at her properly, for she is a woman in every way that matters. Take her for your wife, Fal, bond with her and leave me to the forest."

"I want you. I always have." She could no longer see his face clearly, but despair filled his voice.

"And she has always wanted you," Linnet added honestly, "as I do not. A tangle, indeed. What is to be done?"

"I will tell you what: you are to put these foolish notions from you and accept me now, and the future will be what was always meant."

"I no longer know what is meant."

"I do, Lin. I have always known. True, it has rushed upon us betimes. My father's death has brought it, and your parents push us to it with their absence. But I see in a way they were right to leave us, sorely as I miss them. For it forces us to grow up and accept what we were born to be." His fingers clenched hers, hard. "Bond with me, Lin. Let our strengths become one."

"I cannot." Linnet blinked into the darkness.

"Because you think you do not love me, or desire me as you should? I will prove you wrong, Lin. Once we lie together—"

She could feel his emotions so strongly they swayed her. She distinctly felt her heart break over his longing. "No."

He turned toward her and strained to see her in the gloom. "Lin, love," he said with an edge of passion, "there is naught else for us. We were conceived and bred for this. How can you think to reject it?"

How, indeed? She did not seek to reject the duties inherent in the triad—only him. But she could not tell him that.

"Let me go to the forest," she begged, "and you go speak with Lark."

"No." Now he spoke the word. "I cannot lose you, too, atop all the other losses." Emotion roughened his voice. "Do not do this to me, Lin. I pray you, do not!"

"Fal—"

"Trust me, Lin. Put yourself in my hands. You are like a flower that has never been touched by the sun. I will show you what may lie between a man and a woman. I will win your heart."

Before Linnet could draw a breath, he kissed her, his lips claiming hers and his arms drawing her fast against him.

All his desire lay in that kiss, a vast river of it, unstoppable as a spring flood. It brimmed with sweetness and erotic power. It should have melted Linnet—or, indeed, any woman—to her bones. Instead it left her wracked by dismay.

In that instant, tasting his feelings, she knew she could not hope to lie to him or deceive him in any way. He deserved better, deserved all she had to give. She could at least give him honesty.

Somehow she drew her lips from his and planted both hands on his chest where she felt his heart racing.

"Lin." He dove for her mouth again.

"Wait." She sucked in a painful breath. "There is something more I must tell you, something you do not know about me."

He laughed unsteadily. "I know everything about you, beautiful girl."

"You do not know that I lay with Gareth de Vavasour."

Falcon froze for the span of ten heartbeats, twenty. "What? Say that again."

Linnet forced herself to hold his gaze, even though it cost her dear. "I gave myself to him. We lay together as man and woman, in Sherwood."

Rage blossomed in Falcon's eyes. She felt his body stiffen with it, as with the lash of a whip, and for an instant she did not recognize the man who looked at her.

"In Sherwood?" Being Falcon, and destined for guardianship, he grasped the significance of that. Vows were made in Sherwood and magic garnered there.

He sprang to his feet and glared at her. In that moment he looked so like his father, Linnet experienced a rush of dismay. "You gave yourself to that stinking, high-born piece of shite? For god's sake, Lin, why? You knew you were meant to be mine—you were always and ever meant to be mine!"

"Hush, Fal, please!" Folk all around turned their heads, searching through the gathered darkness for the source of the disturbance. Linnet stumbled to her feet also and reached for Falcon, but he drew away from her.

"Nay, do not touch me with those hands that have touched him. I do not believe it, Lin! Yours is the purest heart I know. I would have wagered my life on your honor. How could you betray me with the enemy to all we are?"

"He is not—"

"His kind killed my mother and Thrush—killed my father! Have you forgotten so quickly the people you said you loved?"

"I have forgotten nothing."

"He has made misery for countless others, he steals the bread from the mouths of dying children. Look around you! He steals the roofs from over our heads."

"Not he, Fal. His kind, aye, but not—"

Falcon went suddenly still with a quiet so intense it silenced Linnet. The darkness quivered before he said, "He *is* his blood. You, of all people, should know that. We are all what our blood makes us. I ask you again"— pain filled his voice—"how you could do such a thing."

"I had to follow my heart."

"Your heart, is it? I thought your heart a true thing, worthy of my worship. I set it high above me. I would have loved you lifelong. Now I cannot bear to look at you!"

"What goes on here? What is all this shouting?" Lark stood suddenly beside them, materialized out of the darkness.

Falcon rounded on her. "Ask your sister. Or do you know already? Has she told you what she has done?"

"No, what?"

"Given herself to the accursed Norman, lain down for him like one of his harlots or the women his kind seize from our villages, only to rape and ravish. She has taken the greatest prize Sherwood had to offer and thrown it at his feet."

"Never!" Linnet felt Lark's gaze sear her even through the dark. "Say this is not true."

"She just told it to me."

"How?" Lark demanded of Linnet. "When?"

Again, Falcon answered for Linnet. "In Sherwood, no less—on that holy ground."

"Lin, is this true?"

"I love him," Linnet said helplessly.

Lark struck out so swiftly, Linnet never saw the blow. It took her in the face and rocked her where she stood. Vicious words, and the hate that accompanied them, followed after. "Love? By the Green Man's heart, you must have forgot the meaning of love—for it is sacrifice. You selfish, loathsome wench!"

"Lark—" Linnet cried, but Lark turned from her and put her arms around Falcon. "She is naught to us, Fal—naught."

Falcon, desperate, spat at her, "She is everything to us—a third of the triad and all we must be." Wild-eyed even in the dark, he rounded on Linnet. "I cannot raise my hand to you, Lin, not ever. But I will repay that Norman cur in full for all he has stolen from me. I swear by the Green Man himself, I shall see Gareth de Vavasour dead."

Chapter Twenty-Nine

"I hope you are proud of yourself. You have shattered the triad before it was fairly formed, and now Falcon has gone off to his death."

Linnet whirled in the face of Lark's angry words, and alarm once more speared through her. All the night long she had lain sleepless, replaying the scene with Falcon, beleaguered by regret. Surely there must have been a better way to tell him the truth. Yet she had always tried to be honest with him, and she loved and respected him enough to grant him that, even in this.

Now, in the first light of morning, her sister flew at her again, eyes wide and her small body rigid with anger.

"What?"

"Falcon. He has gone to Nottingham—alone—with the intention of killing de Vavasour."

All the breath left Linnet in a rush. "He would not be so foolish." Even as she spoke she scanned the open area that used to be the village of Oakham, searching for one wild, fair head. People arose, women lit their fires and children wailed for attention, but she did not see Falcon.

"He is angry. More than that, he is hurt. I spent all the night while you slept peacefully striving to talk him out of it. When I dozed off, he left me." Disconcertingly, Lark's eyes filled with tears. "He left me."

"I did not sleep quietly—" Linnet began to protest.

"Neither did you come to him, argue with him, make him promises." Two tears trailed down Lark's cheeks. So rare was it for Linnet to see her sister weep, it caused emotion to clutch at her heart. "Say or do whatever you must to keep him from going. He would not stay for me—not for me!"

"Nor would he have for me," Linnet put in, distress flooding her. How could Falcon have been so heedless as to go haring off into danger alone? He knew what he meant to Oakham, to the triad.

Aye, just as she, Linnet, had known how important she was to Falcon and Lark before she lay down with Gareth de Vavasour in the forest.

"Stand there as you will," Lark sneered. "I mean to act."

"How? What—"

"I am taking a band of men and going after him. If you had one loyal bone in your body, you would come."

"If he gets himself captured—"

"If he gets himself captured, I will move heaven and the earth itself and slay every Norman bastard in Nottingham so to free him! I barely know you, Linnet. Where is the sister with whom I grew? Where the daughter our parents raised? How could you so much as touch that stinking swine when you could have had Falcon?"

"Gareth de Vavasour is not what you think. He is a man of honor."

"Ha!" Lark spat. "There is no such thing, as bespeaks a Norman. He must have stolen your wits as well as your maidenhead. Stay you here—I do not need you with me to save Falcon."

"Wait." Linnet seized her sister's arm. Lark shrank from her, the action as stinging as a blow. Lark— closest in the world to her, flesh of her flesh—stared at her with a stranger's eyes and flinched from contact.

"Lark, please try and understand. I never intended to love Gareth de Vavasour. It came upon me from nowhere, like a blessing. Can we choose where our hearts decide to bestow themselves? You, who love Falcon, should understand."

Lark lifted her chin a notch. "Falcon Scarlet is fine and just, and worthy of regard. And I would have held all my love for him locked in my heart. I would never have acted on it because I knew the triad—the welfare of our people—must come first. I would have sacrificed him to you—you, Linnet! I would have watched him wed you and bed you, and give you his beautiful children. All because it was what he and Sherwood chose. And what do you do? Throw it all away like it is naught, so you can rut in the forest like a Norman whore."

Linnet fought down her own anger, a rare thing but now rising wildly. "It is not like that, Lark, it is not just a thing of the flesh. Gareth and I have formed a deep connection. We are even able to share thoughts between our minds, just as Ma and Pa do."

"How can you? Do not ever speak of them in the same breath as that cur!" Lark raked Linnet with wild eyes. "I do not know you. You are no longer my sister." She turned to leave, her small body stiff with indignation.

"Wait," Linnet said again. "I will come with you, if

you think it will do any good."

"It may make a difference to Fal," Lark spat in return. "So aye, I bid you come, and I suppose I shall just have to bear your company."

****

My love, are you there?

Linnet formed the words and sent them forth through the stillness of the morning, telling herself they did not constitute a betrayal. The party from Sherwood, of which she made the fifth member, moved almost silently. Around them, birds flitted and the light strengthened. She could feel her sister's anger and resolve, and her desire for secrecy. Was it wrong to tell Gareth they were on their way?

My love. His reply came like a thread of music afloat through the trees and, despite her despair, gladdened Linnet's heart. *Are you safe?*

A strange thing for him to ask—or perhaps not, if he could sense her emotions and the furor that possessed her.

Ah, and how much to tell him? Linnet picked through her thoughts almost delicately, unable to decide.

She trusted Gareth; she had since the moment she first lay in his arms. Yet trusting him with her life was one thing; trusting him with Falcon's another.

Linnet, love? His voice came to her more strongly, as if his concern sharpened it. Linnet lifted her eyes to the trees overhead and the light sifting down. Would they share this ability—the same her parents possessed—were Gareth unworthy of her trust?

I need your help. We are in some difficulty.

Immediately his emotions flooded her, all

203

protective concern. Walking just ahead of her, Lark twitched as if she felt the backlash of his awareness.

Tell me what I may do.

Falcon has learned what took place between us in Sherwood. He is on his way to Nottingham, after your blood. I follow with Lark and a band of our men. I need to protect Fal at any cost.

And had she just done? Or had she condemned him? She trusted Gareth—aye, she did—but no sooner had the words been thought than doubt nibbled at her.

How could she doubt the man who possessed her heart?

Gareth fell silent, which added to Linnet's uncertainty. She had begun to panic before he asked, *What road does he take out of Sherwood?*

Should she tell? Belated caution made her back off a step. *Why?*

Because he is known here in Nottingham. Our guards have instructions to watch for him. If he comes anywhere near the castle he will be seized.

We follow now in an effort to catch him, but he is one man, and moving swiftly.

Tell me how he comes and I will ride out to meet him, try and reason with him, keep him from tossing his life away.

There is no reasoning with him. He is angry.

If it is a confrontation he wants, I will give it to him away from Nottingham. Where?

Lark glanced over her shoulder and flayed Linnet with her golden gaze. Lark felt something of this exchange; her suspicions were all up and warring. How best to protect Falcon? Lark might not believe it, but that was Linnet's first concern.

She hesitated one moment longer and then drew a breath. *The forest path just east of the York road. It is the quickest way, and what he must take.*

That leads to the clearing near Ravenshead, does it not? I will hurry and await him there.

My love, he is armed with his sword as well as his rage.

I will come similarly armed.

Ah, by the Green Man's horns, what had she done? Gareth de Vavasour was a proven champion. Fully healed by her mother's magic, he could well prove an opponent Falcon could not best. Better, perhaps, to let Fal take his chances searching out, in Nottingham, a man he might not find. Had she spared him capture? Or condemned him?

Gareth, my love, I need him. I need him alive. Over the green distance, she received no reply.

Chapter Thirty

"Nephew, hold up a moment."

Gareth paused on his way to the stables and spun in mid stride to see his uncle approaching across the courtyard. No one could ever say Robert de Vavasour did not perform his duties assiduously. Many men might lie abed until the sun was well up, but Nottingham's sheriff had arisen in time to catch Gareth hurrying off in answer to Linnet's summons.

"My lord." He planted a bland look on his face. Bad luck indeed, being intercepted before he could even leave Nottingham proper.

"Where are you bound, so early?" Was the suspicion in Robert's eyes sharper than usual, or did Gareth only imagine so?

"I thought to ride out, my lord."

"Now? Do the young men not await you for drilling?"

Gareth's mind raced. "Aye, my lord, but they are still at their breakfasts. I meant to ride out betimes and catch your night patrol before they seek their beds—one of them is said to be a doughty man with the sword, and I hoped to persuade him to meet me in the Lammas competition."

Robert's gaze sharpened. "Could that not wait?"

"It could, Uncle, but I confess I am eager to put on as fine a show as possible for you, especially should the

King be in attendance." Gareth allowed himself a tight smile. "I have had few takers, as yet, willing to meet me."

"That is because your reputation as a swordsman grows. You begin to earn a name for yourself, as should be, given your name is de Vavasour. Very well, Nephew, go snare your man and do what you can to stage a fine spectacle. Only make certain you win this competition. Do not embarrass me."

Gareth inclined his head. "Aye, Uncle. I had further thought of marking all those who do summon the courage to face me and forming of them an elite band to put pressure on the peasants, perhaps even venture into Sherwood, if need be."

"An assassin squad, eh? I like the idea. Aye, you go about your recruiting as you will and choose your men carefully. Meanwhile, I will continue with my own methods of persuasion."

"My lord?"

"You think I mean to sit still whilst Henry holds me responsible for those lost taxes? Nay, lad, Monteith has his orders. There will be a right reign of terror until those Saxon dogs turn over what belongs to me."

Gareth, flooded with sudden alarm, nevertheless strove to meet his uncle's gaze with a steady stare. "Aye, my lord."

Robert lowered his voice. "You are not the only one, Nephew, capable of scheming."

****

"Halt you right there!" Gareth bellowed the command as soon as he saw Falcon Scarlet enter the clearing. "Do you come looking for me?"

Scarlet skidded to a stop so quickly it was almost

comical, and Gareth stepped out from behind the shelter of the trees, where he had concealed his mount. Falcon greeted him with a stare of astonishment—to his mind, there must be no way Gareth could have anticipated his arrival here, or his intent—and reached immediately for his sword.

Give the man credit, Gareth thought, his wits moved swiftly and well for an untutored peasant. For Linnet's sake, Gareth would need to refrain from killing him. This might prove a difficult battle, but better—far better—to turn Falcon away here, before he had a chance to throw his life away in Nottingham.

"What are you doing here?" Falcon called, standing full in the morning light. It made a nimbus of his wild, fair head, and Gareth saw how well he balanced on the balls of his feet, a fighter born.

Of course, Gareth thought, a moment too late, His father would have taught him, and none but a fool ever underestimated Scarface.

"You come seeking a fight," he returned. "I mean to give it to you."

Falcon shot a swift look around the clearing, no doubt suspecting a trap.

"Nay, it is just you and me," Gareth told him. "Are you man enough to face me?"

No fool, Falcon must be wondering how Gareth had known to intercept him here. But his anger, well-stoked, was enough to overthrow his caution. He raised his sword and charged Gareth with a howl.

And Gareth, moving forward to meet him, heard a voice in his mind. *My love, my love, my love—do not harm him, I pray.*

A difficult proposition, at best, for Scarlet came at

him like a wild wind, sword high and whirling. No drilled maneuver, this. It held generations of pure Saxon bloodlust. Gareth set himself and raised his own blade, just in time to meet the first crashing blow.

By the sweet lady of heaven, who had taught the man to fight? If it was indeed his father, he must have been a brute with the sword. The sunlit clearing rang with the sound of blades meeting again and again. Gareth had all he could do to turn Falcon's blows and no hope, yet, of taking the offense.

Aye, and he had spent countless hours drilling with the sword. But that had been as a squire and, later, the way a knight practices, by rote and by rule. Falcon knew none of that. His eyes glared at Gareth, crazed and wild, and all his rage rode in every strike.

Do not kill him, I pray. Again he heard Linnet's voice in his mind, sounding closer this time.

Aye, and he was lucky if he could keep Falcon from killing *him.*

"Bastard!" Falcon tossed the epithet at him with another pounding stroke, delivered two-handed. Gareth did not know from whence he had come by his sword, but it was a good one, likely gotten from Scarface. He railed at Gareth with every move. "Curse you and all your kind, thinking you can take what you want! Use what you want! Ruin what you want! She was mine, do you hear me? Mine, mine, mine—"

He loves her, Gareth thought. The knowledge jarred through him like one of Falcon's blows. He knows she has given herself to me. And he hates me as much as he loves her.

No time for thought, then. Gareth set himself to endure the fierce onslaught until Falcon began to tire, as

Gareth knew he must. The man had not trained, as had Gareth, for endurance. He had never fought hand to hand while wearing heavy armor. Half a knight's training centered on being able to last.

Yet never before had Gareth been forced to battle with a newly-healed arm. True, he had spent days on end, since his recovery, training the lads at Nottingham, and sparring with members of his uncle's guard, as well. But none of that was sustained, and Gareth's left arm now began to scream at him. It might do well enough holding a shield or even performing light duty, but he found himself forced to meet Falcon's two-handed blows with both hands on his hilt, and felt it. He did not know what magic the woman, Wren, had used to heal his bone in such a miraculously short time, but clearly the miracle proved incomplete.

"Cur!" Falcon Scarlet spat at him. "Thinking you can rape the very flower of Sherwood!"

"'Twas no rape." Gareth gritted his teeth and felt the sweat bead on his brow. "She gave herself full well to me. Had she wanted you, she would have done the same for you." He lifted his blade swiftly, judging the time had come to take the offensive. At the same moment, he caught movement from the corner of his eye—a party burst into the clearing. His awareness told him Linnet numbered one of them, even though he barely dared to spare her a glance.

My love. Her voice pulled at him.

And he replied, *Wait.*

"Falcon!" someone screamed. Lark, it was. With the shreds of his attention, Gareth saw her run forward, closely followed by the other members of her party.

The movement—and perhaps the cry—distracted

Falcon also. He turned his head, and Gareth took advantage, quick to push in upon him. He had to take the man's sword. Short of killing him, it made the only possible end.

"Wolfsheads, wolfsheads!" Another cry, this one from behind Gareth. A party of mounted soldiers led by the captain of the guard, Monteith, burst into the clearing.

Run, Gareth tossed at Linnet, his heart twisting in sudden panic. *Go, go, go—*

Falcon! she screamed.

And then madness erupted in the clearing.

Some of the outlaws fled. Gareth raised his sword horizontally and pushed at Falcon. "Go," he said through gritted teeth. "Get you from here."

The fool stood and stared at Gareth, his greenish-blue eyes wide, even as the soldiers surrounded them— too stupid or too courageous to turn tail and run.

All thought suspended then as an arrow whizzed past Gareth's nose. Lark had also refused to flee. Instead she stood firm and drew her bow for another shot. Her first arrow had split the air between Gareth and Falcon, its aim to end Gareth's life.

Her second took one of Monteith's men through the throat. The man fell and his horse reared in distress, adding to the confusion.

Monteith called out, "Stand! In the name of the Sheriff of Nottingham, I do arrest you."

Another arrow answered him. It missed only because Linnet dragged at her sister's arm.

Go, Gareth screamed at her in his mind.

I cannot leave her, Linnet wept in return, *nor Fal.*

And, quite plainly, Falcon Scarlet had lost all

chance to fight his way free. The mounted soldiers now surrounded him where he stood, his chest still heaving from their battle.

He turned his head sharply toward the two women, as if he had heard one or both of them call him with her mind. Lark? Or Linnet, whose desperation Gareth could see carved on her face? Did Falcon reply through the bonds that joined them? Gareth could not tell, yet suddenly, to his relief, both women turned and fled.

Two members of Monteith's troop started off in pursuit. Lark paused long enough to fire an arrow that caught one of them through the heart. Linnet ran on, and Gareth watched until he saw both of them disappear into the safety of the trees.

"Good work, Sir Gareth," Monteith called to him. "Too bad so many of them escaped." He leaned down from his mount and pointed his sword at Falcon's throat. "At least we have this cur to drag back to Nottingham."

Chapter Thirty-One

"You did this! You betrayed Falcon to your accursed Norman lover, and now all is lost. Fal will surely die. You have condemned the triad and Sherwood, both!"

The bitter words stopped Linnet in midflight and spun her around to face her sister. Lark, as breathless as she, looked transformed by rage, alive with it, and dangerous as a maddened wolf.

They were alone, save for the trees—as alone as they could ever be in Sherwood. Even now, distracted by grief and fear, Linnet felt the presence of the life force that contributed to Sherwood's magic, an indefinable yet vital thing.

In the face of that, she struggled for speech. "I did not betray him. I never would."

"Aye, and I did not suppose you would lie down with that Norman serpent, either, he with the blood of our people on his hands. Have you forgotten, Lin? Do you not remember how Ma bargained for justice? Or what the fight has cost us these last many years— Sally's life, and poor wee Thrush, and countless others?"

"I have not forgotten." Linnet wetted her lips, gone suddenly dry. "And Fal is as dear to me as any of them—nay, dearer. How could I possibly set a trap for him?"

"Easy, I should say." Lark stared at her as she might a hated stranger. "Did you not tell me you and your Norman lover can communicate by thought, like Ma and Pa? Aye, you bragged of it! Deny that you warned him Fal was gone looking for him!"

Linnet went hot and cold by turns. How could she deny it? She had sent Gareth just that message—in an effort not to betray Falcon, but to keep him from harm. Then why had the soldiers arrived in the clearing? Her heart clenched and spasmed inside her chest. Surely her trust in Gareth was not misplaced.

Lark took her silence for answer. She hurled her next words at Linnet like weapons. "Ah, so I see what you are, Sister! And I see what your selfishness costs us—all hope for the future. Without Fal we are lost, the triad is lost, all is lost." Disconcertingly, Lark began to weep, the tears of rage pouring down. She did not bend before her grief but wore it like a fierce battle shield.

"Lark, please try and understand. The triad has always come first with me. Sherwood has always come first. I did not choose to love Gareth, but I do love him."

"Love?" Lark screeched the word so it echoed through the trees. "You do not love. For love is giving, love is sacrifice. Or have you learned nothing all these years?"

Lark's anger, a pure, unstoppable barrage, crashed into Linnet like a visceral storm an instant before Lark launched her small, hard body in attack. Linnet went over backward with her sister on top of her, all arms, legs, and pain. Blows rained upon her from Lark's clenched fists, accompanied by enraged cries. All her life Linnet had known her sister capable of this, but never had Lark's rage been aimed at her. And never had the tight bond between them been so strained.

She raised her arms in defense, tried to catch Lark's wrists to restrain her, but Lark had become an unstoppable fury. And far worse than the blows coming at Linnet was the hate.

My child. His child. Lark, please! The words cried aloud in Linnet's mind. Miraculously, Lark heard, even though Linnet uttered them not. Abruptly, the blows ceased. She removed her body from Linnet's as from a source of contagion and scrambled to her feet.

"Say it is not so!" She gasped and stared. Her gaze raked Linnet where she lay. "You carry that bastard's get? I should kill you now."

Stung and hurting, Linnet cried, "Kill me, and the triad is destroyed."

"It is destroyed already! If you think de Vavasour"—she spat the detested name—"will ever set Fal free of Nottingham another time, you are far too foolish to live. You have cost us all! Take your accursed brat and get out of my sight."

Linnet struggled up, aching in every limb and wounded to the heart by what she saw in her sister's eyes. With a whimper she turned from the hate, and ran.

She fled from, not to, and chose no direction except away. Her surroundings passed in a green blur fogged by tears. When her breath gave out she paused and gasped, doubled over, and then fled again.

She would not have believed she could become lost in Sherwood, where she had grown and played, yet when she went to ground at last, felled by the root of an ancient beech, she lay as a creature stunned and utterly bemused. No sense of orientation, inner or outer, accompanied her. The voices that so often hummed within her mind or her heart—those of Lark and of Falcon, of Sherwood itself—had ceased, and she had no sense at all of Gareth's presence.

The silence terrified her. She lay on the moss where she had landed, aching and straining every sense, frightened of being alone for the first time in her life.

It seemed she had been born with the voice of Sherwood in her ears, the rustling of leaves, the undulating song of the breeze, the chuckle of running water, the constant murmur of life. The voices of her parents speaking together, mind to mind, had been always a soft, whispered presence of which she caught the echoes. Lark's, and later Falcon's, life force had been available to her if she chose to tap into them.

Now she heard only birds singing their eternal music through the deep, underlying silence, and she thought, I am going to die. I cannot live cut off from all that is. This is the end of me.

Something stirred to the right of her, a real and present sound, but when she turned her head she saw nothing there. Again, a rustling beyond her feet. She sat up, so abruptly her head swam and her stomach heaved, and saw a tuft of grass bend beneath invisible feet.

Who is there? She spoke with her mind rather than her lips, for she knew this was no living person. Better anything, though, than the aloneness, and stunted senses.

A fox appeared from the trees and looked at her with Lark's keen, golden eyes. Linnet blinked at it and it blinked back, and awareness nibbled at the edge of her mind.

Deep magic, as her mother might have said.

Sudden longing to hear her mother's voice again convulsed her heart.

"Do not weep, child." The voice sounded in the air, and not in Linnet's mind. She blinked in an effort to clear the tears and saw a woman standing before her where the fox had been.

She had the coloring of the fox, coppery red, and the very same eyes, like Linnet's mother's, like Lark's. She was someone Linnet had never before encountered in Sherwood. Nevertheless, Linnet believed she could guess her identity.

She drew a breath and began to scramble up, but the woman held out a slender hand.

"Peace, Daughter. You need not stir yourself." She smiled, and Linnet gazed at her in wonder. Beautiful she was, her hair half braided and trailing down, her smile as sweet as sunrise. Clad all in green wool and brown leather, she appeared scarcely older than Linnet. But her smile was Lark's, quick and mischievous, and confirmed her identity in Linnet's mind.

"Grandmother." She breathed the word like a prayer. "If you come to me, I must be dying."

"Your grandfather sent me." She smiled again and beauty flashed in her face, as if it flared with the mention of the man. "Robin Hood."

"You are Marian." Stories of her were legion, how she had abandoned her comfortable existence to live with the outlaw Robin in Sherwood, and lived henceforth for him most truly. How she had crumbled upon his death and abandoned his child new born— Linnet's mother, Wren—and later died languishing for love of him in a nunnery, a broken woman.

She looked whole now, and serene. Linnet's

heartbeat steadied. "If you are here," she whispered, "does that mean the two of you are together once more?"

"Together most surely. So long as Sherwood remains free, we cannot truly die."

"You held a place in the triad, the first triad," Linnet said.

"Not the first. There were many before us, but we took ours out into the open, where Robin made of it a means to fight. He has sent me to you now, child, because I once stood where you stand." Her lovely face clouded. "I, too, carried the future."

Linnet pressed her scratched and bruised hands against her belly in an age-old gesture of protection. "My child."

"He will be strong and very gifted, and the most important person ever born in Sherwood."

"How do you know?"

"I know because he is destined. He was meant to be conceived here at this time. He is the future. He is the past, come again."

Linnet swallowed hard. "Lark thinks I have destroyed the future. She thinks I betrayed Falcon. She hates me."

"Lark battles hard. She feels her emotions keenly, especially love. She loves Falcon beyond all reason…" Marian's expression saddened. "Even as I loved your grandfather. Unreasoning that was, almost like a sickness. I would have done anything, sacrificed anything, to be with him. I saw, too late, the one thing he would have asked of me was the thing I failed to do."

"What was that?"

"Carry on. Keep strong and fight, for our daughter's sake. But when he left me, I believed all the light in the world went with him."

"I understand." Linnet thought of Gareth. Would she ever see him again? Ever hold him, watch the quick thoughts move in his eyes, feel his gentle kindness? Or had he moved forever beyond her reach?

"Here, child, your face is beginning to swell." A stream appeared as if by magic at Marian's side. She bent to the water, and her hands produced a soft cloth. She wetted it and approached Linnet quietly, as the fox might.

She means to touch me, Linnet thought. But she is a spirit.

She was not. Marian knelt down beside Linnet and pressed the cold cloth to her face with infinite gentleness.

Once more, Linnet's eyes filled with tears. "Grandmother, what am I to do?"

"That is easy, Linnet, as well as very, very hard. You must do as I did not. Gather your courage and all your strength. Go back and take up your place in the triad."

"Lark—"

"Lark will need to master her feelings also, for the sake of the greater good."

"She despises me." The pain of that bit deep.

"She needs you, though, and Lark is capable of most any sacrifice. What is it your father always says?"

"Sherwood gives, and Sherwood also demands."

"Aye." Marian's gaze became kind. "Sacrifice is demanded of us who are given much. It is a lesson I failed to learn. I was given the most wonderful gift any woman ever received, and I loved." Her voice whispered. "How I loved! But when the time for giving came, I forgot the most important truth."

"That we must give back?"

"No, child—that none of us can ever actually lose another, no matter the lies presented to our eyes. I came here to give you the benefit of that. If you love this man, you cannot ever truly be apart from him."

"Even if I never see him again?"

"But you will, Daughter." Joy filled Marian's face. "He belongs now to Sherwood and will endure with the rest of us, so long as Sherwood remains."

Linnet drew a breath that contained both wonder and pain. "I do not know if I am strong enough."

"You are. You have your mother's strength." Another smile trembled across Marian's face. "And Robin's. You will do as you must to protect the future." She placed both slim hands on Linnet's belly. "It lies here. You quicken!"

Strength, Linnet thought, and sacrifice. But her grandmother promised she would find beauty and reward at the end of it.

"And magic," Marian whispered. "Do not forget the magic." She leaned forward and kissed Linnet's brow. A shower of amber sparks erupted, lending a rush of warmth, before she transformed back into a fox. It winked at Linnet once and then slipped back into the cover of the trees.

"Aye, Grandmother," Linnet vowed. "I will not forget."

Chapter Thirty-Two

"A fine prize," Robert de Vavasour gloated. "I believe, Nephew, you have seized a ringleader of those outlaws who have been making such difficulty for us in Sherwood. One of the same men I was forced to trade away before, is he not? He shall not escape us again. You have done well, Gareth. Very well."

High praise, indeed, from a man who gave it far less than he dealt blows from his hand. Gareth, seated at the high table in the great hall at Nottingham with a goblet of congratulatory wine in his hand, did not look up to meet his uncle's eyes. All night long, ever since Falcon's capture, his thoughts had raced, seeking the best way he could help Linnet, even if that meant helping Scarlet, the man who hated him.

He wondered again why he had lost touch with Linnet in his mind. True, their bonds were sometimes fragile with him in Nottingham and her in Sherwood. But usually he could catch a whisper of her thoughts. Now it felt as if a portcullis had crashed down and severed everything.

Sudden terror twisted his gut. Had something terrible happened to her? Could this silence mean she was dead?

"I will admit," Robert continued grudgingly, "I had my doubts of you when first you came and brought so much trouble with you. But you have done well enough with training the young men and conceiving this contest for champion. And I am gratified you located this wolfshead. Tell me, Gareth, how did you come to encounter him?"

"'Twas chance—or more precisely, whim, my lord. When I did not succeed in meeting the guard whom I rode out seeking, I remembered that clearing, where I met the headman, was close by and is frequented by those in the forest, a kind of pilgrimage place."

Robert crooked an eyebrow. "Aye, and how did you know that?"

"Something I overheard while held in the outlaw camp. Since I was so near, I thought 'twould be as well to take a look."

"That is not chance, Gareth, but good instinct, which has long been an attribute shared by those of de Vavasour blood. Perhaps you prove your father's son at long last. And it seems your time spent in captivity, humiliating as it might have been, was not wasted."

"Uncle"—it nearly choked Gareth to call this man by that name, but he was not thinking of himself, not now—"allow me to go into the forest again. I believe I begin to anticipate the ways of these vermin. I am certain I can snag one or two more of them."

"If you know something of value, talk to Monteith. He will organize a proper pursuit."

Gareth lifted his eyes. "With all due respect, Uncle, a single man can go unseen where a troop of soldiers cannot. I learned much about how these rascals move, whilst they dragged me about with them. Allow me to track them first on my own."

De Vavasour debated it; Gareth saw the doubt in his eyes. "And should you get yourself captured again?"

"I will not."

"I do not wish to have to trade this prize we have just taken for your ransom."

"I promise you, my lord, I will return."

"See that you do. I have just received word that King Henry will be in attendance for our tournament. I want you to put on a fine show. And if you can reclaim his tax money for him—the large coffer that was taken, or the smaller—so much the better." Robert rubbed his chin. "Meanwhile, we will give thought to questioning this wolfshead we have in the dungeons. Perhaps he can direct us to Henry's treasure."

****

Leaving Nottingham Castle later that same morning, Gareth's eyes raised to the motto carved over the gate: *Vivit Post-Funera Virtus.* He had enough Latin to know what that meant: Virtue Outlives Death.

Ah, but he must have seen that message a score of times since arriving at Nottingham, yet never before had it struck him. An apt sentiment, indeed, though more for those who inhabited Sherwood than his own kind, who set themselves above them.

Death, it seemed, swallowed all things. It had engulfed his young, beautiful mother and robbed from him the only love he had ever known. That love, or the desire for it, seemed to have lain dormant inside him until Linnet entered his life. Then it had surged and blossomed and become a vital growth that encircled his heart.

The walls of Nottingham would have him believe virtue survived death. And love with it? Something surely survived in Sherwood, the spirits of folk long dead. Had he not seen and conversed with one of them?

And what if Linnet lay dead even now, somewhere in Sherwood's arms, beneath the green boughs? What if that made the reason he could no longer hear her in his mind? Would her love for him live on? Aye, so it must—for he knew his, for her, would never die.

Sherwood welcomed him with open arms as he slipped into the trees and the green-lit morning closed around him. He stood for a moment inhaling the scents that made him think of Linnet and the warmth, feel, and taste of her in his arms. Overhead, birds flickered like the light. He heard a lark call at a distance, an aching sound.

And what else could he hear? Silence, save for the rustle of leaves, the drone of insects. Sweat gathered and trickled down his back.

He called to her, *Linnet, my love!*

A hare appeared from the underbrush. It winked at him before it turned and disappeared again. No fool, he followed.

A merry chase the hare led him, deeper and deeper into Sherwood. At times he lost sight of the animal completely; always it came back for him. He prayed as he went, not to some far-off entity, a God he had never seen and who dwelt in cold, stone buildings, but to the Being who brought the light to the leaves, who made the stag run and sent the current of life flowing. That same power dwelt here; he could no longer doubt it. And he was more than willing to sacrifice himself to it for Linnet's sake.

Let me find her. Let me know she lives. Let me touch her one more time, and I swear I will ask nothing more all my life long. A dangerous bargain to make, for he knew that men were created for wanting. And he knew he would never stop wanting Linnet.

Champion. The sound spun him around. The man he had met here before, the one called Robin Hood, stood full in the green haze of light, looking as substantial as Gareth himself.

Gareth lost no time in wonder. "Where is she?"

Robin did not answer. He tipped his head, though, as if listening. The light slid over the length of his hair, pricking reddish lights from the brown. Just so, Gareth knew, did sunlight warm the hair of his Linnet. Air invaded his lungs in a rush. This man was her grandfather. And *alive* or *dead* no longer seemed such a vital distinction.

Robin smiled. "Virtue survives death," he said. "Never doubt it, Champion."

"And love?"

Robin lifted his hands. "Need you ask?"

Gareth shook his head. Hushed, he asked, "What is this place? What makes its magic?"

"Sherwood is, and always has been, a repository of belief. Think of it as echoes, my son, the echoes of faith, intent, and longing. They die away but never cease, no more than I. The source of all things has been worshipped, here, for time out of mind. To those who believe, Sherwood gives back again, and gives much."

"The source of all things?"

"Love. Life. In the purest way, they are one. First, my son, there came a thought and then belief in the thought. Belief is all."

"Is Linnet here?"

"She is here forever and always, so long as Sherwood endures."

225

"And if Sherwood does not endure?"

Robin hesitated. His deep blue gaze moved over Gareth with curiosity and regret. "If faith dies, Sherwood dies and all with it. Why do you think I fought so hard? Should our enemies steal our hope, our faith will soon follow. Should they cut down the trees and root up the stones, naught will endure."

"I will not allow that to happen." Gareth said it hoarsely.

One of Robin's brows quirked up. "And who are you?"

"A champion. You have said so."

"A Norman champion? Or one for Sherwood?"

"For Sherwood." Gareth's heart thudded within his chest. "For Linnet. Return her to me."

"Do I hold her?"

"You hold all things. I pray you, my lord—I know I am your enemy—"

"You are no enemy to me." Again Robin smiled. "You are a bridge, a branch, a sprig of green willow. You are proof, walking, that all men born of English soil may someday be one, living equal. That is my dream."

Gareth returned gravely, "And now mine, also."

"Go to her, then."

"How can I find her?"

"Listen."

"I can no longer hear her voice in my mind."

"That is because you have let fear block your senses. Did I not tell you to follow your heart?"

"Aye."

"Then listen to it now."

The sun shifted and the branches swayed, allowing

brightness to blind Gareth's eyes. When he blinked through it, Robin was gone, leaving behind only a faint shimmer of power. A bird lit out from one of the branches overhead and flew away to Gareth's right. He turned to follow and spoke at the bidding of his heart.

Await me, Linnet, my love. I come.

Chapter Thirty-Three

Linnet, my dearest love.

The voice sounded inside Linnet's head like the chime of a bell, an instant before a hand touched her hair. *Gareth.* She would know him anywhere, even blinded and bound.

She roused from the bosom of Sherwood, where she had fallen at the end of her flight. In the newly-descended dark beneath the trees, he looked no more than a dim shadow on his knees beside her.

Gareth?

Linnet, darling.

He gathered her into his arms, and his strength wrapped around her. The agony inside her eased—she did not know how he came here, but his presence answered her every need, and she burrowed into him as she might into the heart of Sherwood itself.

"How did you find me?" Did she speak aloud or in her mind? She no longer knew.

His lips slid across her brow and down her cheek. He gave a gusty, wondering laugh. "I followed a bird, and after that a glint of water, and then a shaft of moonlight. They led me, all, to you."

His hands caressed her gently, as if they embraced glass. "What happened to you? 'Twas as if you fell away from my mind." He drew an unsteady breath. "I was not sure I could endure it, did not think I would be able to go on without you."

"I argued with Lark and she thrashed me soundly. She blames me for Falcon's capture, thinks I betrayed him to you. She will never forgive me." All at once she wept, she who so seldom gave in to tears, as all the pain flowed out of her heart and into his. She felt his great gentleness rise to meet her pain and absorb the hurt with a fathomless depth of patience.

"Let me see." Very carefully, he tipped her face up to the moonlight. Linnet could feel how the tender flesh that surrounded one eye had swelled, and the bruises on her cheekbones. More bruises covered her arms, and her hands were torn. "Fierce little thing, is she not? You look as if you have been in the wars. No broken bones? No pain anywhere inside?"

"My ribs ache. That is naught, though, to the ache in my heart. Gareth, I cannot go home. Lark will have told everyone I betrayed the triad. I will be outcast."

"No. Your folk all know you. You have spent your life taking care of them. They will never believe such a thing of you."

"Gareth, I saw my grandmother." Linnet sought his eyes in the dim light. "I spoke with her, she who is dead."

Gareth made no reply, but his hands, on her shoulders, tensed.

"She told me sacrifices must sometimes be made, and I have always known Sherwood demands them. I thought—" Her voice caught, but she forced herself to go on. "I feared I might be required to give you up. But Lark, also? And Falcon?"

"I know how closely bound the three of you are. It is a hard thing to bear. But I cannot believe Lark could ever turn her heart completely against you. As for Falcon—"

"He is lost. Do not say 'tis not so. Do not lie to me."

"Listen, Linnet. I have spoken with your grandfather, even as you have with your grandmother. He gave me reason to hope. I told him my heart is yours, and because that is so, my loyalty belongs to Sherwood. There may yet be a way to help Falcon."

"How?" She stared at him. "Can you persuade the Sheriff to release him?"

"That I do doubt. But soon the King comes to attend a tournament at Nottingham, and my uncle is desperate to recover the stolen taxes before then. Do you have any idea what happened to the two casques seized along with me? Returning them may be the only way to save Falcon's life."

"Two? I saw but one that day." Linnet shook her head. "And the coin will be long gone, distributed among those in need."

"Are you sure? There was a large box and a smaller one filled with not coin but jewels. If you can recover even part of that, it might go far to ransom Falcon."

Linnet thought hard. Martin had been in charge of the only casket she had seen, back in Oakham. What would have happened to it after his death? "Are you certain there were two?"

"Aye, and I should be, since I was in charge of guarding them, along with the King's tax collector, a thing my uncle never leaves off throwing in my face. The smaller was in the keeping of the King's man. I cannot imagine his attackers would have missed taking it from him after he fell."

"I saw only the casket filled with coin, all small pieces. I do not recall seeing another. Might it have been hidden, and lost when Oakham burned?"

"Gold and jewels do not burn, my love. Who would know?"

Linnet thought hard on it. "Martin did not share control, or knowledge, easily." Her heart sank. "The most likely person to know would be Falcon."

When Gareth said nothing, she prompted, "That is not good news, is it?"

"I fear not."

"They will question Fal at Nottingham, will they not? Torture him… Oh, Fal!" Her cry of grief pierced the darkness. "He is strong, but not as his father was. I know him; I have always known him. He has long tried to follow Martin's ways, as he believes he must, but inside him there lies a great compassion, a softness. I do not know how he will endure."

Again, Gareth remained silent.

"If he does not come back from Nottingham, all is lost. There is no one else to hold his place in the triad. And Lark will never forgive me."

"I have told you: she cannot possibly turn her heart against you."

"Ah, but you do not know her. Lark hates as strongly as she loves, and she loves Fal as much as I love you."

She felt Gareth's emotions come rushing in response to her emotions, a vast well of tenderness founded in determination like bedrock. If others could only feel this in him, she thought, they would never doubt his loyalty. Only she heard, along with

Sherwood, and that must be enough.

"I swear to you, Linnet, I will do all I can to save him."

"I know you will. But how?"

"As I say, there is to be a grand display at arms whilst the King is at Nottingham. If I make Falcon part of it, he might then fight for his life."

The breath caught in Linnet's throat. "Fight—against whom?"

Gareth ignored the question. "He is a good man with the sword. I discovered that much in the clearing near Ravenshead."

"Aye. Martin trained him well, and Martin had his skill from his own father, Will Scarlet, who was once a soldier. But Falcon lacks their instinct to kill."

Irony filled Gareth's voice in the darkness. "In this instance, he may well wish to kill his opponent."

Fear gripped Linnet's heart so it fluttered like a bird in a clenched fist. "And who will that be? Whom will he need to face?" she asked once more, though she already knew.

"Me." The word came low and steady, but Linnet could feel his emotions behind it: doubt and determination she could barely comprehend.

"No," she breathed.

"Aye, love, if I can only arrange for it." The darkness was now almost complete, but she felt his lips brush hers, like the fleeting touch of butterfly wings. Her whole body responded to that touch, leaped toward him in love and desire.

"You see, I must be his opponent, for only that way can I assure his opponent does lose."

"No." She protested it again as a wall of pain

crashed upon her, and she distinctly felt her heart tear in two. She loved Falcon and had been raised in the belief that he was vital to everything she would ever hold dear. Without him, the future was lost, along with Sherwood's precious magic.

But this man who now cradled her so gently between his hands was precious to her also, as dear as her own breath, and the one desire of her heart.

She whispered—or did she only speak in her mind?—*I cannot let you. I cannot hope to go on living without you. If you must fight him, can you not just allow him victory? Must it be a fight to the death?*

Be sure I will try. But 'twill be an open arena and before hundreds of eyes. It must be convincing, and the man already wants my blood.

Ah, no! Linnet cried again, broken.

And he told her, *Sacrifices must be made. Have we not both been so bidden? I am willing, for your sake.* He bent his head in a beautiful gesture of devotion and bowed to her as a knight might bow to his liege, with total, humble grace. Once more she felt the fullness of his love surge upon her, unstinting.

Linnet, I go to do this thing with a whole heart, as your champion.

Linnet, caught and helpless, made him the only answer she could; it came in the form of a kiss, one salted by her tears. They clung together, held fast in the spell of Sherwood's darkness, and their emotions twined and tangled so her fear became his, exchanged for his determination.

When he had kissed her lips, her eyes, and every bruise that mottled her face, he spoke again into her mind. *My love, you will need to be there.*

What? Her terror, only partially soothed by his touch, spiked again. To know he went and did this on her behalf was one thing. To be forced to stand and watch it—quite another.

Relentless, he said, *You need to go to Nottingham with a band of your people to demand justice of the King—should I fall and my uncle fail to keep his word.*

Could she entertain such a possibility, even in her mind? Might imagining it make it so?

Courage, love. I can win for him his chance; I can even tip the scales for him. But it may be up to you to ensure he receives his reward.

Courage, he bade her, when she knew very well she held the better part of that between her hands. All brightness and valor was the spirit of Gareth de Vavasour. And to be worthy of him she must try to be as strong as he.

She nodded in the darkness even as she reached for him with her mind, with her hands, and with her heart.

You win him free, she whispered, *and I will get him free, for Sherwood.*

For Sherwood, he returned.

But first, my love—she ran her hands over his shoulders, against the warm skin of his throat and inside his tunic, desperately craving the taste and feel of him, desiring the comfort and completeness of him inside her—*I would ask one thing for me, just for me.*

And he replied, as he laid her down in Sherwood's holy darkness, *That I am most glad to give.*

Chapter Thirty-Four

"And where have you been? Out running wild in the forest, by the look of you," Lark said sharply, "even while Fal languishes in a dungeon at Nottingham."

"Since when have you ever found fault with running wild in Sherwood?" Linnet tried desperately to control her emotions and disregard all the hurt burgeoning inside her. She could feel Lark's pain, the ache of loss that possessed her at Falcon's absence. Lark's terror for him rendered her very nearly helpless.

And Linnet understood that terror full well: she had just sent the man she loved away, possibly to sacrifice himself. In truth, she could not see a way forward from the tangle in which they were caught. If the promised combat took place, Falcon might not return and the future would be lost. Or Gareth de Vavasour might not survive and Linnet's own future would be too bleak and terrible to contemplate.

She had felt his intent when they parted. He fully meant to lose on purpose if he must—for her and for Sherwood.

She glared at her sister now, both sympathetic and impatient with Lark's habitual truculence.

"Are you willing to put aside your anger with me, Lark, and work for Falcon's sake?"

Lark looked up from beside the hearth place of what had once been Linnet's own cottage, where she had found her. Oh, Linnet thought, what had become of her orderly life, when the worst thing about which she had needed to worry was Lark and Fal spoiling a morning's work? Now morning came again, and the pure light poured through the trees with the same beautiful promise, but all had changed: Martin dead, her parents gone, Falcon's life forfeit, and her sister, closest in the world to her, glaring as at a stranger.

And Gareth—her heart convulsed at the thought of him. Aye, but she must be strong, as strong as he.

"I will do anything to save Fal," Lark declared. "Anything. But what is to be done?"

"In two days there will be held a tournament at Nottingham. We must be there and we must take whatever we can gather up of the taxes stolen at Midsummer, to return them to the King."

Lark came to her feet slowly, as if drawn by strings. "How do you know of this?"

"Does it matter? During the tournament, Falcon may be given an opportunity to win his way free. But the Sheriff will not be appeased unless we can first offer some reparation—"

"Slut!" The word hissed from between Lark's lips. "You have been with him, have you not? Lain with him again. No need to lie about it—I can virtually smell him upon you, the reek of Norman swine."

"I met Gareth in Sherwood, aye." Why deny it now? Linnet knew Lark could feel the truth. "But only so we might make a plan to help Fal."

Lark trembled where she stood, her gaze an accusation. "Why would Gareth de Vavasour choose to help Falcon Scarlet? They are enemies born."

"Gareth acts for my sake." Tears came to Linnet's

eyes. "And for Sherwood."

"For Sherwood, a Norman champion?" Lark scoffed. "Words he gave you, no doubt, to get you on your back." She swept her sister with a punishing glare. "And it worked, did it not? His handprints are all over you."

Linnet lifted her head high. She still tingled from Gareth's touch, and the warmth of him lingered inside her like a treasure, one she might never again possess. Their farewell had been desperate and hard; he had taken the better part of her heart with him to Nottingham. But what remained belonged to Falcon, and to Sherwood.

"Do you want to punish me, Lark, or do you want to help Fal?"

Unexpected tears flooded Lark's eyes. Her emotions assailed Linnet in a wave of anger combined with grief so deep it burned. "I wish for both! That any sister of mine could betray us this way—a child of Sherwood, granddaughter of Robin... You spoke to that Norman bastard in your mind. You told him how he might capture Fal. Now you act for him once again in an effort to reclaim the King's blood money."

"Lark, listen to me." Linnet seized her sister's wrists and received another jolt of feeling as a consequence, an increased sense of Lark's pain. "This is Falcon's only chance. Think not of your anger but of him."

"Think of him?" Lark howled. "I can think of naught else. I can feel him, Linnet! I can sense his hurt and despair as if they were my own."

"Good. That means he is still alive. In order to save him, you must trust me." She gazed full into her sister's face. "Not Gareth de Vavasour. Me."

Lark shivered and shuddered. Anchored by Linnet's hands, she stood fighting an inner battle, its intensity visible in her eyes.

"Lark, Sister, we are lost without Fal. But you are also lost without me, and I without you. It needs the three of us, all three. Go to the forest and pray on it. Let Sherwood speak to your heart."

Lark blinked at her and then gave a hard nod.

"Only, go swiftly," Linnet bade, "and do not be gone too long. Falcon awaits us."

****

"Awake, my son."

Gareth opened his eyes to a dazzle of brightness. The chamber his uncle's seneschal had assigned him faced east, and the new morning sun came in the window and found him where he lay. Pure white, it appeared to him as he lay just called from sleep, and blinding.

Who had spoken to him? He had dreamed of Linnet, but this did not sound like her voice. Yet it was as familiar to him, over the distance of memory.

The brightness shifted, gathered, and took form. A woman stood at the foot of his bed, smiling.

And, oh, he remembered that smile. Every day of his youth it had been gifted to him, the highest reward he could hope to win. It held a measure of magic and beauty so true it even now twisted his heart in his chest.

"Mother?" He sat up, scrambling among his blankets. Ah, but she was wonderful to look upon! Clad in what he now remembered as her favorite gown of spring green, she looked slender as a willow, and her fair hair—golden, with a touch of red—spilled down her back. And her eyes—as a child, Gareth had believed heaven lay in her eyes, and all the love available to him in the world.

But they had laid her in her grave. His heart clenched again. Her presence here could not be real, much as he longed for it.

She shifted, came forward, and sat on the foot of his bed. Her smile deepened. "Look at you. All grown, and so handsome."

He lifted a hand to the scar that now marred his face. "Nay."

"I speak not of your appearance, my son, although that mark takes nothing from you. I speak of the man within. I am so very proud of you."

Hot tears flooded Gareth's eyes. How long had he waited to hear those words? Like a child, he answered, "I have tried, Mother. I remembered all you taught me."

"I know. I have often been with you, though you did not see." She shook her head and the morning light shed from her hair in radiant sparks. "That you could have come through your father's hands, survived, and kept your heart pure amazes me."

Gareth's thoughts leaped. He had not forgotten what morning this was. Today he would fight a contest for Falcon's life, and his own. Was that why she came, to warn him? Did she come because this day he must die?

Much as he wanted that answer, he dared not chase her with a question and end this moment. Almost, he did not care—her presence proved enough.

So he whispered, "You look well." She did, especially since the last time he had seen her she had lain a broken creature, pale and wasted, most of her brightness flown. "You are happy?"

Her smile deepened. "I am. Only look." She lifted both her hands in a graceful gesture and cupped them together. They caught the sunlight and spilled brightness like water. She laughed. "Remember the magic about which I told you, and that I said was everywhere? I am filled with it now; I am made of it. There is, my son, nothing to fear in death."

Gareth swallowed hard. So, that was indeed why she had come. "Mother, am I to die today? If it is for her sake, I will not shy from it."

"Oh, what a son you are! You combine my love and your father's courage." Gareth's heart protested, and she said swiftly, "Nay, do not deny it."

"I despise my father."

"Then you must despise a part of yourself, for he too contributed to what you are. Say what you will of him, he made you strong." She tipped her head, considering him. "Are you strong enough to accomplish what you must, this day?"

Gareth nodded soberly. "I live for her. Should I not die for her also?"

"You will do as you must. Follow your heart."

His eyes widened at the familiar words. She leaned forward and laid her hand against his face. He felt a tingle where she touched his skin. Now he could see her eyes, deep green like the light in Sherwood.

"Therein, my son, lies your strength. It is a twisted, beautiful thing that in his cruelty your father gave you the iron to survive the poison he fed you and somehow keep the ability to love so strong."

"No mystery, Mother. You taught me. *She* taught me."

"Then bless her, and bless you also, Gareth. May the wind come and aid you when you need it, may the fire burn inside, may the purity of the water and the great strength of the earth flow through you. In the name of the Old Ones do I invoke all these for you."

"Thank you, Mother." He closed his eyes with the strength of her blessing. Through his eyelids he saw the light shift and he knew she had gone, even though the memory of her touch lingered. "Thank you."

Chapter Thirty-Five

"Here is your blood price, or most of it." Angrily, Lark thumped the small, heavy casket down at Linnet's feet. For the past two days, Linnet knew, Lark had searched for that chest, unstinting in her efforts.

Now Linnet's gaze flew to her sister's. "How did you find it? Where?"

"Does it matter?" Lark scowled. "Some of it is gone. Yet surely it will still buy Falcon's life."

Linnet's heart rose on a wave of hope, the first she had felt since parting from Gareth in the forest.

"So," Lark continued, "you may speak to your bastard lover in your mind and tell him you have what he seeks. It goes hard with me to turn over to you what might keep the wolves from so many doors this coming winter, but I would do far more for Fal's sake. Anyway, I have prayed on it."

"And received an answer?"

Lark's golden eyes narrowed. "We are lost anyway, without Falcon. So those who dwell in Sherwood do say."

"We are three or we are nothing," Linnet acknowledged. She, too, had done a lot of thinking these days just past. She knew she carried the future in the form of Gareth de Vavasour's child. It was as if she could feel a measure of brightness tinged by magic just beneath her heart. Whether or not she bred the future, she knew she must accept the present in full. She had to step into her place in the new triad—nothing could be more important.

She remembered her mother telling her many times how life shaped individuals to be what they must. Events only defeated a woman if she failed to learn from them.

Quite possibly this day's events would shatter her. She faced the possibility of going into the future without the man she loved more than her own life. Yet if the worst did happen, she would need to walk on, for Sherwood.

"Thank you, Lark," she said softly.

"Do not thank me. I do naught for you—all for him."

Gently Linnet replied, "Anything done for the three of us is done for Falcon. I only pray he lives still."

"He does." Again Lark's eyes flashed. "I have spoken with him; I have been with him where he lies and upheld him, even as he endured the questioning. Nay—they have not tried him too sorely yet, but I have felt what he feels." Wonder touched her, strong and visible. "In his time of need, I have lent him my strength." Her chin tipped up. "If he survives this day, he will be mine."

The fierceness of the declaration explained much, including the chest at Linnet's feet. She nodded. "Then let us assemble our band of men and make haste to Nottingham."

****

My love, we come. We have the casket you sought. Will it be enough to buy Falcon free?

Gareth straightened where he stood, sword in hand,

when the words entered his mind. Already was the contest, which had begun at sunup, well advanced. The lads Gareth had spent weeks training had put on a fine show. The day—one of deep azure skies and white clouds streaming before a strong breeze that unfurled also the pennants on the royal pavilion—could not be more perfect. Robert de Vavasour, seated with the King, appeared pleased, and even from where he stood at the edge of the field Gareth could see that Henry looked content.

Now, with the sun high in the sky and the hour nearing noonday, came time for the major events. Gareth drew a deep breath and thought of the woman who spoke to him, and not whether this bright day might be his last.

Where are you, Linnet?

We are at the outer gate—myself, Lark, and four of our men. Where is Falcon?

He has not yet been brought forth. Gareth pictured her passing through the gate. *Virtue survives death*—he must believe all higher emotions did so survive, especially love. *He will be here when the moment comes.*

First, he knew, he must do his part, defeat all comers in order to win the privilege of facing the man he meant to name Nottingham's worst enemy. For he must face Falcon as the champion in order to claim that right.

He flexed his left arm. Already it pained him. The bone Wren had fused by magic, in Sherwood, had perhaps mended too quickly. How many men could say they had a broken arm that healed in a matter of days?

True, it was not his sword arm. But with his shield

upon it, he needs must take the brunt of every blow meant to fell him, in defense of his life—at least until he could face his last opponent of all.

What is it, my love—what is amiss with you?

Ah, and she could feel his disquiet. Could he hide anything from her, including the desperation in his heart? He answered, *I would play my part carefully, and true.*

We all take our lives into our hands and do as we must. Her strength touched him a mere instant before her love came rushing, filling and uplifting him like light. Despite the circumstances, it brought him fierce joy.

But I wish to see you, she said, all her hope and longing in the words.

If all followed his plan, she might see him die. He would spare her that if he could, but did not know how. *Aye, love. I come to meet you now, at the gate.*

Then I can keep breathing.

With a nod in the direction of the pavilion, Gareth hurried off, after sheathing his sword in one swift movement. People thronged the grassy area just west of the castle proper, where the contest was being held. Moving against the stream that contained peasants, tradesmen, and nobles alike, he searched for the party from Sherwood.

And found them by feel.

They looked no more than another group of woodsmen. Even Linnet went clothed as a male, and they all wore their bows on their shoulders. Gareth did not think he had ever before seen Linnet with a weapon.

She wore leggings and a leather hood with a wide-brimmed leather hat that shadowed her face. But he need not see her face to know her, for her spirit reached for him, a stark contrast to the hostility of Lark, at her side.

Even as he approached, Lark stepped forward. "Well, Norman, you had better intend to deal with us in good faith, or I swear you shall live to regret it. If Falcon does not survive this day, I will find and kill you myself."

Gareth met her fierce, golden stare and spoke the truth. "Should your Falcon survive this day, my life may well be forfeit."

Her eyes widened, and he went on, "If you would give him a chance to be away out of here, you needs must be clever in it, and we shall have to work together—no matter how much you hate me."

That took her aback. For one of the few times since he had met her, she looked less than certain. "It is a matter of trust, Norman. How am I supposed to believe you willing to sacrifice yourself for Falcon?"

"Not for Falcon." Gareth moved his gaze to Linnet's face. All his being, as he now knew, lay with her. And he would do all he must for her sake.

Her eyes met his and, again, the love came rushing upon him, a sense of claiming so strong it steadied his resolve and his heartbeat.

Her voice sounded in his mind, a caress. *Forever, beloved.*

Lark twitched, almost as if she heard.

Gareth looked at her again and then swept the grim-faced men who accompanied her with a glance. "Listen to me. Falcon will need to fight for his life. I can wrest for him that chance, and I can try to tip the scale—little more. Follow my lead, and above all else get Falcon away after the contest ends, no matter what condition he may be in."

Lark's chin tipped up. "If you can imagine I will not—"

"I can imagine you losing your temper and spoiling our chances."

" 'Our'?" she sneered.

"Were I not with you, Mistress Lark, I would not make this attempt. Look around you. Do you think I can do more than sway these events? Now hold your tongue and come to meet the King."

All six of them stiffened.

"You do mean to betray us," Lark hissed.

"He does not." Linnet laid her hand on Gareth's bare arm. The last time ever she would touch him? Ah, but his whole body strained to her even as her love flooded through him again.

I will be with you, she whispered in his mind, *in the sunlight, the breeze, and the grass beneath your feet— in the strength of your heart.* It was so like the blessing his mother had bestowed upon him, he caught his breath.

He nodded at her once. "Come," he said again. "And, all of you, be as strong and wise as ever you have been."

Chapter Thirty-Six

"Sire, I have grand news. I bring the return of your stolen taxes, lost here in Nottingham some weeks ago."

The words caught the attention of the mild-faced, sandy-haired man seated in comfort in the pavilion, and brought the Sheriff of Nottingham to his feet.

Linnet had never before been quite so close to the dreaded Robert de Vavasour, and had never before laid eyes on the King. Now she stood under a silk canopy surrounded by guards and nobles, one of whom was the Sheriff's captain, Monteith.

Would Monteith recognize them from the encounter near Ravenshead? But no, his gaze slid off both her and Lark, no doubt dismissing them as unimportant peasants.

King Henry crooked an eyebrow. "What is this you say, Sir Gareth? And are these varlets the fellows who stole it?"

"Nay, my liege." Gareth bowed deeply, and his golden-brown hair spilled over his brow like liquid sunlight. So handsome did he look, stripped down to fighting trim in his leggings and boots, he nearly distracted Linnet from the situation at hand.

Nearly.

"These are your loyal subjects, my agents, who have been working on my behalf among the forest folk."

"What?" Monteith straightened at that, and Robert de Vavasour looked taken aback.

Gareth spared a look for neither of them. "My liege," he said again, "there are folk who work on your behalf, always."

"Well!" Henry sat up straighter, and a smile curved his lips. "We are impressed by your devotion, Sir Gareth." He waved a hand at Linnet and her companions. "And by that of these faithful subjects. Not everyone in Sherwood has forsaken his King, eh, de Vavasour? And it seems your young nephew has succeeded where you failed. We are pleased, indeed. Not only a fine entertainment provided us this day, but the return of what is our due."

Beside Linnet, Lark twitched violently. Linnet prayed she would control her indignation; she knew very well how many weapons Lark carried about her person and just how quickly she could draw that bow on her shoulder. They stood, here, in the very heart of danger. If Lark gave in to her impulses, they would never leave the pavilion.

Robert de Vavasour grunted, "My nephew should have come to me with this information."

"Or me," Monteith put in.

"My agents," Gareth made a sweeping gesture toward the party from Sherwood, "have only just succeeded in finding what they sought."

"Well, where is this prize?" Henry asked.

Edward Fletcher, who made one of Linnet's party, stepped forward and set the heavy casket at Gareth's feet. A big man, Edward, brawny and usually fearless, he now appeared struck dumb. But then, none of them had expected to be hauled before the Sheriff and the

King.

Gareth lifted the lid of the small chest. Everyone gathered in the pavilion strained forward to see, and Robert de Vavasour spoke incredulously. "How did you manage that, Nephew, when the captain of my guard could not?"

Again Gareth gestured to Linnet's group. "My lord, I made some useful connections while captive in the forest."

Lark twitched again, and Linnet almost tasted her fear. Her sister believed Gareth used them to his own glory, in this moment. Yet, miraculously, she held her tongue.

"A true champion, eh?" Henry cocked an eye at de Vavasour. "Working for his King even in captivity. We are well pleased. And I trust you will put on another fine show for us this afternoon?"

"I hope to, my liege, finer than you can imagine."

"Then go." Henry waved a dismissive hand, the casket of riches that could have fed the poor of Sherwood indefinitely already forgotten. For an instant Linnet experienced, in full, Lark's anger and resentment. Then Gareth turned, and she saw the look in his eyes.

Magnanimously, Henry added, "You have my thanks. And perhaps ale all 'round for your stalwart helpers."

"Thank you, my liege." Another bow and Gareth led them away down from the sheltered pavilion and back into the sunlight. It made a halo of his hair and burnished his deeply tanned shoulders.

At his left shoulder, though, Linnet could see the ugly, puckered scar from the wound she had tended.

Her mother had healed that—or had she? Linnet sensed something in Gareth, a hesitancy or possibly pain. But so many sensations rushed upon her here, including Lark's suspicion and anger, her senses were nearly overwhelmed.

"You had better be dealing in good faith with us, de Vavasour," Lark spat. "Else, as I have promised, I shall make you pay."

Gareth gave her a long stare. "Best leave that to Scarlet, eh?" His mouth tightened. "You have a long afternoon ahead of you before I can wrangle his appearance. Choose for yourselves a place from whence you can see everything yet still get him away when the time comes."

Lark tossed her head and tried to scoff. "As if I believe you truly will deliver him to us."

"If you did not believe it, you would not be here. Whatever happens, when your opportunity comes you must get him out through the gates and back to Sherwood. Understand?"

Lark nodded once, and Gareth turned to Linnet.

Her heart seemed to lift and then shatter into pieces at the tangled love and resolve she saw in his eyes. He spoke not aloud, but into her mind. *What I go to do, my love, I do for you, and for Sherwood.*

I know.

You have brought me joy, more than ever I dreamed.

She reached out and grasped his wrist. Warm from the sun, the feel of him beneath her fingers seemed, in that moment, to hold all life and all hope. *I bid you return—to me, and your child.*

His eyes grew wide with amazement. She felt the

joy and the pain of it engulf him, all one emotion. And in that moment she knew for certain he did not expect to survive this afternoon's work.

By God! That makes all the more reason for me to act as I do, my love, in the hope that our child may someday live free.

"Sir Gareth!" Someone called him from across the field. Linnet felt his pain as he turned—the physical kind, this time—raw and hot at shoulder and thigh, bone deep in the arm that had been broken. Sheer terror engulfed her. He was not whole, and he went to fight to the death.

She drew a breath and almost—almost—called him back. But Falcon's life hung in the balance, and the triad, and Sherwood, all things she had been bred and born to defend.

I love you. Fight well. They were her last words to him as he stalked away from her across the bright green grass.

****

"Your man—Norman or not—can fight, I will say that for him." The words came from Lark, uttered almost beneath her breath, honest and grudging. She stood as she had for the last interminable stretch of time, taut as a bowstring, watching every move on the field before them, completely enthralled. She had not missed a blow or sword stroke, and her eyes glowed.

At her back the others of their party muttered. Linnet could hear them, and Lark, and the cries and cheers of the crowd, but she could no longer look at the center of the arena where Gareth de Vavasour—her love, her heart—fought for the name of supreme champion. She only knew he had agreed to take on all comers and had fought, already, six members of the Sheriff's guard and taken them all down with wounds that rendered them incapable of fighting on.

"A costly proposition for the dog de Vavasour," Lark had grunted at one point. "These must be his best men, and now all hampered."

And what of Gareth? He must be hampered, as well. Linnet knew his beautiful body, so graceful beneath the sun, was now streaked and spattered with blood, some of it his own. She could feel his weariness, ever-increasing, and the unbearable ache in his left arm. Facing the last opponent, that arm had nearly failed him and he had almost lost his grip on his shield. The whole crowd—now entirely behind him—had cried out in anguish before he had managed to disarm his adversary.

Even the King, still undeniably enjoying himself, was on Gareth's side. Linnet had heard Henry call out, as well. But she could not look. She could no longer watch her love endure.

"He is earning his title, no doubt of it," Lark ground out now.

"No more takers," said one of their men, also completely engrossed.

And Lark breathed, "What of Fal?"

What, indeed? Against her better judgment, Linnet gazed through the haze of afternoon sunlight and watched as her man—*her man*—lowered his sword at last and stalked toward the pavilion where sat the Sheriff and the King.

"My lord and liege," he called. Was she the only one who could hear the exhaustion in his voice? "It seems I am fresh out of opponents."

"You have fought well," Henry returned most

graciously, "and earned the title of Champion."

Gareth bowed, and Linnet received another taste of his pain. "Thank you, my liege. But I confess I would fight on."

Even from where she stood, Linnet saw Henry raise his hands. "How, when you have answered all comers?"

"There is one more I would face, sire. He languishes in your dungeons."

Lark's breath caught hard. She reached out and caught Linnet's forearm strongly enough to leave bruises. "Fal! Ah, but surely your brute will kill him."

"Hush. He keeps his promise."

"What is this?" Henry called, and glanced at Robert de Vavasour.

"My liege, one of the miscreants who took part in thieving that which my nephew has this day returned to you has been captured and awaits trial. It seems your champion would choose to face him."

Gareth bowed again. "I would, my liege. I say let his trial take place here and now, before your eyes. Should he defeat me, he may win his freedom. Should I defeat him, my blade shall deliver your justice."

And Henry called, "As if he could defeat you, and he an untrained peasant! Aye, Champion, let the rogue be brought, and do well my work for me!"

Chapter Thirty-Seven

Go carefully, love.

Gareth heard Linnet's voice in his mind even as he stood awaiting the arrival of Falcon from the dungeons. He dared not look at her, though his entire being longed for it and he could have pinpointed her effortlessly in the crowd.

He felt her fear for him, even as she must be able to feel his weariness, which now went bone deep. He ached, and a buzzing filled his head the way it sometimes had after his father had beaten him and he was forced to walk back to his chamber on his own two feet. Pride had kept him upright then. Devotion kept him on his feet now. One more opponent to face, and this time he did not have to win.

The pain in his left arm was a blinding thing, so raw it felt as if the bone had given way again. Yet the limb still served. The new cuts and abrasions merely stung; he would spare them no heed now. But both his healed wounds, at thigh and shoulder, burned, and the scene blurred intermittently before his eyes.

Not enough to keep him from seeing Falcon, though, when he appeared flanked by two guards. Falcon looked much the worse for wear—he would have been questioned about the whereabouts of the tax money—but he was still on his feet and moving with his usual lithe strength. Gareth tried to imagine the shock of being hauled from one of those stinking cells without warning and brought out into the bright sunlight before this great, eager throng. Falcon came with his head up, his wild, fair hair alight and haloed, and his eyes everywhere.

Gareth felt the emotion coming from Linnet's direction spike. *For you, love,* he told her, *I do all for you.*

Helpless, loving, her feelings tumbled through him. *Beloved.*

The guards brought Falcon to the center of the field, where Gareth waited. Gareth had to credit the man—he did not look half as frightened as he should.

In the pavilion, Robert de Vavasour got to his feet. "Wolfshead," he addressed Falcon, "you are accused of crimes against your King." Beside him, Henry leaned forward eagerly. "Your trial will now commence. Give him a sword."

Falcon shot the Sheriff one long, disdainful look before his gaze swept the crowd. He fixed his blue-green eyes on Gareth, and his lips curled in a grimace of hate.

"So," he said for Gareth's ears alone, "you are to have your wish after all, the chance to face me with a sword in your hand."

"I do this for Linnet, and for Sherwood. Fight well."

Robert de Vavasour's voice overrode Gareth's. "Wolfshead, you fight for your life and freedom. Should you defeat the King's champion, you may walk free from this place. If you go down to his blade, your life will be forfeit. Do you accept the challenge?"

In answer, Falcon spat in the direction of the

pavilion. The crowd muttered and stirred, and Robert made a haughty gesture with his hand. "Let the contest begin."

One of the armorers standing near placed a sword in Falcon's hand. The onlookers drew an expectant breath. After the day's events, they thought to see this opponent felled, and quickly. How else should it be, between a peasant and a trained knight?

But Gareth had faced Falcon in the clearing near Ravenshead and knew too well the man was no stranger to the sword. And by the way Falcon reacted now, head up, back straight, eyes full of hate, Gareth could tell that, of all the men in the world, Falcon would choose to face him, Gareth.

So it would be a fight to the death, then. Deep regret touched him that he would never kiss Linnet's lips again, nor see the green light sifting down through Sherwood like magic, nor hold his child in his arms.

The armorer handed Falcon a shield. Gareth took up his own, and his abused left arm screamed at him in agony.

"Come on, then, Norman cur," Falcon growled. "Have at it!"

Beloved. Linnet's voice whispered once more in Gareth's mind. But he could not let himself be distracted now. His entire world narrowed to Falcon's green-blue eyes and the hatred that reached for him. He could not afford to make a mistake.

His sword met Falcon's with a clang that shook him to the roots of his teeth. Aye, and he had not remembered the Saxon's power wrong—even fresh out of captivity, Falcon showed his training. No wild blow this, but one measured and delivered with deliberate intent.

Gareth turned swiftly and set his feet in the grass. Falcon Scarlet was no man to underestimate. As a member of the three that included Linnet, he might well be invested with a measure of Sherwood's magic.

Falcon raised his shield and brandished his sword in a flurry that ended in another crashing blow. Gareth met and turned it with difficulty, and shook the hair out of his eyes. The crowd gasped. Aye, Falcon had good training behind him. But Gareth had drilled countless afternoons under brutal scrutiny. And even hurting and half spent he could put on a proper show here today before he let Falcon win.

He braced himself and began dealing blow for blow, enough to rattle Falcon's bones but always directed at the man's shield rather than behind or beneath it. Falcon met him with bright eyes narrowed and mane flying in a glorious nimbus. They paced before all those eyes in a deadly dance while the breath began to come short in their lungs and Gareth's body protested in earnest. Falcon's sword was far quicker than Gareth liked, and the pain in his left arm had progressed into borderline numbness.

Another turn, another step, and Gareth's injured thigh threatened to steal his leg out from beneath him. Falcon, quick to take advantage, all his instincts running high, pressed in and delivered a tremendous blow directly to Gareth's shield.

Gareth never even felt the fingers of his left hand fail him, but he saw—as from a distance—his shield fall and clatter onto the trampled, green grass. The crowd cried out, and there came a call from the pavilion that Gareth could not quite hear for the loud buzzing in his ears.

An unholy grin spread across Falcon's face. He raised his blade again with murderous intent. Gareth saw the glint of light as the sword swung for him and set himself to take the strike, endure the wound, and end it, as he must.

But at the last instant, Linnet screamed in his mind, *Love!* Instinct acted without his permission and brought his blade up somehow to meet Falcon's. The two weapons met with a screech, and the impact tore a groan from Gareth's lips. He did not have the strength to hold.

Falcon bared his teeth and disengaged in a movement worthy of a trained sword master. He rounded on light feet and attacked Gareth again before Gareth could turn.

"Norman dog!" Falcon growled, a heartbeat before his blade hooked Gareth's and tossed it wide. With a glint of light, that same blade then found its place at the side of Gareth's neck in a deadly kiss.

Everything stopped. For an instant, time itself froze: the sunlight ceased to beat down on Gareth's head, his heart seized in his chest, and even the beads of sweat he could see on Falcon's brow arrested. He knew what Falcon felt at that moment, could read it all in the man's eyes—the victory and the ownership of it, all laced with gratitude. It mattered not how Gareth's wounds burned or that his left arm felt limp as a length of rope. He regretted only for Linnet's sake, and prayed only that he might live on, like those other, blessed spirits in Sherwood.

"Do it," he spoke into Falcon's face.

Something moved in Falcon's eyes. His sinewy

arms flexed, and Gareth felt the bite of the blade. Curiously, there was no pain, or perhaps it was merely lost in the welter of other agonies that engulfed him.

He fell.

It seemed as if he descended backwards into a bottomless chasm. Darkness enfolded his sight, but he could still hear. Screams and cries and, aye, some cheers from the onlookers, for all were not nobles, there.

And one shattering call that he knew not whether he heard with his ears or his soul, straight from Linnet's heart.

No, no, no, my love.

Chapter Thirty-Eight

"Does he live?" Linnet caught at Falcon with hands like claws and arrested his flight. The rest of their party halted also, breath searing their lungs. Already they were well away into the trees, though Linnet did not remember running nor, in truth, leaving Nottingham. She remembered only seeing Gareth's bright head go down.

Falcon whirled to face her. "Do not touch me, Lin. I am stinking from that place."

"Do you think I care? Tell me if you left Gareth de Vavasour dead, if you slew him even as you have wanted this long while." She watched Fal's lips while her heart pounded in her ears, willing him to deny it, to speak the impossible.

Instead, his mouth twisted in a grimace. He said, "Did you expect me to spare him?"

A sob caught in Linnet's throat, a terrible, raw thing. It seemed she must have harbored some such hope after all, for she felt it die now, and her soul came apart in pieces, a scorching pain. "He fought that fight for you. He sacrificed himself for you!"

Falcon stared. The other men of their party looked away. It was Lark who stepped forward to face her sister. "You are wrong, Lin. Whatever your champion just did, 'twas not for Fal. How should he care for one wolfshead? What he did, he did for you."

"Aye." All her breath stolen, Linnet struggled for air and then crumpled with pain, collapsing in bits where she stood and sinking to the floor of the forest.

"Come, Sister." Lark's voice softened with compassion, and the hands that gathered Linnet up felt kind. Linnet did not know if Lark could sense what she felt, or even part of it. She hoped not, for she would spare even her worst enemy this pain.

"Get hold of yourself," Lark whispered. "You can give in to grief later—not now. We must get Fal away, or your man will have died for nothing."

"Is he dead?" Linnet looked into Lark's face through tear-filled eyes and saw a reflection of her own sorrow. Her stubborn heart still hoped, amid its agony. "I fear he must be, for I can no longer feel him, in my heart or mind."

"The Lady save us!" Lark muttered, and caught Linnet close, as she might a child. Over her head, she looked at Falcon. "Help me with her. We cannot linger here lest those at Nottingham fail to honor the bargain, with de Vavasour dead."

Dead. The word echoed in Linnet's ears. Was this how her grandmother, Marian, had felt when Robin fell? This wrenching, unbearable loss that made every heartbeat a hollow agony and changed the future into an unimaginable wasteland? No wonder Marian had retreated inside herself, unwilling to carry on.

Linnet had not realized that for days she had existed on Gareth's love for her and hers for him, exchanged and ever flowing like a current between them even when they were apart. She had lived on her acute awareness of him. Now stark terror replaced that awareness. She had never felt so alone.

"Listen to me." Lark whispered the words even as she drew Linnet closer. "What of his child you believe you carry? Will you not be strong for his or her sake?"

"Lark, I cannot."

"You must. The love is still with you, Lin. Sherwood is all about love."

"You lie! Sherwood is all about sacrifice."

"Help me with her," Lark appealed to the others again. "We must away."

Strong hands bore Linnet up, and her grief with her, and carried her on.

****

Somewhere, someone wept. The knowledge of her grief enfolded Gareth amid the darkness where he lay. Deep black it was, and paralyzing. He wanted desperately to break free of it and comfort her, but he had not the strength.

"Help me." He spoke the words to no one in particular, or rather to everyone and everything: to his mother with her bright beauty, to Robin with his strong kindness, to Sherwood itself. It felt as if a crowd of spirits surrounded him, those he knew and some he did not. Their essence began to flow into him, a mere trickle at first, and then a flood of strength.

Champion.

Robin's voice it was, calling him with insistence enough to rouse the dead. Was he, Gareth, dead? Or had Falcon, for some unimaginable reason, held his stroke? It would take inestimable skill to do so in the heat of the fight. And Falcon, who hated him, had no reason.

A form materialized beside the place where Gareth lay. He did not know how he could see it, for his eyes remained closed. Composed of light gathered from separate, glowing particles, it coalesced into the form of a man who laid his hand on Gareth's brow.

Sherwood takes. The voice, Robin's voice, spoke again. *But it also gives much. If you might have one thing, lad, what would it be?*

To ease her pain. For it caught at him, called to him even as had her love, drew him back from the pit of darkness into which he had fallen.

He felt Robin smile. *Then arise and go to her.*

Gareth's eyes opened. He lay on a hard surface in a dim, cool room, with his arms spread wide. Light slanted in through an open doorway built of stone.

The castle, then. He was somewhere in the castle. He drew a breath that expanded his lungs, and brought a hand to the left side of his neck.

His fingers met with wetness, the sticky residue of blood. It had happened then, and truly—Falcon's blade had taken him there in the sunshine, with all those faces looking on. Beneath the stickiness he could feel the edges of the wound, now joined together like a seam in a leather pouch.

From beyond the doorway came the sound of voices.

"Here, my lord. You will no doubt want for him to have a hero's burial?"

"Why should you suppose so?" The voice of Robert de Vavasour at its harshest and most impatient. It might have been that of Gareth's father, coming to him from out of his childhood. A shudder shook Gareth from head to toe.

"My lord Sheriff, he fought and defeated all comers."

"Aye, save for the last." Shadows blocked the sunlight and caused it to flicker as the two men came in. The castle seneschal it was, in company with Gareth's uncle.

Robert de Vavasour paused beside the stone slab where Gareth lay sprawled.

"Prepare him for burial," he told his man, "and put him in the ground before sundown."

Aye, Gareth thought, and did his uncle still suppose him dead? Was he dead after all, even while possessing this awareness? For though he believed he had opened them, he realized he lay with his eyes yet closed, and Robert saw not how the breath filled his lungs.

But Gareth could see the anger and disdain in his uncle's face when the man leaned close.

"So, you failed me," Robert ground out, too low and vicious for the seneschal to hear. Or had the man gone? "Failed me, our family, and your King. You could not take down one lowly peasant with a borrowed sword when it mattered. Better you are dead, and I need not disgrace myself in dealing with you."

De Vavasour spat. The spittle touched Gareth's cheek like a curse. Robert spun on his heel and marched out without a backward look.

Aye, and the seneschal had gone; Gareth found himself alone save for the sunlight. He sat up. A shower of what he recognized as magic surrounded him as he did so, silvery green droplets like dew. His head swam violently, and he still could not tell for certain whether he lived.

He sought for Linnet in his mind but could not find her. He needed to leave this place; he no longer belonged here, if ever he had. All strength and all love lay in Sherwood.

He slid from the stone and stood on his feet, swaying. If someone came now, what would he think? Might he run from Gareth, screaming?

But no one came as he walked to the doorway of the chamber. No one saw as he took himself from that cold place and out into the light.

I come to you, Linnet, my love, he called with his spirit. *Sherwood, I come.*

Chapter Thirty-Nine

"Linnet, listen to me." Falcon knelt at Linnet's feet and took both her hands in his. The light of the new morning flooded over and around him—green light, Sherwood's light. Linnet sometimes felt she had been raised on it, had drunk it like mother's milk. But she found little comfort in its presence now. The endless night might be done, her first without Gareth since she had bonded so completely with him in body and mind, but her pain had not abated.

Falcon's fingers squeezed hers hard enough to hurt, and his eyes captured her gaze persistently. "Do not go away from us. We need you, Lark and I."

Behind him Lark stood on one foot and bit her finger viciously. Linnet should be able to feel what Lark felt, but all her senses seemed stunned by grief. She felt little even from Fal, who touched her.

She blinked at Lark and then tried to focus on Falcon's face. She saw sorrow in his wide eyes, and something that might be fear.

"We cannot do this without you, Lin," he said, and bowed his head over her hands. "Do not hate me."

She felt a stir of emotion then, the deep pull of the ties that bound the three of them together. She sighed, restless as the wind in the trees. "How could I ever hate you? You are part of me." She blinked still harder. "But you slew him. Did you slay him?"

Falcon clenched her fingers, crushing, and refused to lift his head.

Lark stepped forward and laid her hand on Falcon's shoulder. *Mine,* the gesture said.

Of course he is yours, Linnet told her, in her mind. The communication worked sluggishly, but it did work. Perhaps in time she would come back to herself.

A measure of the tension went out of Lark. "Come, Sister," she said, gently for her. "Falcon acted only as he had to. Let us travel deeper into Sherwood, to where we can get you some rest and decide how best to carry the magic among us. It is all that matters now."

You have your love, Linnet returned, mind to mind.

Have I? Lark's gaze fell to Falcon, still poised at Linnet's feet.

In answer, Linnet reached out and laid both hands against Fal's face, lifting it to her. "You go with Lark," she bade him. "Make for her a good husband."

"Aye."

Linnet felt something pass between Falcon and Lark, a question asked and an answer given, acknowledgement of what had been forged between them while Falcon languished in Nottingham's dungeon.

"I will remain on my own for a while," Linnet added softly.

"But we need you." This time Lark protested.

"I will rejoin you anon," Linnet said. "But first I need what answers Sherwood can give me."

Falcon freed her hands and got to his feet. He and Lark exchanged speaking glances.

"We will not abandon you," Lark said then. "Did not Ma always say abandonment is the very worst of things? You come with us or we do not go."

So that was how it was to be from now on, Linnet thought. She must live for these two, for the triad, and for the child who might one day assure the guardianship of Sherwood, or not at all. A lesson learned early: Sherwood gave much, and took much.

Even though it felt as if her heart had been torn from her breast, it beat still, and so she must go on.

****

Beloved. The word shimmered through Linnet's mind like a stray shard of moonlight and woke her from her uneasy sleep. She aroused with a start to find herself surrounded by magic.

The three of them—she, Falcon and Lark—had migrated back to the place where her parents had once held Gareth de Vavasour, deep in Sherwood's heart. Not fifty paces from where Linnet lay was the moss bed where she and Gareth had consummated their love with wild abandon and conceived the child that now rested, so precious, beneath her heart. She awoke to find the clearing aglow all around her, every leaf rustling beneath a full moon, and every spirit whispering in awareness.

He comes!

He is here.

The champion of Sherwood.

Linnet's heart leaped painfully. She sat up, her senses alive and quivering.

Not far away, Lark and Falcon lay sleeping, tangled together like two hound pups. Lark's head rested on Falcon's chest and his arms encircled her the way a tree's roots hold the deep soil of Sherwood.

Beloved.

Linnet's head turned sharply. She saw nothing save the flicker of moonlight, yet her heart opened, the pain loosening for the first time. She knew she heard his voice in her mind. If he came only in spirit, that was better than not at all.

She got to her feet and stood quivering. She strained to hear him again.

"Linnet? Are you unwell?"

Her sudden movement must have roused Falcon from his sleep. He put Lark from him with great care, slid from her grasp, and got to his feet, awash with moonlight. She felt his concern wrap around her even before he reached her side.

"I awoke," she said helplessly. "I heard his voice."

Falcon hesitated and then touched her shoulder. "I have thought I heard my father's voice many times since his death. They are all here with us, Lin. Is that not what makes Sherwood worth our blood and our allegiance?"

Linnet sought his eyes in the magical, silver light. "They are all here? Even an accursed Norman?"

An odd look came to Falcon's face. Linnet knew that for Fal's father, Martin Scarlet, life had been black or white, right or wrong. But try as he might, this man before her was no Martin Scarlet. He was capable of seeing as many shades of color as Sherwood had to offer.

Slowly he shook his head. "I cannot say."

"You faced him, Fal, with a sword in your hands. You fought him. Could you not feel what he was? He chose that combat, arranged for it, in order to free you from that dungeon. He sacrificed himself so the three of us could go on together. His love did that, for me."

"I faced him, aye, Lin, and I fought him. But I know not what I felt." Moonlight flickered in Falcon's eyes. "From the first I met the man he wanted naught more than to face me with a sword in his hands. How do I know he did not just arrange for that chance?"

"Because I tell you so, and you should believe me, if you are to believe anyone. You are a fine man with a sword, Fal, even better with a bow. But do you truly suppose you could best a trained knight?"

"He had already faced many before me, so Lark says, and he underestimated my skill." Falcon drew a breath. "Does it matter now, Lin, with him dead? The three of us must go on, as was always meant."

"Aye, it matters." Tears filled Linnet's eyes and she pressed her hands to her belly. "I carry his child, Fal, a child conceived here in Sherwood. You know what that means."

"I do," Falcon acknowledged. Children begotten in this place were special, even sacred. Had not the three of them been conceived here also?

He reached out and captured her hands in his warm ones. "I will welcome the child, Lin, if that is what you ask. No blame for its father. The three of us will raise it together in the knowledge it will need." Deliberately, he added, "It shall never hear an evil word from my lips about its sire."

"Thank you. You are a good man, Falcon Scarlet."

"I am what my father would call soft." He tossed his wild head in a rueful gesture. "But as we take up the burden of the triad, we must find our own way with it. So long as we keep the magic safe, I do not believe those who came before us can dictate how."

"And Lark, do you think she will offer this same

kindness?"

He cast another rueful glance at the place where Lark lay still sleeping. "Who can measure Lark's heart? She is all passion and mercy tangled up together, is she not? To think I never knew her, even though I knew her all my life." His voice grew hoarse with emotion. "When I lay in Nottingham, helpless and hurting, she came to me. She upheld and saved me. I need to be with her, Lin. It does not mean I love you any less."

"I know." Just as Linnet's eternal love for Gareth did not mean she loved Falcon less.

His hands squeezed hers still more tightly. "She is inside me now, in a way I cannot even begin to explain. I need her fierceness and her strength—they complete me."

That, too, Linnet understood: the need answered, and the heart finding its one home. "She has loved you long."

"And I too blind to see the great gift she offered. But, Lin, the three of us together must find a balance. We need to take up Robin's fight and advance our people's lot. It is no longer enough merely to survive and steal sustenance from our overlords, or win a few running battles. We must win a legitimate place. I thought much on this, also, when I lay in Nottingham. We must win rights, rather than just battles. Things in Sherwood, and in England, need to change."

Linnet felt it then, the force gathering above and around them as if all the spirits of Sherwood drew near to listen and hear Falcon's words. The trees tossed in an invisible wind, magic trailed and skittered across Linnet's skin and, where she lay, Lark stirred and came half awake.

Everything responded to the call Falcon made, and Linnet's awareness heightened almost unbearably.

"We need," Falcon declared forcefully, "a means to claim our God-given rights, not as Saxon peasants but as free Englishmen."

And a voice spoke out of the stirred and enlivened darkness. "Perhaps you will allow me to help with that."

Chapter Forty

"My love!"

Linnet spoke the words with both her lips and her mind. Gareth heard, and knew them the way an infant knows its mother's voice. Gladness arose to enfold him, wild in his breast. He had come to her through the forest, blind in all his senses but one. As never before, he had followed his heart.

She and Falcon stood with their hands linked, a dim glow of radiance around them. Both had turned startled faces to him when he spoke, and their eyes widened like those of two children beholding a miracle.

After a single glance, Gareth dismissed Falcon from his awareness and focused on Linnet. "I come," he told her softly, "even as I promised, as Sherwood assures. I return to you."

She gasped, drew her fingers from Falcon's and extended them to him. The radiance he saw around her brightened and changed color, streaming pure gold. Gareth knew if he could reach that radiance, if it flowed into him, he could exist for eternity.

He could not feel his feet against the ground. An unknown force seemed to buoy and uphold him. If he touched her hands, would he be able to feel her? Reality seemed to have bypassed him, all sense of time flown. For he had floated rather than walked through the trees, straining always for her. Aye, and if he touched her now, could she anchor him?

He reached out for her and saw that a dim glow also surrounded his hands: silver it was, the pure color of moonlight.

"Linnet—" Falcon said hoarsely.

She ignored him. All gladness, now, she leaped forward and grasped Gareth's hands the way a drowning woman might grasp for land.

And oh, he could feel her! His fingers met hers in a rush of golden-silver sparks that fused fast in an elemental bond. Everything within him rejoiced and cried aloud, a wealth of gladness. Sherwood demanded much, aye, but it gave so very much...

Bliss enfolded him, and a sense of total belonging. He drew Linnet hard against him, into his arms, and his spirit exulted riotously.

"You are alive, alive, *alive*—" She poured the words into his mind even as she spoke them aloud, and her hands explored the reality of the assertion. Her fingers caressed his naked chest, slid across the skin of his shoulders. One of them came to rest against the slash at the side of his neck. "How can it be?" She wept now, tears of pure joy. "I believed you dead; I thought you lay slain."

"There is no such thing as death," he told her with absolute certainty. "Surely you know that. And"—above her head his eyes met Falcon's—"my opponent pulled his stroke. He delivered no death blow."

Falcon stood quietly and said nothing.

"And so," Gareth concluded, "I come to offer my services, the King's man no longer but a champion of Sherwood."

Falcon hesitated and then inclined his head, a liege

lord accepting a vow of fealty. Gareth looked into Linnet's dark eyes and saw there every hope for his future.

"You, here? How can it be?"

Gareth and Linnet spun together, as one. Lark stood on her feet, trembling, one of her many weapons—a knife—clutched in her hand.

"Love brought me," Gareth told her. "Go ahead, Small Fury—attack me and do as you will. I shall not be parted from her again."

"You are supposed to be dead." Lark's nostrils quivered, and she threw a look at Falcon. "I thought you finished it."

"It is finished, Lark—or, rather, I suspect it is just beginning anew. She loves him, even as I love you."

"I understand that." Lark's fingers clutched the hilt of her knife still harder. "And I regretted her sorrow at the loss of him, when I believed him dead. But does that mean we are supposed to accept his presence amongst us, even at this most holy place?"

Gareth answered her before Falcon could. "It is Sherwood brought me here, Sherwood that led me."

She glanced around at the trees and the stirred, living darkness. She must be able to feel the magic gathered, that shed from Falcon and Linnet, and even from Gareth's own skin. Now that he looked, he could see a faint haze of it surrounding her, as well, in a blush of crimson.

"That may be so," Lark said with a hard toss of her head. "But to suppose you belong here at the very root of all we are—"

"He belongs." Linnet tightened her grip upon Gareth. "If I do, then so does he. One does not refuse a miracle, Lark, and it is a miracle that he lives."

"So it is," Lark acknowledged, "and that he has found us—if he actually lives at all and we do not behold a spirit."

And in those words, Gareth realized, lay the essence of Lark Little. All battle and fight, she nevertheless possessed such an affinity for the magic of this place she did not doubt she might be standing and speaking with a spirit. And aye, before his hands had met Linnet's, had he, himself, not doubted?

Gravely, he told Lark, "I promised Linnet I would come to her, alive or dead, and so I have done. But I am living. Let me prove it to you." He reached out for her, but she shrank back, staring.

"I see magic around you. But I also saw the blow that felled you. How can you be other than spirit?"

"Let him prove it." Falcon gave Gareth a long look. "As he gave me a chance to fight for my life in Nottingham, now I will give him a chance to win his place at Linnet's side. Are you up for it, Champion?"

Gareth met Falcon's stare steadily. "Swords?" he asked.

Falcon shook his head. "Ah, no. We have done that. This time the combat will be on my terms."

****

The longbow felt awkward in Gareth's hands. He had trained long and hard with the sword and for the lists, but rarely with the bow. Under the best of conditions, he might be a passable shot.

This could never be described as the best of conditions. Too many things beat at him—his own exhaustion, the debilitation from his wound, the awareness coming from those who surrounded him and from the forest itself. Magic moved everywhere, a potent distraction.

But Linnet filled him. Even when he stepped away from her, he could feel her love holding him, vital and unflagging.

"You have only to best me," Falcon gave him a smile that contained a hint of mischief.

"And do so fairly," Lark chimed in immediately. She had taken the place beside Falcon and now virtually jumped up and down with the intensity of her emotions. She darted a look at her man. "You are not to let him win."

"To be sure, not," Falcon agreed. "If he is to own his place, he must do so fairly."

"I always deal fairly," Gareth told Lark. "It is something you will learn of me."

Her eyes narrowed at him. "Other than my father, Falcon is the best archer Sherwood has to offer."

Gareth believed it. Falcon had the grace of an archer born, and Gareth remembered the skill with which he and Sparrow had brought down game when he was with them in the forest.

"He deserves his chance," Falcon declared, "even as he offered me. But no favors. Look you there, Norman—do you see that tall ash tree some hundred paces off?"

Gareth peered where bidden. He could not be sure what he saw in the uncertain light that flitted through the trees.

"And see the beech beyond that, almost in a straight line? And the broad oak past it?"

Helplessly, Gareth shook his head.

"Those are your targets. Three"—Falcon grinned—

"to match the magic of Sherwood."

"I need something at which to aim," Gareth protested. "Some marker."

"Only listen to the dog whine." Lark tossed her head. "Let me." She drew something from her pack and then hared off. Gareth watched in amazement as she swarmed up the first of the trees and fastened a square of fabric in place.

Linnet took Gareth's hand in both of hers. "You do not need to do this. My love does not rest on their approval."

"I know that full well, Linnet. But my place at your side does," he told her softly, "and that I am no longer willing to yield."

Chapter Forty-One

"There, Norman." Lark came racing back from setting the target, not a bit breathless. "Is that good enough for you?"

He looked her in the eye. "My name is Gareth. I hope when this is done you will pay me the honor of using it." He knew to the roots of his soul just how important these two were to the woman he loved. The three of them stood linked by the magic of this place that he had only begun to understand.

"Use my bow," Falcon bade, and caught it up. "Lark's will be too light for you, and we are almost of a height. We will take it in turns—does that sound fair?"

"Aye, but I pray you shoot first." Maybe if he followed the flight of Falcon's arrow with his eyes, he might have some hope of finding the target. He did not doubt Falcon would hit the first, and probably all three of them.

Falcon snagged an arrow from the quiver that lay on the ground and posed himself. For an instant he stood so, breathing deep, and Gareth saw the magic gather round him, pure green-blue. Falcon inhaled it like air and then made his shot.

The arrow flew with exquisite grace, arced through the near darkness, and embedded itself in the tall, ghostly form of a tree.

"Ah." The sound came from Lark's throat, a sigh

of pure satisfaction.

Falcon turned and handed Gareth the bow. Gareth glanced into Linnet's face, aglow with faith in him, and wished desperately he had the skill needed to accomplish this—for her sake, if not his own.

All is given, for love.

The words sounded in his head clear as a bell, a voice he knew. *Stand, son. As you give yourself now to Sherwood, so shall Sherwood give itself to you.*

A flare of magic surrounded him. He heard Linnet's breath catch, saw Lark stare, and saw Falcon smile.

A spirit not his own lifted the bow and notched an arrow. Eyes not quite his sighted, hands not his corrected the aim, the precise and barely definable amount needed for the distance.

The shot loosed and flew true in a shower of pure white sparks. The arrow entered the target so near Falcon's the two were indistinguishable from where Gareth stood. Once more Lark went racing off to see, and returned as swiftly with a curious expression in her eyes.

"Both in the very center of the target."

Falcon slanted Gareth a look. "The next, then, if you wish to continue?"

Gareth nodded, no longer sure what voice might issue from his lips, should he dare to speak.

"I have secured the next target," Lark dared him. "Let us see, Sir Champion."

Not yet his name, but no epithet either. Gareth gave Falcon the bow.

So acute had Gareth's senses now become, he could feel Linnet holding her breath, could feel the air flowing through the trees in a veil of power. And he could feel the spirit waiting inside him, strong and patient.

Virtue survives death, it whispered with a hint of humor. *And virtue recognizes its own, even in the guise of a Norman.*

Gareth replied, *But I cannot see the target.*

No worry, son. I can!

Falcon shot in another shower of aquamarine sparks. Lark, whose eyes must be much keener than Gareth's, crowed in delight.

Aye, he is good, said Robin inside Gareth's head, even as Falcon returned the bow. *But I am better.*

He raised the bow and shot. This time Gareth felt the full power of it, the rush of strength and certainty. His heart bounded.

Lark, apparently tireless, ran off again. She came back scowling. "Both arrows beside each other once again. I have placed the last target but—it lies in the deepest darkness. Fal, I do not know that even you can find it."

"That," Falcon told her, "is what makes it a challenge." Almost respectfully now, he took the bow from Gareth's hands and notched his final arrow. "This one flies by faith."

Falcon raised the bow, notched the arrow, and sighted long. He shot and his arrow disappeared, even its trail of magic swallowed by the darkness.

Lark went after it more slowly this time. When she returned, she shook her head sorrowfully.

"I am sorry, Fal—your arrow missed. But he will not be able to make the shot, either."

Falcon handed Gareth the bow. "He will."

"How can you say so?"

"Look at him, Lark. Do you not see who that is?"

Giving her no chance to respond, the spirit within Gareth raised the bow. High above, in the darkness, the trees stirred. Magic came flowing, streaming down in great rafts like moonlight. It surrounded the arrow and enfolded Gareth's hands when they released the shot.

For an instant everything stilled. All four of them were able to hear the solid *thunk* as the arrow found its impossible target.

"Nay, Lark—do not bother to chase it." Falcon seized her arm when she would have dashed off. "You need not look. There is no doubt."

Uncertainty now filled Lark's eyes. She peered at Gareth and her face twisted in wonder. "But why? Why would Sherwood take his part?"

"Because." Linnet stepped to Gareth's side even as that other spirit lifted gently from him and arose like breath to disperse among the trees. "If ever we are to achieve our dream, all must be one—Saxon and Celt and Norman alike. One England, one people. Sister, if it cannot happen in Sherwood, it cannot happen at all."

****

"Please kiss me." A smile colored Linnet's voice as she turned and lifted her face to Gareth's, safe within the circle of his arms. He smiled in response. The night just past should have wearied him. He had lost count of the number of times they had coupled. But he lived on the remnants of magic and the fullness of his need for this woman, and felt as if he held eternity between his hands.

"No need to ask." He bent his head and brushed his lips across hers, a whisper of devotion. "Tell me you love me," he bade in return.

"Let me show you, instead." She pressed her body against his and delight curled through him, slow and languorous. Already drunk on the taste of her, he took her lips once more and drank deep.

They stood together in the dawn forest, alone but very much not alone. Following the contest last night, Falcon had clasped Gareth's arm like a brother before leading Lark off to Gareth knew not where. It had not mattered then and it barely mattered now.

He slid his hands over Linnet's slender back and drew her still nearer. She left off kissing him long enough to gaze into his eyes, her expression both wise and mysterious. He pressed possessive palms to her buttocks and parted them slightly so she fitted him better. "Show me, then."

"Wicked lad!" She bit his lip temptingly. Her luscious, soft mouth had been all over him this night. Just thinking on it had him up and ready for her again.

He tangled his fingers in her hair and a shower of magic erupted, glittering mellow gold. "'Twill take me some time to get used to that," he said ruefully.

"Not too long, I trust. For Sherwood wants you here, as do I." She punctuated the sentiment with another kiss. "My champion."

"Just try and chase me away. I only hope I can prove worthy of the place your grandfather chose for me." A bridge, Robin had called him, a branch—a Norman champion taken to Sherwood's service. "I hope I can make a difference and strive for a united England."

"So do I." The wisdom in her eyes deepened. "The welfare of our child relies upon it."

He drew a breath and urged,. "Tell me once more; I cannot hear it often enough." Wonderingly, he ran his hands over her again. "You carry our child, my child? You are certain?"

Her face lit with joy, making her even more beautiful. She nodded. "It will be a son. Strong and true of heart, like his father."

"Ah." His joy caught from hers and gladness filled him. A reason to live, this, as if he needed any beyond the woman in his arms. A reason to fight, and a continuation of the precious magic that had saved, uplifted, and brought him home.

"Now," he said in rampant delight, "there is a gift come straight from Sherwood's heart. There," he added more gravely, "is a piece of the future."

"And, I do not doubt, the founding of the next triad. If I do not miss my guess," she cast him another look, this one tangled with mischief, "Lark and Falcon are off somewhere even now seeing to the founding of the second part of it. From whence, I wonder, will come the third?"

"Only kiss me again," Gareth said joyfully, "and we will leave the future in Sherwood's keeping."

A word about the author...

Born and raised in western New York, Laura Strickland has pursued lifelong interests in lore, legend, magic and music, all reflected in her writing. Though her imagination frequently takes her to far-off places, she is usually happiest at home not far from Lake Ontario with her husband and her "fur" child, a rescue dog. Currently she is at work on the third book of the Guardians of Sherwood series.